D0993629

By the same author

*Diary of a Manhattan Call Girl*
*Diary of a Married Call Girl*

# TRACY QUAN

# *Diary of a Jetsetting Call Girl*

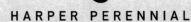

**HARPER PERENNIAL**

London, New York, Toronto, Sydney and New Delhi

Harper Perennial
An imprint of HarperCollins*Publishers*
77–85 Fulham Palace Road
Hammersmith
London W6 8JB

www.harperperennial.co.uk
Visit our authors' blog at www.fifthestate.co.uk

This Harper Perennial edition published 2008
1

Copyright © Tracy Quan 2008
Internal illustrations © www.joygosney.co.uk
Tracy Quan asserts the moral right to be identified as the author of this work

A catalogue record for this book is available from the British Library

ISBN 978-0-00-724938-1

Set in Minion by Palimpsest Book Production Ltd, Grangemouth, Stirlingshire

Printed and bound in Great Britain by Clays Ltd, St Ives plc

This novel is entirely a work of fiction. The names, characters and incidents
portrayed in it are the work of the author's imagination. Any resemblance to
actual persons, living or dead, events or localities is entirely coincidental.

*For my mother*

*O for a beaker full of the warm South ...*

JOHN KEATS

# CONTENTS

# ACKNOWLEDGEMENTS

My heartfelt thanks to Charles Peck for being such a tenacious editor and vigilant reader, and for sharing his delightful insights.

I am very grateful to Essie Cousins, my patient yet persistent editor at HarperCollins. Her encouragement and guidance are deeply appreciated. Joy Chamberlain, Ilsa Yardley, Natasha Law, Joy Gosney, Lizzy Kingston, Rebecca McEwan, Georgia Mason, Mark Johnson and Kate Hyde: thank you for applying your talents to Nancy Chan's checkered existence. Doug Pepper's blessing is noted with pleasure.

Paul Shields has been a dear friend to my project and to its wayward author—I'm fortunate to know him. Nora Rety and Barnaby Lewis have inspired a great deal of mischief.

Katinka Matson, Russell Weinberger, Karla Taylor, Max Brockman, Michael Healey, and John Brockman of Brockman Inc; Peter Benedek, James Kearney, Craig Losben, Howard Sanders and Gary Gradinger at United Talent Agency; Dana Friedman and Chad Matheny of Dragonfly Technologies: thank you for taking care of me.

A special note of gratitude to Lloyd Grove.

Stephen Lee, Andrea Piccolo, Mike Godwin, James Wolcott, Ralph Martin, Carole Murray, Matt Weingarden, Steve Richardson-

Ross, Nomi Prins, Pico Iyer, Melissa Ditmore, John Dizard, Noel Vera, Cynthia Connors, Richard Porton, Darren Star, Mark Farley, Steve Wasserman, Laura Agustin, Gretchen Soderlund, Rebecca Kaye, Gerard S., David Sterry, Mari Alden, Richard Adams, Giovanna, Lily, Joe Lavezzo, Bowie Snodgrass, Desmond Mervyn, David Andrew, Eliyanna Kaiser, Adrian, Frances, Rachel Aimee, Sylvia Federici, Louise Aibel, and the New York Society Library have been helpful in diverse, unexpected ways: thank you.

Will Crutchfield climbed a mountain with me, helped me find the byways, and made this possible. I'll never be able to thank him enough.

CHAPTER ONE

# France: A Session in Provence

*Thursday, July 4, 2002 Villa Gambetta, Saint-Maximin-La-Sainte-Baume*

Dear Diary,

This morning, Milt surprised me with a special request, as my lips were approaching the base of his manhood.

"Suzy?" Sometimes, I wonder if I've outgrown Suzy, but there's not much I can do about it now. Milt's been calling me that for years.

He placed his hand on the side of my head, ever so lightly, and stroked my hair. Although he's a self-confessed sleaze, he knows when to be polite. So, while my mouth became more relaxed, his fingers grazed the crown of my head, then retreated. I went a little deeper—a reward for his good manners—and came up slowly for air.

"I want you to promise me something."

OMG. Is that the Viagra talking?

Reluctant to interrupt this blow job, I forced myself to look up. With an inquisitive smile, I warned my favorite customer: "A woman will promise you anything when you're hard."

I filled my mouth again and put more energy into what I was doing.

"I want you to promise you'll get me off—" he was trying not to come "—in every room of the house, before you go back to New York."

With the head of his cock resting against the tip of my tongue, I giggled softly. I could hear the wooden shutter in the en suite bathroom swinging loudly on its hinges. A cool breeze, followed by the faint aroma of fresh lavender flirting with cypress, entered Milt's bedroom and stiffened my nipples.

After he came, I scurried to the bathroom and looked—in vain—for a washcloth. Filling the bidet with hot water, I draped a large hand towel over the side to soak. I bundled the used condom into some tissue and checked myself out in the mirror. My bra was still on, though my thong had slipped off. More to the point, my hair's holding up, forty-eight hours after leaving New York. (Must email Lorenzo a thank you note ASAP. A hairdresser needs to know his travel-proof blow-outs are appreciated.)

Minutes later, as I wrapped one corner of the hot towel around Milt's cock, we resumed our negotiations: "How many bedrooms again? Eight?"

"Ten," he said proudly. "But I didn't say every BEDroom. What about the other rooms? We could have a quickie in the solarium tomorrow afternoon."

"We didn't discuss *that* in New York."

I tried to look both saucy and stern.

"Come on, I work like a dog all year. And this renovation cost a fortune! Don't I get a reward?"

"The library's a possibility," I offered. "But the wine cellar's kind of impractical, don't you think? All those hi-tech temperature controls." *Anything more than a quick hand job would surely play havoc with the artificial climate.* "And the solarium's totally exposed! What if Duncan sees us?"

Milt's cook lives in Tanneron—a bit of a trek, so he's been

sleeping in a guest room downstairs . . . right next to the solarium. Duncan's politely enigmatic, and acts like he has no idea what I'm doing here. Whether or not that's true, why ruin a good thing by making a spectacle of myself? Even though he's gay—so it's not like I'd be giving him a free hard-on—I need to maintain some decorum around the staff.

"I'll find something for Duncan to do at the post office. He'll be gone for at least an hour. And the gardener can stay home. Only a few wild rabbits will see us!"

If I do Milt in the solarium, have I got enough SPF 90 to cover my entire body? And what if the sunscreen comes in contact with the condom?

"Well . . ." I don't want to rain on Milt's parade. "Wait till Allison gets here. I'll see to it that you get off in *almost* every room. With one of us, or both of us . . . Allison *loves* going down on me."

But Milt doesn't know I've been trying to reach her ever since she landed in Barcelona. All he knows is he paid for her ticket! Allie wouldn't stand us up—would she? I've put in a call to Isabel, but I doubt any of Isabel's girls will be up for the solarium when they find out there are ten perfectly nice bedrooms—six with en suite bath and bidet.

"I like the way you're thinking!" he said. I reached under the small of his back to retrieve my lace panties. Duncan's SUV was pulling into the driveway. "You're the perfect houseguest," he added. "I think I'll jump in the pool while Duncan unpacks the groceries."

### Friday, July 5, 2002

The light in this part of France is, indeed, special. Last night, I forgot to close the shutters in my room and woke when the sun began to rise. After checking my cellphone for a message from Allie, I tried to go back to sleep. Instead, I spent two hours hiding with the door locked, treating my eyes to an oxygen mask.

I've known Milt for longer than I care to admit. I knew he kept Wall Street hours, but had no idea he'd be such an early riser when I agreed to come to St-Maximin. Isn't he on vacation? He gets up at eight-thirty, and calls that sleeping in! Still, if he finds out I'm capable of waking before he does, he'll be disillusioned. I am, after all, a luxury.

I tiptoed around the bedroom, terrified of being overheard. Then, I spent an hour perfecting my natural look for our poolside breakfast, keeping one eye on my silenced cellphone.

I hope she gets here soon, because Milt needs a threesome—and so do I. When he doesn't have an extra girl (or three) to distract him, he stays hard forever. If I could figure out where he keeps the Viagra, I would totally hide it! Coordinating this trip with Allie is turning into a major headache. Speaking of which, by the time I was dressed, I had been awake sans caffeine for hours and was feeling the symptoms. But headaches are another no-no. A smart call girl never feels unwell. She mysteriously disappears until she's better. No explanations. Well, she might claim to be visiting her mother. Polite code for *out of town with a man possibly richer than yourself.*

Keeping all this straight comes naturally in New York: normally, I spend no more than two hours with a customer. It's more of a challenge when Milt's around all the time. The trick is to appear comfortable without becoming too comfortable.

From my bedroom window, overlooking a cluster of olive trees, I monitored the sunniest corner of the swimming pool. I waited until Milt was stretched out on a wooden lounger with his *Herald Tribune* and a croissant, then wandered downstairs, determined to look like a carefree princess. Not a sleep-deprived working girl with a head full of enlarged blood vessels.

Milt was reading the paper with his shades on. I guess it's generational? He finds sunshine invigorating. When Duncan began opening my table umbrella, Milt leapt up from his cushioned lounger and took over.

"Uncle Miltie to the rescue!" he said. "Damsels in distress are my thing."

The aroma of Milt's croissant, sitting on a plate nearby, made my eyes go wide, but I forced myself to inquire about fresh fruit.

"Blackberries," Duncan informed me. "The figs are just right, and the croissants—"

Yikes. "Not for me, thanks! I'll come get some black coffee. Then I'll organize my berries and figs."

I followed Duncan back to the kitchen where a breakfast buffet had been arranged on a red-tiled counter top. As I poured my morning fix from the half-empty cafetiere, I took him into my confidence.

"Just between us? I have the tiniest headache coming on. Is there anything like Tylenol in the house? I don't want to bother Milt while he's reading the paper."

"What's in Tylenol again?" Duncan was rummaging through a drawer. "How about some Prontalgine. Twenty milligrams, codeine, works like a dream."

"Don't you have something, you know, over-the-counter?"

"Codeine *is* over the counter." As he handed me the box, our eyes met, and I tried to place his accent. New Zealand? "Welcome to France," he said, with a twinkle. "I have the cure for your mal de tête."

Gosh. Could Duncan be . . . my surrogate hairdresser? Not for my hair, of course. But for my general well-being. He really is a treasure. And his coffee is excellent.

## Later

The countryside is ten times trickier than Manhattan.

First, if you're going to be seen at all hours of the morning by a john, fourteen days in a row, you need to do some sort of clarifying mask *every day*. Bare skin's a high-maintenance look. You can't be walking around in full make-up with a vineyard next door—lip gloss is out of the question—so you'll need to cultivate a natural glow.

Okay, the Chemin du Moulin isn't exactly hardcore countryside. We're minutes from the town center, but you'd never know it. Milt's house is set back so far we can't hear the traffic and is protected by a wall of hundred-year-old pine trees.

I'm trying to limit our shared activities: sex (different position each day), meals, the occasional excursion. Milt's never spent this much time with me, so my inherent mystery is at risk. He's been my favorite customer—forever, it seems. But if I become a too-familiar presence during this vacation—his, not mine—there's a chance his frequent visits could peter out when we return to New York.

Duncan was right. My headache's evaporated! Is codeine really available over the counter at this strength?

Instead of the solarium, I've promised Milt an appointment in the nursery. The guest room down the hall is equipped with two single beds, a child's wooden rocker, a chest of drawers with large blue butterflies for knobs, and a toddler's denim armchair. I've taken the liberty of moving the chairs, so Milt won't knock them over.

My frilly white panties (open crotch) seem to work with that decor, but do I misunderstand his request? If middle-aged perversion is setting in, I should put my hair in pigtails and wear the white bra as well.

Or is Milt just being territorial about his newly acquired *domaine*? In which case, my white panties, and nothing else, will be more appropriate. More alluring to greet him bare-breasted, stretching out on one of those small beds with my legs apart. He can discover his late afternoon quarry in masturbatory solitude.

. . . Too bad I have no bedroom toys to bring with me to the nursery!

Packing for this trip was a delicate, sometimes terrifying, operation. I was much too nervous about getting through customs (and airport security) to even *think* about packing my dildos. When I landed at Nice, I discovered that my fears were misplaced. They barely noticed my bags and waved me right through. If only I had known.

But, if Allie gets here soon, this won't be a problem. Didn't she say something about bringing her Pyrex love baton to Barcelona? In her carry-on?

## Saturday, July 6

Just woke from a remarkable dream.

Duncan, beckoning from the far end of the swimming pool, was waving something in his hand. A box of codeine pills? Fully clothed, he floated toward me, as if he were a rather efficient angel, sliding across the water's surface on a pair of invisible waterskis. On closer inspection, I realized he was holding an electric shaver. (*No wonder he's so clean-shaven*, I thought.) As he drew nearer, I was disturbed by a buzzing sound.

My phone, vibrating under the pillow.

When I came to, the buzzing had stopped, the shaver was beginning to make sense, and my unknown caller had disappeared without leaving voicemail. Of course, it would have to be a private number. Isabel calling back with her international menu? But I really need to straighten things out with Allison before I start making plans with Isabel.

Allie's silence is worrying, and I don't want Milt to sense that I'm stressed out. I certainly don't want him having any doubts about buying her ticket! I, after all, have been paid handsomely to monitor his girl-supply without letting the seams show. If something goes wrong with Allie, why should he trust my dealings with Isabel?

Milt's going to Nans-les-Pins to play golf, and Duncan has promised to take me to the internet café. "Milt's rather old school," he explained. "He doesn't want a computer in his hideaway."

## Later
## Maison de Thé, Place de l'Hôtel de Ville, Saint-Maximin

Now I understand why Milt's too lazy to drive his BMW to the golf course.

Behind the wheel, Duncan's responsible yet fearless, unfazed by sudden curves and regional customs. Even the local hunters, who prowl around in the woods, drunk on Pernod, before getting into their pick-up trucks don't worry him. He really is the ideal country concierge! As we neared the Sainte-Baume golf course, I was tempted to turn my phone on.

But there are so many callers I must avoid, starting with Matt who thinks I'm in La Croix-Valmer today. Milt has no idea Matt's my husband—he assumes we're still engaged—and he'd love to hear me snowing my "fiancé." I haven't got that much nerve, though.

And what if Allie calls with bad news?

Instead, I succumbed to a much safer temptation: checking out our driver from the back seat, while Milt, sitting next to me, checked his calls.

Duncan's neat sandy hair, cut so close to the nape of his neck, underscores his boyish appearance. In tidy jeans and a crisp navy T-shirt, he's impeccably casual. Not absurdly buff. Built just right.

What a waste! But—I never think this way. I'm too practical. Too concerned about my own looks to be eyeing a man who is, by definition, unavailable. Perhaps it's a change for the better. Part of coming to terms with your thirties and being less self-centered.

Milt, of course, has no inkling of Duncan's sexual orientation. He believes in a part-time "girlfriend" sharing Duncan's house in Tanneron. Gaydar isn't part of Milt's vocabulary. If a guy's not really obvious and swishy, he might as well be straight. Another one of those generational things.

"Your visitor from Barcelona. Do you know when she's due to arrive?" Duncan asked.

Milt, supposedly engrossed in his voicemail, looked up discreetly and wiggled his eyebrows at me. Visions of a *ménage à soixante-neuf* (well, it's a multiple of *trois*) were dancing through his head.

"She flies into Marseille next, um, Wednesday," I said. "We're just waiting for her to confirm the flight."

If she doesn't? I'll have to worry about that later. There's no point revealing my insecurity, when the prospect of our next threeway is keeping Milt erotically stoked.

And the prospect of Milt productively occupied for the rest of the afternoon is reassuring to *me*. Calling home when I'm staying in a customer's house seems dicey, but I'm anxious to send some conjugal email soon.

Unfortunately, when we drove back to town, Ste. Maxiphony—the Cibercafé-Teleboutique which claims to be open from 15H00 till 22H00—was still closed at 15H30. A resigned-looking teenager was standing outside, smoking a pungent cigarette, waiting for them to re-open. I coughed and moved away from the door.

"C'est toujours comme ça," the boy was telling Duncan. He shrugged, then he inhaled. "Ils font ce qu'ils veulent." Smoke drifted toward me.

"Omigosh," I muttered, as we walked back to the SUV. "They smoke in there, don't they! I'd forgotten all about that. I'll find an outdoor café while you do your shopping. I need to call Allison."

Miraculously, Duncan's actually got a list of all the smoke-free venues in the area.

"Not that there are so many," he warned. "Sit up front, I'll drop you near the church. There's a salon de thé where you can relax. A New Yorker's idea of paradise."

He's right. The No Smoking sign is gigantic, by French standards. In the kitchen, someone's listening to Barry White, but the music is so faint you have to know the melody to actually hear it: *You're playing a game . . . it's so plain . . . you want me to win.*

The walls are lined with jars of linden honey and anchovy-fig pesto, bottles of Coteaux Varois rosé and artisanal vinegars. A cliché, perhaps, but an attractive smoke-free cliché.

A positive argument for Duncan's surrogate hairdresser potential.

The tables are tiny, and the gray-haired lady to my left is lost in her Michelin guide while her husband pours black tea from a glass pot. I feel conspicuous. The only customer not part of a cozy couple. Trying to leave a businesslike voicemail for Allie without raising my voice: "Milt's cook is coming to pick you up, but he needs advance notice—the airport's a two-hour trip. Don't worry, he's a gentleman, you'll be in safe hands. And he's cute! But you have to leave a message because I can't always answer. And don't block your number! I'll pick up if I know it's you! I'm counting on you to be here Wednesday. And remember. Milt has no idea what you're doing in Barcelona. Let's keep it that way. And don't forget to call me Suzy."

10

Should I really be alerting Allie to Duncan's looks? I feel a twinge of guilt about dangling him in front of her—without telling her the whole story—but I MUST use whatever psychological weapons I have at my disposal to get her onto that plane. Reminding her that she's expected in Provence might not be enough. She might linger in Barcelona, rush back to New York or . . . who knows with Allie?

In any case, this little slice of solitude really hits the spot. Here comes my chestnut crepe. And this glass of rosé sure beats—

I can hardly believe it.

Last month. Was I really reduced to ordering *a white wine spritzer*?

## CHAPTER TWO

# New York: A Sinner in the City

*One Month Earlier*
*Monday, June 10, 2002 Manhattan*

This afternoon, after dropping off $500 with Trish—her cut from my date with Terry—I met Jasmine for drinks at the Mark.

Dressed for a summer quickie, in a pale green wraparound skirt, uncreased linen blouse and Chanel flats, she had just finished doing a call across the street at the Carlyle. From a distance, Jasmine's a deceptively conservative brunette. Until you get within earshot. When you might also catch a glimpse of her eighteen-carat Bulgari knock-offs.

"A spritzer!" She was indignant. "When did you start drinking THAT?"

"Today, actually. Just in case." I tried not to look at her dry martini.

She swallowed some of her Grey Goose vodka, placed the cold glass on the table, and gave me a long, thoughtful once-over.

"I'm six days late!" I told her. "That makes me what? Three weeks pregnant? I haven't told Matt yet. It's too soon."

"I thought you were on the pill again."

Matt has no idea about my secret stash of birth control pills. Jasmine—and Dr. Peele—are the only ones who know. And the Duane Reade pharmacist, of course. But only Jasmine knows it's a secret.

"I was. Then I wasn't. Then I—"

"Six days? Hard to tell. At this point, you're late. That's all we know."

I shook my head. "It's never happened before. My cycle's always been as reliable—"

"As a clock," Jasmine said. "I remember. Maybe your body's taking a stand. All this on-again off-again pill-popping! So where'd you get the idea you can drink spritzers? What do you think? You're 'a little bit pregnant'?"

"As a matter of fact, yes." I tasted some bland fizz. "That's exactly what I am. One tablespoon of white wine can't possible harm a developing baby."

"No! But imagine the harm to the mother! Spritzers are so eighties." She wrinkled her nose. "I'd rather go cold turkey. Actually—" Another sip of martini, and she was almost mollified. "Any child exposed to spritzers in the womb HAS to be a moderate drinker. That's a good thing!" She frowned. "So let's say you're more than a little bit pregnant."

"You mean pregnant."

"Right. Have you decided what you'll do with your phone?"

"My business isn't for sale, if that's what you're asking."

My secret apartment is close enough to the East Side pre-schools—but not so close that I risk being spotted by the other mommies. I've got a plausible strategy for my child's education, but I still have to figure out how to avoid answering my phone without losing all my customers. The mommy track's starting to look like the mommy *tightrope*.

"You're not going to be like Trisha!" Jasmine said.

"What exactly have you got against Trish?"

"Nothing. But she married a bum! He's constantly getting fired—well, that's what she says. I sometimes wonder if he's ever *had* a job. Your husband's in a different league."

I don't like the sound of Trisha's husband either, yet feel an obligation to defend her. It's tacky to trash someone who sends you business—and there's more to it than that.

"Nobody knows what goes on in another girl's marriage," I said. "You can't judge from outside. I've never asked Trish what the deal is with her husband."

And she doesn't ask what the deal is with mine. Every marriage is based on a secret code. Married hookers respect that; single girls like Jasmine just don't get it. A call girl who's never been married feels comfortable expounding on the most excruciating details. Things you instinctively shy away from when you're married.

"You don't have to hustle the way Trish does." Jasmine reached toward the bowl of nuts. "Soon Matt will be earning enough to hire a nanny for your nanny! Let's face it, Trish stays with that guy because he IS the nanny."

"He's the father of her child," I said tersely. "What they do is none of our business."

"Whoa. You're pregnant for all of THREE MINUTES, and already you're closing ranks with the other mommies! Soon you'll be shopping for baby clothes with your sister-in-law! Have you been stroller-shopping yet?"

"I won't be discussing my pregnancy with Elspeth. She's very big on vaginal delivery."

Even though she had twins!

"Vaginal WHAT?" Jasmine looked horrified. "Where do people GET these crazy ideas?"

"Well, actually . . ." Vaginal *was* the default setting for most of human history, but I know what she means. "Childbirth isn't our biggest area of disagreement. Schooling is. Elspeth's planning on sending her kids to Dalton. When she found out I was looking into Loyola, she started talking to Matt behind my back!"

"Isn't Loyola . . . a Catholic high school? You're talking about an *embryo*."

"It's co-ed and Jesuit. We have to plan ahead," I explained. "And I need Matt's help. He has to find out if anyone at the office has a child at Saint David's. Or Sacred Heart. I want to get started at a Catholic pre-school, but Elspeth's telling Matt we should take advantage of her Dalton connections. Trying to brainwash him against my plans! I have no intention of running into Elspeth every morning and afternoon when I—"

"Hang on a sec. You'll send your kid to parochial school just to avoid your sister-in-law? You can't let her intimidate you like this!"

"Elspeth was a prosecutor," I pointed out. "Have you forgotten she worked for the DA's office before she had the twins? She's always asking me to invite my single friends to her parties. And she's trying to find a girlfriend for her favorite bachelor—that guy with the new sailboat? He's a prosecutor too! And what about Elspeth's husband? I'm trying to keep my distance from Jason," I reminded her. "Elspeth wants to know why she's never met *you*."

"You're right," Jasmine said abruptly. "We don't need Elspeth OR Jason fixating on your single friends! The less contact you have the better."

"There's no way Elspeth will even consider the pre-schools I've scoped out," I assured her. "And if she continues to oppose my commitment to a Catholic education, I have every right to avoid her. I'm protecting my pregnancy from stress!"

"Maybe you're not even pregnant." She signaled for the bill, and flipped her phone open to check the time. "But if you are?

I bet you can't have just one. Nobody has just one these days. Especially bankers."

Amazing. There is no aspect of mating that eludes Jasmine's expertise. And the less she knows about it firsthand, the more opinions she has. How many years have I known her? In all this time, she's had a grand total of one relationship. Jasmine has never even lived with a man.

"Matt's not just any banker," I told her. "He's my husband, and he cares about my well-being."

"I always said he was a catch! But when you start reproducing your DNA, you enter the primal rat race. You have to keep up." She pulled a small mirror out of her tote bag. Using the bag as a shield to hide the mirror, she peeked quickly at her lipstick. "If you think you'll have time to see your johns on the sly, you're deluding yourself. In case you haven't noticed, Wall Street's experiencing a DNA boom. Bankers' wives don't do small families anymore. They're thinking Bumper Crop. They're as wedded to that reproductive plow as they are to their husbands. A lot of these mega-mommies have powerful ancestral memories. From when their great-great-grandfather was a potato farmer."

"Where did you hear all this?"

"You're too close to the situation to see it clearly. Strollers are the new handbags. And children—" she put the mirror away "—are the new potatoes. I follow all the markets, you know. Not just my own."

She might be right about handbags, but I hope she's wrong about "new" potatoes. Is she implying that the young bankers are *potato farmers*?

"And meanwhile, our business is getting more competitive every day." Jasmine smoothed out her skirt as she stood up. "You'll be keeping up appearances on two fronts. Trying to be a MILF *and* a MIFF."

Okay, I know what a MILF is. A "mom I'd like to fuck." Fertile, fit, conceivably available, but—

"MIFF?" I asked. "What the hell's a MIFF?"

As we left the bar, I realized that my phone was vibrating, but I didn't want to draw more attention to myself by answering while the uniformed staff eyed our legs. Jasmine cocked her head to one side and whispered: "A mom I *frequently* fuck." On the sidewalk, she adjusted her sunglasses and said, in that dark tone which precedes one of her flights of wisdom, "No woman can serve two masters."

A man in a very good gray suit wandered past the hotel, and she swept some hair behind her ears, with a little smirk. Losing her previous train of thought, she followed his progress to the corner of Seventy-seventh and Mad, where he turned around to gaze at us—even though his light was green. Jasmine seemed to be daring him to walk back to the hotel entrance. In summery heels (me), and ladylike flats (her), we appeared almost the same height. God knows what he was thinking. He was certainly the right age for us. A pampered sixty-something.

"Cut that out," I hissed. "We're way too dressed up for you to be doing this. The doorman's looking right at you!"

In the cab, on the way home, I checked my voicemail.

A message from Matt about our dinner plans with Elspeth and Jason. "He's got a meeting, so it'll be a threesome. Want to meet at their place?" It would be nice to have Jason at the table to dilute Elspeth, but the less I see of him, the better. Ever since I ran into him in front of my health club, following Allie around like an infatuated puppy, I've been afraid to have more than a five-minute conversation with him. As far as Jason knows, Allie's just a girl I know from Pilates class: he thinks he's protecting her secret from ME. And, if Jason finds out how much I know about his very private midlife crisis, my entire cover will be blown.

Followed by a message from Charmaine, alerting me to the status of our Seventy-ninth Street time-share: "I'm leaving at seven for an outcall. I changed the sheets, in case you need the apartment, but I have to come back for a ten-thirty." Ever since we had that disagreement about her new customers, she makes a point of giving me extra time in the apartment.

A final voicemail, from Etienne, promising to call this week with his travel plans: "I am on my way to Cologne, cocotte. When I have my schedule for New York, you will hear from me."

If I'm pregnant, I hope he shows up before I start to show. It's been almost a year since his last visit!

## Tuesday, June 11

Last night, I miscalculated.

Although I timed myself to arrive on the late side—so Matt would be there to protect me from his sister's questions—I was early. Elspeth's front door was open, which seems rash, even in Carnegie Hill with a twenty-four-hour doorman. I never leave the door ajar when I can't actually see who's coming in. As a hooker, I'm *supposed* to be paranoid. The minute you're not, other hookers think you're losing your marbles. But shouldn't Elspeth be cautious, too? When she was an assistant DA, she worked on some high-profile murder trials—what if someone with a grudge sneaks into her building? How can she be so confident of her safety?

While I stood in front of the hall mirror, powdering my nose, I could hear her, in the back of the apartment, chattering with the au pair in the twins' bedroom. One baby was making a happy gurgling sound. For the first time, I felt sure this was Bridget. Usually, my niece and nephew sound alike. The fact that they often gurgle in unison doesn't help, but this time, when Berrigan joined in, I could pick out two distinct voices. My maternal antennae must be emerging!

As I listened to the boy-girl duet, I stared at myself in the mirror, and looked for some obvious signs of impending motherhood. I suppose it's too soon, but they say your hair becomes fuller. Will I be able to throw out my Velcro rollers?

"Nancy!" Like a thief caught in the act, I jumped at the sound of Elspeth's voice. "Sit down, you look GREAT, honey, I didn't hear you come in, that's what happens," she cackled, "when you get lost in the BACK ROOM! Where's darling hubby? Mine can't make it."

"Too bad," I lied, feeling smug about my ability to avoid Jason.

As I maneuvered past the double stroller—Elspeth's "baby Hummer"—it occurred to me that strollers are more like handbags than Jasmine realizes. You fall in love with one designer's perfect model, only to find you don't really like their colors. And you can't have exactly the same bag or stroller as everyone else—especially when everyone else is your sister-in-law.

My search for a houndstooth Peg Pérego baby carriage has been fruitless, but I'm not giving up.

I intend to own this pregnancy! Unlike Elspeth, who covers all her baby furniture with gingham, I'm never allowing that stuff to darken our door—and I intend to keep working. Even though, as Jasmine says, I don't have to hustle like Trish.

I waited quietly for Matt to arrive. Jasmine's the only person who knows I might actually be pregnant. Should I tell him tonight? Maybe I'm not ready for that. *Remember when he tried to throw out an entire case of tinned tuna? To protect the developing fetus? We were still using condoms at that point!* I need to keep this pregnancy a secret for at least a month, while *I* adjust my diet. Perhaps that'll discourage him from getting so involved in the process.

While Elspeth buzzed around the living room, picking up magazines and cushions, I envisioned the magazines as petty criminals—they were being handled rather casually—and the cushions as felons. She sidled up to me with a small felon in her hand, and nudged my side with the edge of the cushion. I arched my back politely, and the cushion was completely imprisoned under my torso.

"Thanks," I said, wriggling to adjust the cushion.

"So!" She was in the kitchen now, talking at the top of her voice. "Matt said you guys are thinking about Sacred Heart! If you have a girl, I mean."

"He did?"

I was pleased to hear him put it in those terms. The other night, when we were alone, he didn't seem so convinced. Maybe he's being loyal to *us*. But, almost as soon as I had opened my mouth, I was wondering if Elspeth might be bending the truth, to hide the fact that she's campaigning AGAINST Sacred Heart, and recruiting my husband as her ally.

"Have you looked at the SAT scores?" She came out of the kitchen with a large watering can in her hand. "I applaud you both for considering single-sex education, especially if you have a girl, but you have to look at the bigger picture, and if you plan on having one child—" *I don't recall telling her that. Did Matt?* "—don't you think it'll be nice for all our kids to be at the same school? So yours won't be all alone?"

"I haven't decided—"

"We'll have a buddy system!" she continued, heading toward the window. "It'll be so much easier for us both. You know? I can pick yours up—or whatever. You'd better hurry up and get pregnant though! We don't want them too far apart! And we'll all have a chance to get to know each other better!"

By the time Matt arrived, and Elspeth had finished watering her plants, I was a nervous wreck. Strangely enough, she didn't say one word about school during our dinner at Island.

Though I tried to muffle my anxiety in crab cakes washed down with mineral water, I was beginning to feel less smug about Jason's absence. He sometimes puts in a good word for Loyola. Was he excluded from this dinner on purpose? And my husband's lateness—whose idea was THAT?

In the cab, on the way back to Thirty-fourth Street, Matt squeezed my shoulder gently.

"What took you so long?" I asked.

"What do you mean?"

"Getting to Elspeth's! I don't think we should discuss our plans with her when I'm still trying to get pregnant." As he looked into my eyes, I felt like the object of a scam. "You have no idea how insensitive she can be!"

"Come on, honey." Matt drew me closer, and I took refuge in my latest secret. "She's just having a conversation with you."

Something in his confident manner made me quite sure he was late on purpose. To please his sister, or persuade me to listen to Protestant reason.

But—what if Elspeth decides to go back to her job? Is she setting me up to become the babysitting aunt who ferries her twins home from school? Motherhood—the way *I* see it—is going to be an airtight cover for my business. The whole idea is to appear not to be working so I can work! But Elspeth may have other plans for me.

Later, I made a point of being the first in bed, so I could be asleep.

I was dozing on my side when Matt pulled back the sheet. Waiting for the cotton to slide back over my torso, I smiled and reached out. Touching him made me forget our conversation in the cab. He placed a tentative hand around my waist and lifted my pajama top. I turned around to lie on my back and pulled him toward me. His hand moved slowly across my stomach. As his

21

fingers went lower, my mood was disrupted by a troubling question. *Will the news of my pregnancy give me more leverage? Or—* horrible thought, but I have to consider it—*less?*

### Wednesday, June 12, 2002 79th Street

Today, a call from Trish, trying to persuade me to see a new customer. "I know how you feel about new people, but he's not from New York."

Last year, when Trish stopped calling, business slowed down, and I became impossible to live with.

"He's from Philly," she told me.

"Are you sure?" I asked.

Thank God Trish is calling again, because it's not easy to work at night when you're married, and most of her business is in the daytime. Her dates are kinky and tiring, but lucrative. Without them, I barely meet my quota.

You aren't a pro unless you have a self-imposed quota, you feel like a failure if you can't *make* your quota, and the heightened security in hotels has made it harder to keep up. I was starting to feel like a shadow of my single call-girl self—until I lowered my weekly quota to a level I can actually meet. Though Matt isn't aware of my job, he totally benefits when business is good, and suffers when business is slow. Perhaps not financially, but in other ways.

Come to think of it, my earnings can't possibly hurt our bottom line. Unless I get caught, which would be awful. That's why I'm afraid to see new customers—though I sometimes make an exception for Trisha's.

"Okay," I agreed. "I just don't want to run into anyone who knows my husband. Or his family."

I can't bring myself to tell Trish about Elspeth's former profession—which she could return to, if she ever runs out of

Ubermommy juice. Trish might never work with me again if she finds out my husband's sister was a prosecutor.

"I hear you," she said. "Can you bring those handcuffs? And a few changes? Something pastel and innocent for the first hour, and something bitchy for the second hour. Do you still have those black boots? The ones that lace up the back?"

This new customer sounds younger than most of our dates, which makes him risky. Older guys (like Etienne or Milt) aren't likely to be part of Matt's circle. Should I really be doing this?

"He's calling in a few days to confirm," she said. "His schedule's crazy. He might have to cancel."

I crossed my fingers, feeling torn. If he cancels, I'm off the hook. I don't want to get caught, but I don't want to turn down business—especially from Trish. This might be my last chance to really work a lot.

Time to get ready for Chip. I won't get caught seeing *him*. He's been in my book for years, a known quantity, and I knew his father for much longer—though Chip, of course, has no idea.

## Wednesday, later

When Chip walked into the apartment, the memory of his father's face was, once again, playing tricks with me. It never fails. I still miss his dad, though he's been dead almost six years. He was gentle, quick, always happy to wear a condom.

But Chip Junior is nothing like Chip Senior. In the bedroom, he's determined to get his money's worth—which means holding back for as long as possible while I straddle, doing most of the work. Just before I slid the condom on, he made some obligatory caddish noises about being "clean as a whistle, and-I'm-sure-you-are-too," in an effort to dismiss the rubber.

I, in turn, smiled pleasantly, as I always do, and made my

obligatory comment about birth control. "And," I chirped, "I'll have you know I'm *much* cleaner than a whistle."

Abandoning the chirp, switching to sultry insistence: "I want you to wear this. So I can get you inside of me. It's been too long since I felt your cock."

This routine has been going on for so long it qualifies as a tradition. I don't trust Chip around the New Girls—I mean, *real* newbies who might not have professional manners. They're liable to give in because he's good-looking (if they're softies), or lecture him about STDs until he can barely get it up (if they're sanctimonious college girls).

As I rode on his cock, I closed my eyes and played with my breasts. My nipples were getting hard. He reached up to touch. I bit my lip, made some hot little sounds, and moved his hand away, allowing it to rest on the side of my ass. I tried to keep my hands busy so he wouldn't be able to get at my nipples. There's something about his hand. He's too forceful—not a brute, just intrusive.

Sometimes it makes me think, "If this were a boyfriend." But why should I come with this jerk? All his banter about money, condoms, cleanliness—I think the only reason I see him is his father. I miss those visits.

But the involuntary connection between nipple and clitoris was making itself felt. I reached down to finger myself as he pushed his cock into me.

I won't be able to have this kind of sex for much longer. And he won't be the first customer I want to see after I—

Omigod.

How exactly do you deal with the evidence of a c-section in situations like this? *The alternative is, um.* Suddenly, my hips stopped moving. *Vaginal delivery?* Yikes.

Chip, feeling teased and slightly frustrated, began seeking his own kind of delivery. *There is just no way,* I thought, forcing myself to concentrate on his cock. *I must sort this out.* And is that why Trish has such kinky dates? So she never has to get completely undressed?

Later, as I tidied him up with a hot washcloth, I was tempted to quiz him about his children. He's got two from his first marriage, and rumor has it he's re-married, because he no longer sees girls at his apartment. The apartment, just off Park, where we've all cooed over the crayon art on Chip's bathroom wall.

If I didn't know any better, I would assume he's too waspy to send his daughter to a school like Sacred Heart, but I know more than I should. His Episcopalian dad knew me as Suzy and saw me twice a month. He sometimes talked, with a hint of exasperation, about an ex-wife who wanted their marriage retroactively annulled, so she could re-marry. That "temperamental Catholic" was Chip Junior's mother. But, if I ask Chip where his kids go to school, he'll probably think I'm trying to blackmail him.

After seeing him to the door, I retrieved five hundreds from the top of my dresser and put them in my money drawer.

It's really too bad. I can't ask any of my regulars to help me get our forthcoming child into one of the top Catholic schools! It might be what everyone else does, but asking the people you know isn't an option for me. The downside of being in this business is having to rely on my husband's connections.

Relying on Matt is safe, sane, consensual—but rather unsatisfying. I probably know more guys who are plugged into the private schools than he does, but I know them too well, in the wrong way. To Chip, I'm Sabrina: a little bit classy, a little bit slutty, perpetually twenty-five (twenty-seven, tops). If "Sabrina" were to broach the delicate matter of getting her child into a Jesuit prep school, Chip would be dumbfounded. Doesn't he come here to escape those conversations?

### Friday, June 14

This morning, as I was leaving Thirty-fourth Street, already running late for my blow-out with Lorenzo, I was ambushed. I rushed back upstairs, thankful to be wearing black jeans, and opened a fresh box of tampons. So much for that!

As I sat in the pneumatic chair, staring at my non-pregnant self in the full-length mirror, Lorenzo tousled my damp hair with his fingertips.

"What's wrong?" His thumbs were caressing my scalp. "You look . . . almost haunted."

"I'm *totally* haunted. I've spent the last ten days looking at strollers! Ordering Dr. Seuss books. Arguing with my husband about pre-schools. And worrying about how my body will look after a cesarian!"

Of course, I don't want Lorenzo to know what I was up to when the c-section dilemma introduced itself.

"Relax," he told me. "You'll ask your doctor to make the incision very low. If you start wearing a more natural look down there, your hair covers the scar. Unless—you haven't had laser, have you?"

"Certainly not."

"Good." His lips went into an opinionated pout. "Laser in the back, never in front. It's called keeping your options open. There's a time and place for everything."

Today, there's a soft layer of dark fuzz on my outer lips because I wax every three weeks. I remember how abundant my pubic hair was, during my teens. I was trying, then, to look more womanly. Is it now time to grow it back?

"How do you know so much about . . . all that?" I asked.

"It's my job." He rolled his eyes. "Hair is hair. And hair is every-where. And wherever there is some hair—" he adjusted the chair

"—I am right there. Don't haunt yourself. I'm excited for you, darling. You get to be a total diva for the next—"

"But I don't!" I said. "I just found out I'm not pregnant!"

"Not?" He pulled a hairbrush out of a drawer. "Did you—? Are you okay?"

"Oh, I don't think—you can't call it a miscarriage when you're only ten days late, can you?"

Lorenzo faced the mirror, a brush in one hand, a blow-dryer in the other.

"If you want to be dramatic," he said, "you can call anything a miscarriage."

CHAPTER THREE

# New York: The Loyal Opposition

*Friday evening Manhattan*

This afternoon, when I got to Seventy-ninth Street, I called Jasmine to announce my news. Actually, my lack of news.

"Hallelujah," she replied.

"Oh?"

"Now we can move on! You were in the seventh circle of limbo! 'A little bit pregnant' is not a good look for you. Or anyone!"

"I see."

"Either you are or you aren't," she said. "If you are, you should be drinking elderberry tonic. If you're not, have a Kir Royale, for God's sake. Not a fucking spritzer! You must be dying for a real drink. I'll meet you after my five o'clock."

I could hear Charmaine's key in the front door of the apartment.

"I don't think so," I replied coolly. Perhaps calling Jasmine was a mistake. Charmaine, in her spinning class shorts and floppy sweatshirt, disappeared into the bedroom.

"It's okay to have ONE DRINK during your period," Jasmine was saying. "Then you'll go back to cultivating potatoes with your husband. You know what I've been thinking? You should talk to your doctor about this. Isn't there some way you can tweak things in favor of conceiving a potential buyer?"

"A potential what?"

"A male child! I think we'll all be happier if you have a boy."

Christ. Not this again. If Jasmine had her way, there would be ten males for every one of us!

"I think *I'll* be happy if I deliver a healthy baby," I told her. "I really don't care whether it's a boy or a girl."

"No hooker in her right mind wants to give birth to a girl. Your *sister-in-law* might love you for it. But your *real* friends will just resent you! For spawning more competition."

"More . . . *what*? You're talking about my future children!"

"Oh." I wondered if Jasmine was coming to her senses. "I almost forgot. You're planning to send yours to Catholic school. Well, of course. Everyone knows there are no Catholic hookers!"

"I don't appreciate—"

"Listen, I almost forgot. Harry wants to see us together. Can you be here at noon on Monday?"

"Are you out of your mind?" I asked her. Does she think we can just go back to discussing business? "You have some fucking nerve!" Then I hung up.

Charmaine emerged from the bedroom, in her exercise bra and nothing else, looking startled.

"What happened? Who was that?"

"Jasmine!" I unclenched my teeth. My cellphone was starting to chime. I turned it off and threw it into my bag. "Jasmine has *crossed a line*."

"Oh." Charmaine can't raise her eyebrows because of the Botox, but the devilish expression in her eyes said it all. "Jasmine? In my opinion—"

"Don't say it," I moaned. Charmaine has kept her distance, from the moment they laid eyes on each other two years ago. But Jasmine and I have been trading dates since our twenties. She helped me when I was in trouble and needed a lawyer. "We've known each other forever," I said.

"I don't know why you put up with that girl."

Charmaine's bare pussy—lasered to match her smooth, Botoxed forehead—was staring me in the face. Her up-to-the-minute enhancements were spilling out of her exercise bra. It's not just that she's twenty-three—her entire body looks like it was invented two years ago. She really is a New Girl, in more ways than one.

"Well—" I was beginning to feel like a hypocrite, but now I wanted to change the subject "—*you* don't have to put up with her, and I don't want to talk about it."

She's too young to understand my friendship with Jasmine, but she has her own business, pays her rent on time, and never seeks my advice. She looked, for a moment, like she was on the verge of giving *me* some, and I didn't want to hear it.

When I was sure that Charmaine was completely immersed in the white noise of the shower, I checked my messages.

"Call me when your hormones stabilize. We can't let your period stop you from seeing Harry!"

What is Jasmine thinking? Does she really think I have no idea how to disguise my period? I have two diaphragms—one for each apartment—and a year's supply of cosmetic sponges from Duane Reade.

Which part of "You have some fucking nerve" does she not understand?

### Saturday, June 15

This morning, as soon as I knew Matt was safely en route to his squash game with Jason, I bolted the apartment door and turned my phone on. With my right hand, I checked my messages. With my left, I emptied the dishwasher. Etienne, now in Frankfurt, managed to intercept one of his own voicemails while I was shaking a few remaining drops of water from a miniature whisk.

"Bonjour, petite mignonne." His elderly purr was reassuring, but it brought disappointing news. "I regret this trip is delayed. I'm glad you finally answered your phone," he added. "I tried to call you from Cologne. Don't change your number!"

"Of course not," I said. "Why would I do that?"

"So many things are changing these days. I take nothing for granted. Tell me, how is New York? Do the girls still remember me? Is it true? Nobody wears high heels anymore?"

"What? Oh. Don't worry. We're all wearing heels again."

"Not just in your bedrooms?"

"Everywhere," I said with more confidence. "I wore my favorite pair to dinner the other night."

"Really! Can you describe them?"

"Not right now," I said firmly. Etienne has never been a phone freak, and I would hate to be responsible for spoiling him.

Some would say I've been guilty of that for at least five years! I don't tell other girls that I come when he goes down on me. You never know what another pro might think—or say—about a working girl having real orgasms.

"Why don't you come back to New York?" I said in a warmer voice. "We can discuss my heels in person. I might even wear them!"

"That would be my preference, cocotte. A live appearance. But—" He paused. "There is something I haven't told you. Something which prevents me from examining those pretty feet in person. Not to mention the rest of your delicious body."

Oh dear. There comes a point in every girl's career when some of her best customers start dying or faltering for reasons of age—and stop visiting. I held my breath. Not his prostate, I hope.

31

"I have tried to enter the country three times in the last eight months," he told me. "It seems my name is on one of those bothersome new lists."

Another one of Etienne's polite fictions?

"Or perhaps," he continued, "my name resembles the name of someone else who is really on this list. But you have no idea. When this sort of thing happens, reality is beside the point. I haven't been to London in six months either!"

"You're . . . on more than one list?"

"Yes," he sighed. "I can travel anywhere on the continent, as long as I don't fly! Or try to cross the channel. My American lawyer calls it House Arrest Lite."

"You have an American lawyer?"

"And a French lawyer. And a Brit. You don't want to know. I hope your life never becomes this complicated and tedious, mignonne."

"The city isn't the same without you!" I was trying to sound light-hearted.

"And vice versa!" he exclaimed. "Germany is quite boring. I promise you will hear from me when I resolve this."

As we hung up, another call was coming in. "I've been trying to reach you!" Allison, sounding breathless and distressed. "Did you get my emails? What's wrong?"

"Wrong? Nothing's wrong."

"Jasmine said you weren't feeling well."

"You can tell Jasmine I feel fine."

"Oh." Now Allie was puzzled. "Maybe I misunderstood. I thought she said 'acute medical symptoms.'"

It is just like Jasmine to assume that this rift is the result of some *biological* malfunction, when it's really a consequence of her own demented—and completely insensitive—worldview.

"I have no idea what she's talking about," I said calmly.

"Does that mean you can work?"

"Of course."

"Ron's coming over Monday, at five. He wants two girls."

"I'll be there."

"Honestly," she sighed. "I must be hearing things, because I'm sure Jasmine said you were turning down business and not answering your phone."

"Only where she's concerned."

"What . . . happened?"

"She *crossed* a *line*. And that's all I wish to say."

"Omigod, does she KNOW you feel this way? You have to tell people how you feel."

"I don't have to do anything of the sort! Jasmine is totally oblivious to anybody else's feelings, including mine. Why should I discuss them with her?" I looked at the clock and excused myself from Allie's impromptu sermon. "I have to go," I told her. "I'm making a cheese soufflé for dinner. I need to concentrate."

"It's only eleven A.M.! What time are you having dinner?"

"I've never made this before. I want to get it right."

But I don't expect Allie to understand. Her idea of cooking is opening a box of soy burger mix from the health food store and trying to turn it into a cake.

## Tuesday, June 18, 2002

Yesterday, when I arrived at Allison's apartment, her client was running late—and she was still tidying up. A pile of New York Council of Trollops T-shirts sat on her coffee table, next to some unopened bills and a stack of zines I haven't seen before. The cover of *Queer Diaspora* features a group of naked girls and guys holding up a rainbow banner: "Straight for the money! And gay for pay! Get used to it honey!" Roxana Blair, NYCOT's founder, was the only familiar face—thank God Allie hasn't been persuaded to undress for the cover of *Queer Diaspora*. Roxana's one of those out-of-the-closet zealots who believes the truth will set us free (which any sensible call girl knows to be wrong), and she's tried, many times, to recruit me because NYCOT needs more "sex workers of color."

Allison poured the zines and T-shirts into a huge Duane Reade shopping bag, along with some bright pink Safe Sex Ho buttons, condom-covered pamphlets and other political detritus from her last NYCOT meeting. Then she disappeared into the kitchen.

The transformation was impressive. Her grandmother's rosewood furniture lends a grown-up quality to the room . . . when it's not buried beneath back issues of *Whorezine*, *Rentgrrl*, and now, *Queer Diaspora*.

While Allie dressed in her bedroom, I changed in the bathroom. By coincidence, we had both decided to wear balcony bras —balconies without railings, so our nipples were completely exposed to the breeze from her living room air conditioner.

"Maybe we should turn that down," I said. "I feel like my nipples migrated to the North Pole! We'll both catch cold."

"You're right." Crossing her arms over her breasts, she scampered toward the AC in her heels and fiddled with the controls. She adjusted her shiny pink panties. "But Ron likes it cold. He's got high blood pressure!"

Allie and I have similar bodies, but her stomach has always been flatter than mine. I'm closer to a C-cup and she's closer to a B. Her pubic topiary is fuller than mine. She used to wear it shorter, but lately it's edging toward naturalism. Funny how Allie's boyfriend, who's so open-minded about her work, is also kind of bossy about her bikini line. He wants her to stop waxing altogether. Whereas Matt's quite happy leaving this policy decision to his wife.

We've never been attracted to the same guys. It's a problem and a blessing, that our lifestyles are so at odds. Despite our differences—her extreme blondeness, our opposite taste in men, her love affair with activism—we manage to see a lot of customers together. Clients like being around us. We fit. And she has enough sense to hide the "sex work" propaganda when they come over.

When the doorman announced Ron's arrival, Allie turned up the chill again. It's not my style to rush someone else's customer, but I moved him into the bedroom, away from the AC. He didn't object.

Kneeling on Allie's bed, I held his cock and teased the head with an alert nipple. As she pulled my panties to one side, I felt, on the back of one thigh, a pair of soft lips. Then her mouth got much closer to my pussy and, before I knew it, Ron was coming on my neck. Perhaps he was aiming for my breasts or my face? I wasn't sure, but I extricated myself quickly, to rinse my hair clean, while Allie took care of everything else. I had done the heavy lifting, after all.

Like most five o'clock dates, Ron had no time to linger. "I'd love to go twice," he told us. "But there's a family dinner . . ."

Allie, still dressed in her pink bra and panties, looked appropriately disappointed. "Next time!" she said, as she helped with his jacket. "You can't be late for that!"

While she saw him to the door, I stuffed my undies and heels into Ziploc bags, and tucked them under the bed. Then I changed into married hooker camouflage—slightly faded jeans and a plaid blouse.

As I walked down Eighty-fifth Street toward York, I checked my phone messages. A call from Charmaine—"The cable bill's in your condom drawer"—and another from Milt, sitting in his car: "If you get this before five-thirty, call me back, kiddo. I'm a prisoner of the Garden State Parkway for the next twenty minutes."

The sun wasn't ready to set. In my bright yellow sneakers, I felt like a small town schoolgirl playing hooky on a warm afternoon. York Avenue has that effect on you during the summer.

Damp hair brushed against my neck. Uh-oh. Will it be dry by the time I get home? This might be hard to explain! I stopped and dabbed my hair with my sleeve.

Then I heard a man's voice—"Nancy is right here"—slightly formal, yet warm and familiar, that made me turn around. Allie's boyfriend, Lucho, was standing near the entrance to Arturo's talking into his cellphone. His free hand held a slightly dog-eared copy of *The Nation*. "Of course," he said, beaming at me. "I will do that, my dear. See you at the bar."

Lucho must know I just left Allie's apartment. What do you say to a guy who's waiting for his girlfriend to tidy up after a session that you've been part of? And he obviously knows it! I stared back at him and felt myself blushing as he put his phone away.

"Lucho!" My voice was unnaturally high. "What are you—" *doing here* sounds wrong, rather hostile. As if he doesn't belong here. But he doesn't! Why can't she meet him on the West Side, where he lives?

The last thing I need is to be running into a best friend's boyfriend on the corner of York Avenue when I've just turned a trick with her, and my hair is still damp from—did he see me doing that? When he cuddles up with Allie, later tonight, my bra will be right there, in its plastic bag, hiding beneath her bed.

Suddenly, I felt naked. His polite nod was almost a bow, and there wasn't a trace of discomfort in his eyes—or flirtation, either—as he greeted me. "How are you doing, Nancy?" He gestured toward the restaurant door, as if nothing strange had just happened. "Will you join us for dinner? We can wait for Allie at the bar."

"Oh—I—um—I can't!" I said, taking in his knit tie and his summer suit. His dark wavy hair is well-managed, though it falls below his ears. I felt not just naked, but silly and immature in my jeans and sneakers. Allie must be getting a little dressed up to meet him for dinner. "I've got a loin of pork marinating in the fridge!" I exclaimed.

"Allison tells me you're a very accomplished cook." He flashed an affectionate smile. "Another night then. Perhaps we could all go out. We would both love to have dinner with you and Matt."

"I'll think about it," I said. "You know, Matt—Allie—I'm not sure about Matt's schedule."

Allie's been trying to engineer a double date with Matt and Lucho for the last six months!

Last year, when we ran into Lucho and Allie at a party, Lucho was unfailingly discreet. And Matt's always hinting that he'd like to hang out with them because, well, you don't meet a lot of trendy Latin American professors on Wall Street.

But the whole idea of Matt dining out with three people who know something he doesn't? I can't. No matter how discreet Lucho is, I can't put my husband at a table with people who know he's being deceived.

There are times when a wife must quietly become her husband's loyal opposition.

Allie doesn't get it. There's no room on her romantic hard drive for these tricky nuances of infidelity. *Because the New York Council of Trollops has taken over her personal life!* Sometimes she forgets how normal people actually live.

On days when Allie's not *working*, she's chairing NYCOT meetings, planning the next conference, or distributing condoms in Hunts Point. I used to think activism was a phase she would outgrow—until Allie met Lucho at a harm reduction conference. Any "phase" that yields a devoted boyfriend isn't something Allie can be expected to take leave of lightly. Bohemian courtship has its own rules—I'm afraid to find out what they are—but it's still courtship. It still, somehow, works, when the right people are in the right place at the right time.

A double date with my best friend and her boyfriend? It's just another one of those things everyone else does—but not me.

### Wednesday, June 19, 2002

"Honey?"

This morning, Matt was surprised to find me in the kitchen wearing cotton panties and a work-out bra. He gave me an appreciative but quizzical look. I'm almost never up first.

I was in a cautious mood, because the last time I had an appointment with my ob-gyn, Matt wanted to be there too. I will never get used to seeing other women's husbands in a gynecologist's waiting room—is nothing sacred anymore? And I refuse to contribute to this trend.

"I forgot to organize the coffee last night!" I lied. Matt's coffee is a built-in excuse whenever I need to rise early. As I filled the coffee maker, he came closer. I felt his bare skin against my back, boxer shorts against my prim white briefs. "There's a new class I want to try."

His hard-on was distracting, and so was his right hand on my panties. I was tempted to turn around, but a quick glance at the clock made me stop. *Dr. Peele's office agreed to squeeze me in early.*

Matt kissed my neck while the coffee brewed, and teased the cotton-covered parts of me with his finger. I was beginning to swell and relax. *If I'm late for Dr. Peele, she'll make me wait two hours. I'll have to cancel my quickie with Ted. And Dr. Peele's receptionist will be furious.*

"Your exercise class can wait," he whispered. "There's another one tomorrow. And you want this."

"I—I do, but we can't," I told him. "My period . . ." Though it just ended, I insinuated that it was just beginning. As I turned around, I felt his hands in my hair. "Can I do this instead?" I tried to lower myself to the floor and felt my panties tugging against my pussy. My mouth was already half-open. I felt like that playful Mafia wife in *Goodfellas* who takes care of her husband in *her* kitchen.

"No." He was holding my upper arms, firmly enough to stop me from moving. I was breathing harder. "It's better when you have to wait."

"But—"

I was beginning to regret that my period "just started." I like to think I can do anything I want with my period—hide it, fake it, or have it. Now I've outsmarted myself, and waiting three days seems more like an ordeal than a successful parry.

Though I was on time for my appointment, I was battling the sensations of unsatisfied arousal as I changed into my paper gown. The stirrups on Dr. Peele's examining table are never left uncovered. Today, they were dressed in soft, inviting cashmere booties which I was eager to feel against my bare feet. When she entered, I was already on the table, day-dreaming about what might have been if Matt hadn't stopped me from getting on my knees. Though I felt pampered by the booties and tantalized by our skirmish, it's just not possible to stay turned on during a transvaginal sonogram.

"Is there any such thing as a *mini*-miscarriage?" I asked. "My last period was ten days late. Was I twenty-four days pregnant?"

"That's hard to say." She was looking at the screen. "We may never know. Long cycles are more common than miscarriages." I felt the probe moving to the left. "Which are also common," she added.

"So, if I have a c-section . . ."

"Yes?"

"I've been thinking about the scar. How low can you make the incision?"

"Most women find that a bikini covers the scar."

"Is it true it can double as a kind of tummy tuck?"

"There are easier ways to obtain a tummy tuck. Not that you need one."

"Thanks, but—" When I turned my head, I was staring at a portrait of blond identical triplets playing in a garden. "—can you actually get rid of the scar?"

The probe moved to the right.

"Nancy." Dr. Peele withdrew the probe. "Childbirth is not cosmetic surgery." I *suppose* she's right. "We can discuss vaginal deliv—"

"I don't think so!" I tried to sit up.

"Don't panic." Dr. Peele was holding up a speculum. "One more thing to do here." I tried to relax. "Breathe through your mouth. Good. Many women are having voluntary c-sections. It's safer when you can prepare for a c-section. But you have to realize, it's major surgery. And some of your questions should be answered by a dermatologist."

I glanced at the triplets, then averted my eyes. "Maybe I need to postpone this project."

"You mean pregnancy?"

"Yes." When she removed the speculum, I took my feet out of the stirrups and sat up slowly. "When I thought I was pregnant, I was excited. But when my period started? I was disappointed at first, and then I was so relieved!" Dr. Peele was perched on a stool, looking at my medical records. "The other day, I was visiting a girlfriend." I bit my lip.

"Go on," she said. "How many children does your friend have?"

"None. And she's single."

"Ah." She placed the paperwork to one side. "I think I see."

"I was walking down the street," I told her. "It was so nice out! I felt sort of naughty." Dr. Peele doesn't know anything about my job, but I told her what I could of the truth. "And I felt free. I was wearing my size four jeans. It took me six months to get back into those!"

"And?"

"I don't think I want to be pregnant. I want to wear my size four jeans!"

"Then you should not be. Pregnancy is more dangerous for your health than being a size four."

Dr. Peele—closer to a fourteen than a four; founder of an A-list fertility boutique—said *that*?? I feel so vindicated.

On my way to Seventy-ninth Street, I stopped at Duane Reade to drop off my new prescription. I had just enough time to change into a miniskirt and get ready for Ted's mid-morning blow job.

### Thursday, June 20, 2002

A call from Milt. For the first time in weeks, he insists on seeing me solo when I want him to spring for a threeway! I was hoping to pay Allie back for Monday. Normally, he's more than willing to be my currency du jour. But not today. "We have some important business to discuss." More important than MY business? But I didn't protest. Sexual book-keeping should always be invisible.

### Later

I was wrapping a hot post-coital washcloth around Milt's cock when he announced, "My house in France is almost done. You should come over with me."

"With you?" I adopted a dreamy tone and pressed the damp

cloth against his lube-drenched groin. Some girls long to visit the Riviera with a rich guy in exchange for massive amounts of shopping money. I fear being away from New York, beholden to some guy who has paid for an oversized chunk of my time, unable to retreat from a diplomatic nightmare. "I should?"

"Yes!" His hand stroked my rump. "It would be nice to have this in my bed," he mused. "Your skin's so smooth. And you can practice your French." As he felt my body pulling away, he said, "Don't worry. I promise not to abuse my privileges!"

"What exactly are you planning on my behalf?" I asked with a skeptical smile.

"I'm going to spend a few weeks in the new house," he explained. "Make sure everything's in working order. Get out of my wife's hair for awhile. They're working on the pool as we speak. You'll have a great time breaking it in with me."

"It's in the Luberon?"

"An hour and a half from Nice. Right next to a vineyard . . . off the beaten track . . . we had the pool rebuilt."

"But I don't swim! I'm not much of a poolside girl, you know, and I'm allergic to sunshine. Are you sure I'm the . . . houseguest you have in mind?"

"Of course I'm sure! Stay in the shade, then. It's a fully equipped house. I just installed a new exercise room. I converted one of the dairy sheds into a media hut. There's a nice library with a fire-place . . . What's wrong?" he asked.

"You might wear me out! I need my beauty sleep, eight hours minimum, and I don't think I can sleep in the same bed as—"

"You'll have your own bedroom," he promised. "I may be a dog, but I'm a well-trained dog. If you want, you can sleep in a separate *wing* with the door locked. This place has more bedrooms than we need. You'll have first choice."

"How many bathrooms?"

"Who can remember? Six? Anyway, the upstairs rooms all have their own."

"They do?" My body relaxed a bit. "The next time you invite a girl to your house, tell her about the en suite bathrooms upfront, Milt. You'll save her a lot of anxiety."

"That's my point!"

"Your point?"

"You're the one who knows how to talk to girls! And I'll make it worth your while."

"Really? Should I find someone to keep us company?"

"Now you're talking. She'll have a very nice room." Milt sat up and looked at his watch. "I'm flying to Nice via Paris. I can try to get you both onto my flight or—"

"I have to think about it," I warned him. "I haven't promised you anything."

"I know. But the last time you said that . . ." My favorite customer appeared to be suppressing a smirk. "You came around to my point of view. Remember?"

"Now look here!"

"Never mind," he laughed. "Take your time and think it through. Tell me what it's going to cost. I'm sure you have to get all your ducks in a row and make a few calls. I leave the third member of our house party in your capable hands. It's all up to you."

"My fiancé—" I began. "I can't just go to France without—"

Milt placed his hand on top of my wrist. "It's okay, kiddo. I know you've got a life." His touch was light and reassuring. "So do I. When you have it figured out, call me." He reached for his boxers. "That boyfriend of yours doesn't know how lucky he is. A two-week break will keep the guy on his toes."

Milt doesn't realize that Matt's my *husband*. Would he still do business with me if he knew?

On my way out of the elevator, I spotted Charmaine in the vestibule, coming in from the street.

Ten feet away, the super (who isn't "supposed" to know she lives here) was hauling a recycling bin toward the back of the building. Charmaine's a perfectionist about the apartment. Given that we could both be evicted for violating the rent stabilization laws—never mind the business we're conducting—she's the model roommate. As she passed me in the hall, I nodded silently, and she winked in the deliberate, labored way Botox-users must when seized with the impulse to wink. Every facial gesture's a major decision with that girl!

If I take this trip with Milt, should I bring Charmaine? I can count on her to keep all my secrets. But first, do I really want to spend two weeks with a customer?

I've never spent more than a night with a john, and overnight calls make me claustrophobic. Milt assumes I've taken lots of well-paid journeys to far-flung destinations—that's what high class call girls do, isn't it? I won't puncture his illusions by telling him about my origins. The Yellow Pages escort agency that got busted by the NYPD. A handful of hotel bars. And the nightclub (almost in Mayfair, not quite) where I hustled champagne. I've come a long way from that, but never lost my taste for the quick finite transaction.

In a perfect world, I'd rather turn five tricks in one day than spend five hours with the same date. My clients don't realize this, because (they think) a girl who prefers quickies can't hold a conversation, pass in polite society, or disguise the fact that she's rushing you.

It's not that simple. When you see five customers in one shift, you're building your business. Each new date—even a guy you barely tolerate—makes you less dependent on any given client. Everyone has a favorite john, the phone call that makes you smile, but that doesn't mean you can trust him with your future.

You see more of the world and retain more independence, when you're in hustle mode. But you can't stay like that forever. The price of success is losing some freedom. I now have a handful of good reliable dates I can't afford to lose. I certainly can't start over again in this business! And this is what I actually wanted when I began my career. So I have no business regretting my comfortable predicament. Do I?

### Later still

Putting business aside, I'm never at my best when vacationing with a man. That trip to Wyoming with my husband last summer? It felt rather crowded, actually.

Thank God New York bankers only take two weeks' vacation!

CHAPTER FOUR

# New York: Jamais Provence?

*Friday, June 21, 2002*

This morning, two messages on my cellphone from Milt, playing it cool while applying a subtle flattering pressure. "Did I tell you how good you're looking? You can wear your bikini indoors, kiddo. I'm ordering a busload of poolside umbrellas, just in case you decide to honor me with your presence."

Minutes later, he called back, sounding a more practical married note. "Can't talk this weekend, though. In-laws! Get in touch Monday."

Can I really get away with such a prolonged session chez Milt? It might, as Milt says, be good for my relationship with Matt— but only if I have a convincing alibi. (Spa vacation with one of my girlfriends? Minibreak *en famille*? But where? Pretend to be in the Caribbean when I'm really in the south of France? *No, I don't think so.*)

This calls for a consultation with Liane. There are times when you need a madam's friendship more than you need her business.

## Later

Must break down my current dilemma. What to tell husband? How to avoid flying with customer, so he won't find out real name? Or age? (Can't let Milt see my passport!) But the first thing I need to sort out is the third person in our—in Milt's—bed. I can't do this trip to Provence alone—now that Milt's on Viagra!

Sometimes I wish my favorite john were an easy hand job. One of those customers you can do in your sleep. You have to "dance with the guy that brought you," and Milt, for better or worse, is that guy. Long before I met my husband, there was Milt, reliable and financially faithful. Three years ago, when I had that huge tax bill, I was afraid my problems would just scare Matt away. Milt came to my apartment with all the cash I needed, in one payment. We called it a season ticket. In return, he persuaded me to do something . . . unprofessional. Then we bickered about whether to call it a pound or a gram of flesh.

When I was alone with him, I allowed Milt to kiss me—a real kiss, just a few times—but I prevented this from becoming a habit. After a steady diet of acrobatic threeways, he seemed to forget we had ever kissed.

Until yesterday!

Is Milt hoping I'll bend my rules again? Do something unprofessional when I'm off the grid? Away from Manhattan?

Even so, he'll never try to kiss in front of another working girl. That much he understands. And his appetite's too much for one woman to handle on a daily basis. Clearly, I can't even consider Provence without some very appealing reinforcements.

The question is: Who?

## Later still

Charmaine?

Milt's only heard about her, and never pushes me to arrange a session, thank God. Two weeks in the company of my bionic twenty-something roommate might get him looking at my body in a whole new way.

She's methodical, easy to work with—and much too ambitious for this gig. But Charmaine knows all the New Girls. For a finder's fee, she can introduce me to someone brand new.

How tempting to bring in a newbie—someone who doesn't yet have much business sense—to do the heavy lifting. Everyone has to be that girl at some point, and we've all paid our dues.

Is it my turn to collect?

When *I* was the New Girl, I met a thirty-something call girl who took a fifty percent cut. Belinda would literally walk around the bedroom in her underwear and heels, smoking a joint while I did the session. I was the energetic, naive bait, willing to get on top of a customer and wear myself out, by riding up and down while faking one orgasm after another. A more diplomatic girl makes an effort to arouse her own regulars, and takes a smaller cut—forty percent might do it—just to keep a hard-working apprentice in a good mood. It's only ten percent less, but it can make all the difference to a young hooker's attitude. Within two months, I got wise to Belinda, did the math, and started slipping my number to some of her best clients.

Perhaps a New Girl isn't such a good idea after all. Better to do business with another girl who knows how hard you work to cultivate your regulars. Someone like . . .

Jasmine? Out of the question.

There's Trish, of course. If any girl can micromanage a two-week escape from two different husbands and two different zip codes, it's Trish. As with Charmaine, I trust her to keep all my secrets, but—having even more to lose—she's even more trustworthy.

But way too kinky.

Once every ten years, a pro-domme like Trish encounters a manageable sleaze like Milt and flips his switch, turning him into one of her legendary creatures. An insatiable perv who can't get enough pain, whether it's his own or somebody else's. Who knows what Trish might do to Milt's psyche if I allow them to meet! I can't afford to find out. Could she transform him into one of those mentally exhausting slaves? A golden shower addict?

He already takes too long to come. *That* I can handle, but kink takes its toll in a different way.


### Later

As my insecurities climb the wall of my pragmatism, like so much virtual ivy, it's all becoming much too clear. There's only one person unambitious enough, pretty enough, yet old enough to bring on this trip. She's safely in her thirties, and she won't steal my best client or warp his mind.


### Monday, June 24, 2002

This morning, when Allie returned my call, I was in the computer nook, dusting my husband's college souvenirs.

"Have you heard from Jasmine?" she asked.

I aimed the can of compressed air at Matt's shot glass collection.

"No," I said. "Why would I?"

"You're not still—you have to make up with her!" Allie insisted.

"What are you talking about?"

"She's—she asked about you yesterday."

"Oh? What did she want to know?"

"Something to do with your hormones," Allie said in a sheepish voice.

"And THAT'S SUPPOSED TO MAKE ME WANT HER AS A FRIEND? Cunty remarks about my hormones?"

"They weren't c—it wasn't like that. Stop using that word!"

"Is there a better one?" I asked.

"It's just her way of saying she misses you! Anyway, I'm sick of running interference."

"Then give it a rest. Nobody asked you to."

"But . . ." There was a strange pause. Allie's voice was wobbling out of control. "Sh—*she* did. She asked me to call you and find out—I don't think Jasmine was held enough as a child! She has trouble expressing her feelings!"

"I'll call her," I lied, anxious to stem the teary tide. As usual, Allie's feelings come first—even when she's delivering an insult from another girl.

"Please do that!" she begged me. "I've seen Harry at her place, twice, and I think he misses you. I don't think I'm really his type."

"Well," I reminded her. "You're Milt's type. Don't you want to know why I called you?"

After outlining the situation in Provence, I offered a special incentive: "I'm only taking twenty percent. I really don't mind." Allie, at least, wasn't on the verge of tears anymore.

"Omigod," she sighed. "I really wish I could."

"What do you mean?" I said. "You have to! I can't go to France alone. And you'll have so much extra cash when you come back, you'll be able to spend an entire month doing NYCOT stuff."

"I know, but NYCOT needs me in Barcelona!"

"Barcelona? What the—"

"It's the international AIDS conference. Bad Girls Without Borders is hosting a shadow conference, and Roxana's chairing a panel on medical ethics, so I have to present for NYCOT during mobility rights."

"Can't you work around this? There must a way."

"My panel's right in the middle of the AIDS conference! I can't just—I'm sorry, Nancy! Roxana NEEDS me, I'm the only person she trusts at this point. She's counting on me to represent NYCOT at Barcelona. Sex workers are coming from all over Europe and Asia! I gave her my word! Besides," she said, "we don't want to disappoint the Cambodians."

I might have known—when I actually need Allie to come through, she's got a date with Roxana to save the world.

"And," she said, in a breathless voice, "it's a historic moment for me. I'm finally part of the solution!"

"Part of—what did you just say?"

"*Sex workers are part of the solution.* That's our new T-shirt! It's all part of our HIV awareness campaign," she explained. "We're bringing a hundred T-shirts to Barcelona! Roxana picked out the font, and I chose the colors."

They must be very pink.

And now they're part of a much larger problem!


### Later

This afternoon, as I scrolled through my inbox, I spotted one of Darren's boyish BlackBerry messages:

*re: as marvin gaye likes 2 say . . .*
*LET'S. so, are we ON? Thursday, 3:30?*

While I typed a businesslike e-ply—

*ok, I GET IT. Confirming 3:30!*

—a rambling apology arrived from Allie.

*Re: HIV & me!*

*Hey Nancy? I'm sooooo sorry about the conflict with our shadow conference! Roxana says it's crucial for NYCOT to be on lots of panels because the Europeans don't appreciate how international we are. It's, you know, the most global HIV event in the world! The Russian outreach workers are coming. There's going to be a very radical keynote address about HIV research from Miguel X. He's a former "rent boy" from Brazil, and it's MY JOB to introduce him! Gretchen was supposed to, but something happened, I don't know what exactly, but now I REALLY have to be there because we want a New York sex worker to introduce Miguel. Pleeeeease tell Milt: I really wish I could be in two places at once but I have to be at the HIV shadow conference!*

Does Allison think she's the only girl in town? Of course, I'll tell Milt nothing of the sort, about Allie OR this conference. When I DO find a girl for him, he must never suspect she's my second choice. As for Allie's conference, Milt must never hear about her activism.

The very thing that makes Milt feel safe—a successful call girl with a secret life, quietly snowing polite society—is also what turns him on. Allie's attempt at a militant new look, complete with HIV slogans, would surely have the opposite effect?

A huge message from my mom with a slightly misleading subject header:

*Re: Normandy Postcard*

Brief—with enough JPEG attachments to fill a scrapbook.

*Having lovely time looking at farmhouses. Let me know what you think. Currently rather enthused third from top. Take note goats and half-timber. Sebastian's at Renascent House again. Thought you wd like to know. Best decision he's made this year, I think. Dodie sends her best. Love to Matt.*

Mother does what she can to put a positive spin on my little brother's crack problem without getting pulled in. Last month, when he tried to move into her B&B in the Welsh countryside, she closed the house and took off on a road trip to Mortagne-au-Perche with her best friend Dodie. Ever since Grandmummy died, Mother's siblings have been renovating or selling up. Not one of these rustic Norman properties is less than twice the size of her farmhouse in Wales. All those rumors about the will, which Mother won't discuss, may actually be true. And her timing couldn't be better, given Sebastian's rehab needs.

An email from Liane—at seventy-something, still newly excited about the internet—startled me:

*Bernie's in town! He's on fire to see you, dear. I know JUST how to spice up your visit to Provence. Will you be near St-Tropez? I have a number for you. Let me know when you get this message. I'm trying to add a return receipt but the silly thing won't cooperate!*

Liane, who began turning tricks when call girls had rotary phones, has had email for less than a year. It makes me nervous to see her talking so freely about business while she's still learning how to send messages. Yesterday, when I called to ask for her advice about Milt, I never imagined she would be careless enough to talk about my plans in email. How can I tell her this isn't what you'd expect from a reputable madam? Lectures about discretion and etiquette have always been HER métier. Besides, she's older than my mother!

## Tuesday, June 25, 2002

Today's session with Bernie was only one part of Liane's solution. As Bernie "introduced me" to the rigors of sex on my hands and knees, Liane was taking a call in the other room from her contact in St-Tropez.

For a few years, Bernie's been under the impression that he's my first—or only—customer. That said, he's not entirely deluded, since he's one of the few who knows about my marriage. Liane raised our fee on the grounds that it was the only way he could coax me out of newlywed bliss for an hour.

When we met, I was supposed to be a college student—now I'm a twenty-something bride married to her college boyfriend. His ideas about college girls and young couples must have been formed thirty years ago watching porno movies about wet co-eds. As I steadied myself on the edge of Liane's bed, I slid my hand across the sheet, so Bernie could see my wedding band.

"You need to get fucked," he told me. "I can tell. Does your husband ever take you from behind?"

"Oh! Not yet," I said in a demure voice. "We haven't tried that. I think he's afraid to hurt me."

"He doesn't know what a hot little cunt you've got," Bernie muttered. He was thrusting quickly, and I reached underneath to discreetly check on his condom. At this point, I was glad the engagement ring was tucked into my make-up bag. "That's right, play with your clit, baby. I'll bet he has a big cock, though. Does he know how much you like to suck cock?"

His hand was resting on my right buttock, and I felt a light pat that seemed to flirt with the idea of a spanking.

"Y . . . yesssss," I moaned. "He does! I love sucking his cock . . ." When Bernie collapsed against me with a loud gasp, I held onto the condom and wriggled away from him, hoping my precautionary measures wouldn't seem too professional.

After seeing Bernie to the door, Liane burst into the bedroom, looking unusually animated. I was still dressing.

"Isabel is your answer," she said. "She's got a new apartment in St-Tropez and a group of lovely new girls! You must call her before you fly. This is a *much* better choice. Allison would have been a mistake, dear."

"A mistake?" I adjusted the zipper on the side of my dress, and followed her into the living room, where a pot of mint tea was brewing. "Allie would have been ideal!" I protested, though I didn't tell her *why* Allie's unavailable. "She's someone I know and trust."

Liane's enthusiasm is making me nervous. What's happened to her innate insularity?

"How do we—" sounds nicer than *you* "—know Isabel's discreet enough?" The chatty emails. Her new contacts in St-Tropez. Do I detect a loosening of standards? It's worrying to think that Liane, of all people, would let an economic slump affect her old-school values. "I hope you don't mind me asking, but it can't be safe for me to do business with someone *you've* never met."

"Dear, I don't mind at all." Liane, in her favorite armchair, leaned forward, extending a delicate, tapered hand toward the teapot. "Some girls are much too greedy to stop and ask the right questions." As she poured, a diamond bangle sparkled discreetly against the sleeve of her blouse.

"I'm glad you care," she said. "That's why we're talking. After my girlfriend Hilary—" Liane looked away for a moment. "She was a little older than I was, and lived most of the year in Cannes.

We sent each other a lot of business back then . . . You've met some of Hilary's people, you know. Isabel bought her business. Hilary moved back to Edinburgh to take care of her aunt." I wonder if there was more to Hilary's departure than her ailing relative. Is she still alive? "Anyway." Liane smiled gently at her teacup, then looked up. "We can trust Isabel. She moved to France a few years ago, and sends me new business sometimes. Hilary always liked her. They met in London."

"Isabel doesn't have a website, does she?"

"I can't imagine why she would!" Liane said. "Dear, why are you always talking about these websites? It seems to be an obsession with you."

"Because! That's what so many people do these days. You never know if they're advertising behind your back, and not telling you. Imagine the risk!"

"People do what they have to do, and we mustn't judge. But," Liane insisted, "we don't know anybody who would have to do that!"

Oh yes we do, but Liane would freak if she knew about Charmaine's site.

"Well," I explained. "Some girls have a very *nice* website, and they're careful about meeting new clients. But you never know *how* careful. Do you?"

"No," Liane agreed. "But there would be no reason for Izzy to do that. She inherited Hilary's customers. And this is much better for you! If this gentleman's an important client, you should keep him entertained with girls who won't be calling when he returns to New York. Staying in that house with him might give Allison ideas."

She paused to refill my cup.

"Men will be men," she said. "Don't take your best people for granted, and don't underestimate your best friends. Allison might grow jealous of your good fortune. What if she tattles to your husband? Or your client? Did you say he's in the dark about your marriage? Isabel doesn't know you're married, and her girls won't know a thing about you. It's dangerous to rely on a girl who's close to you."

Madams are sometimes hard to read. Is Liane promoting Isabel because she owes her some business? Or because she wants to remold me into the best mini-madam I can be?

"There's a lot at stake," she pointed out. "Izzy will provide the gentleman with variety. That's what keeps your relationship with him stable and secure." She reached into the pocket of her long slim skirt, and handed me a small white card. On one side, in her graceful handwriting, a phone number. No name.

"This makes me quite nostalgic!" she said. "Hilary was a beautiful girl in her prime. When we strolled up and down the Croisette in our summer dresses, everybody used to stare at us. She had a friend from Monaco who stayed at the Hôtel du Cap at Antibes. He sent a car, and I went for a week. It's wonderful to be in your thirties, still passing for twenty-five!" Liane sighed happily. "Make the most of it, dear. Of course, it's up to you, but Isabel's expecting your call."

Exiting Liane's building, I felt my hair wilting in the damp air. As I walked toward Madison, I checked my phone and discovered two impatient voicemails from Trish: "That guy from Philly? He just called from the St. Regis. Call, okay? He wants to see you!"

It's unprofessional to keep hoping he'll cancel again, but I don't trust new customers under forty. Trish has only seen him once or twice. How does she know he lives in Philadelphia? What if he's some married Wall Streeter? Maybe I've met his wife at one of Matt's corporate barbeques. So many of these guys fudge their whereabouts, to protect their own house of cards, never realizing they might be endangering ours!

"Can you make it tomorrow at noon? I don't have anyone else who's your type, and he's totally fixated on Asian!"

Yikes. If a customer's counting on a girl to supply my type, it seems inconsiderate—downright rude—to ignore her pleas. Especially when I'm her only Exotic.

## Wednesday morning, June 26, 2002

At six A.M., Matt got out of bed to meet one of *his* clients. My head started buzzing with the logistics of a kinky nooner in midtown involving three changes of costume. I couldn't even *pretend* to sleep, so while he showered, I started the coffee.

I was standing in the kitchen, in PJs and bare feet, chopping an apple, when my husband appeared in the doorway wearing a towel around his waist. "Honey," he protested. "I'm having *breakfast* with this guy at his hotel."

He looks disarmingly heroic like that, but I forced myself to overlook his dewy biceps—and his slightly damp chest hair.

"When you're meeting a client at this hour, you want to keep an eye on your glycemic index." I handed him a vitamin pill and a small glass of pear juice. "Where's he staying?"

"Peninsula." He swallowed his juice. "What's wrong?"

"Nothing." The Peninsula's practically next door to the St. Regis. Should I be doing hotel calls at this point in my marriage? Trish has her own worries, but running into her husband at a Manhattan hotel isn't one of them. Thank God it's a breakfast meeting! I spooned some sheep's milk yogurt into a bowl. "This'll prevent your blood sugar from crashing."

"Is that?" Matt peered into the bowl. "Some kind of cereal?"

"Two chopped brazil nuts, half an apple and a tablespoon of yogurt," I said, daring him to ignore my nutritious snack. "Now you'll be totally alert when you meet him. If your client's still waking up," I added, "so much the better!"

He chewed slowly and gazed into my eyes—a bemused, longing look that made me forget my job, my monthly quota, and today's obligations . . . for about two minutes.

Now to marshal my resources.

Those black lace-up boots are truly a pain—I worry about lacing them too tight against the back of my thighs—but they are, as Trish points out, effective. I always need help adjusting them, and guys appreciate it when you've got a gimmick.

Charmaine's Wednesday guy is pathologically prompt, sometimes early. Must get to Seventy-ninth Street NOW.

## *Wednesday, later*

When I arrived at Seventy-ninth, Charmaine, dressed in lace bicycle shorts and a matching navy bra, was vacuuming the living room carpet.

I closed the bedroom door so I could concentrate. Then I put my boots in a large Duane Reade bag, which I placed at the bottom of yet another bag. A big purple Bergdorf Goodman shopping bag is perfect for getting a pair of thigh-high boots into a midtown hotel without arousing the security guard's curiosity. Makes me look less like a working girl, more like an out-of-town guest on a spending spree. (Duane Reade bag screams Local Schlepper—a tactic that should only be used when trying to throw your *husband* off the scent.)

I packed some lingerie—innocent pastels for our first hour, vampy black corset for the second—and a few pairs of colorful strappy heels. My final touch was a convincing layer of white tissue paper. Now I really look like I've been shopping. Then I changed into a loose ladylike blouse, soft black pants, and low heels—the kind you wear to go shopping. I was ready, or so I thought, for a wrinkle-free journey in the midday heat.

My first miscue was an SUV-wielding cabbie who thought I

really was an out-of-towner, confusing the St. Regis with the Regency. "No!" I insisted. "I know where I'm going! How long have you been driving?"

"A week," he said. "Where is the Regis?"

"I'll show you." I was trying to locate the pillbox in my make-up bag so I could hide my rings. "Don't take Second Avenue!" Instead, I stashed my diamond ring and my wedding band in a case of powder. When we arrived at Fifty-fifth Street, I felt so guilty about my frantic, bossy directions that I overtipped. As I struggled to get out—still not used to the heavy, sliding doors on these new cabs—the pressure on one fingernail made me squeal with pain.

I adjusted my sunglasses and managed to glide past the doormen into the lobby. I've executed this elementary move thousands of times in my career, but everything about this day was conspiring against my nerves. Matt's meeting across the street. My fears concerning Trisha's new customer. My bag of incriminating outfits. My lack of sleep. My newly cracked fingernail.

And now, to my horror, talking urgently on his cellphone, scanning the lobby with expectant eyes—Elspeth's husband, Jason! My brother-in-law was standing in the lobby of the St. Regis, guarding a thick, boxy briefcase, and peering at the entrance. I froze for a second, but he was too involved in his conversation to spot me in the crowd.

Grateful to be wearing my shades, I turned quickly, and walked as casually as I could. My heart began to race. Underneath my demure blouse, I was perspiring. Now I was in a corner where he couldn't see me. I pulled out my phone so I could pretend to be engrossed, and looked up cautiously. Jason was pacing while he talked, looking toward—no, away—yes, away from me. Thank God!

But now, he was deciding to sit down in one of those red chairs! And he was putting his phone away, staring around the lobby with a sense of purpose that made me want to run. Instead, I forced myself to breathe slowly. I turned again so he wouldn't see my face, and pretended to be deeply involved in a phone call of my own.

I can't get to the elevator without walking right by him! What if I call his cellphone repeatedly? I have a blocked number, he'll never know it's me. Get him distracted. I could sneak past while he tries to figure out what's wrong with his phone.

But I don't actually have Jason's cellphone number! We never have any reason to talk, outside of his living room or mine, damn it.

Jason reached into his briefcase, pulled out a copy of *American Lawyer* and settled into his chair. His legs relaxed as he studied the magazine. I studied my route to the elevator, while trying to look like a cellphone user studying her missed calls. Jason picked up his phone again, and the magazine went back into the brief-case. He was looking in my direction. I bent over my shopping bag, so my hair would cover my face, and fiddled with the tissue. A bulky man in a suit—security, for sure—began walking toward my corner of the lobby.

If it weren't for my brother-in-law, I could face down the secur-ity, as I've done in the past, and have them call the room. But— what choice did I have? I walked quickly toward the hotel entrance, making sure Jason would only see my back. I could feel security closing in as I reached the front door. When I hit the street, I walked faster, afraid of what might happen if I made the mistake—like Lot's wife—of looking back.

When I reached Fifth Avenue, I hopped into a cab. "Thirty-fourth and First," I said, without thinking. As we neared First Avenue, I suddenly realized—I can't bring this bag into my home! "I'm sorry," I told the cabbie. "I have to change my destination. Can you take me to Seventy-ninth and First?" *The one place where*

*I feel safe, but I can't go there right away—Charmaine's seeing her regular.* "Ummmm." Staring at my compromised fingernail, I amended my trip once more. "I'd better go to York Avenue instead."

Not until I was safely installed in the waiting area of the nail salon did I realize: OMG. I have to call Trish! How could I have forgotten to call her from the cab? As soon as I turned it on, my phone began chiming.

"Where are you?" Trish said in a low voice.

"I'm—I had a terrible thing happen!" I explained. "I can't really say—I'm in the nail salon—"

"THE NAIL SALON?"

"It's not what you think—I saw someone in the lobby—I had to avoid—and I panicked—I had to come here because I can't get back into my apartment and since my nail got—"

"YOU'RE GETTING YOUR FUCKING NAILS DONE?" Trish was talking over me. "HOW COULD YOU FORGET ABOUT OUR SESSION?"

"No!" I said. "Please listen—I have to call you back—wait, wait." I got up, slid the purple shopping bag into a corner, and headed for the door, so I could talk on the sidewalk, away from the other customers. "I saw somebody in the lobby—I couldn't—"

"I don't care what happened! I've been here since noon, and you can't even be bothered to CALL me? It's almost one o'clock! What kind of—is this how you do business?"

"You know it's not! I was so scared I forgot to call! My brother-in-law—"

"I wasn't born fucking yesterday!" Is Trish yelling like this in front of her client? Omigod. "Whatever your fucking excuse is, this is the last straw, okay? Lose my fucking number, you stupid bitch!"

"But—"

"Don't ever call me again! I will have you fucking blacklisted—"

I had to hang up. When I returned to the waiting area, and my perfectly organized bag of tricks, I was trembling with fear and shame.

### Later still

How could I screw up so badly? It's not the first time I've experienced Trisha's temper. If only I had called from the cab! She might have listened, tried to finesse things.

What was I thinking? My problem is—I wasn't. I was reacting. Like an amateur. Like a part-timer! Reacting to the immediate crisis when I should have been thinking about the bigger picture. This is what I'm known for. Thinking ahead. What Liane says. "Asking the right questions."

Christ.

Am I losing my professional edge?

### Even later

And if I've lost it, can I get it back? Or is it gone for good?

My husband, exhausted from a day of successful, back-to-back meetings, is snoring in the bedroom, blissfully unaware of my insomnia. Not to mention my catastrophic afternoon, and the career path that got me here.

To think that I built my own business out of nothing. I started out in this city as a scrappy teenager with no customers or contacts of my own, and two pairs of shoes! I managed to become one of the best-connected private call girls in Manhattan.

And now I'm being insulted—blackballed—humiliated by a pro-domme who lives in *Westchester*.

What went wrong?

Could Milt's offer be my salvation?

### Thursday afternoon 34th Street

After knocking myself out with Tylenol PMs, I slept until noon. Still groggy from prolonged sleep, the first thing I reached for was my cellphone, a lifeline to the career I once had.

A voicemail from Milt made my heart sink: "Something came up, kiddo, call me. It's about our trip." Oh no. Provence . . . canceled? Did Milt's wife decide to go with him? Never count on salvation, especially in the form of a john.

Followed by a message from Allie. "If you haven't booked someone else for Milt's vacation, I think I could—should—maybe I can leave Barcelona early. Can you call me? I have an idea!" she burbled. She sounds so upbeat (as usual) that I feel like crying. No matter what happens, she's afflicted with a chronic optimism. How does she do it?

A message from Jasmine—"Roberto wants to see you Friday"—caused a pang of regret. He's an easy hand job—my share, $400—and he's always in a hurry. But more to the point, I can't tell Allison, Liane or Charmaine what happened yesterday. It's bad for my reputation, and totally embarrassing. Jasmine—always skeptical about Trish—is the one girl I *would* confide in, if I were still speaking to her.

I'm no longer working with Trish, but I won't go crawling back to a former best friend just to replace some lost business. Were the situation reversed, Jasmine—like me—would stick to her guns.

I don't have the heart to call Allie or the nerve to call Milt!

CHAPTER FIVE

# New York: Escape from New York

*Friday, June 28, 2002*

Early this morning, after spending yesterday in hooker purgatory, I forced myself to answer my cellphone.

"Where've you been, kiddo?" The concern in Milt's voice touched me in a surprising place. Perhaps I'm not quite ready to retire from the only day job I know.

"I—uh—just dealing with some family stuff," I riffed. "Sorry! Tell me about France!" I added, trying to sound cheerful.

"I'm flying on Sunday. Something came up. I've been trying to talk to you about nailing down the dates at my house. Do you think you can join me?"

"I thought you were canceling!"

"Why would I do that?" Milt paused. "Suzy, are you sure you're okay?"

"I'm fine! Really!" It was hard to suppress my sudden mood shift. "I have our additional playmate—playmates—all figured out. It's a surprise," I added.

"Good work, kiddo. You sound like yourself again."

Being offered big bucks to spend time with a guy as successful as Milt is rather ego-enhancing. Puts what happened on Wednesday in a *quite* different light.

In Provence, I'll get ahead of my quota. Never have to worry about running into my in-laws. Stock up on fresh lavender oil. Figure out my next move. (Should I try to get pregnant *next* year?)

Perhaps I'll even have a chance to relax.

I called my husband at his office and left a message on his voicemail. "Honey? I really need your advice. I don't know if I should try your other phone." If I disturb him on his cell, that's even better. I'm less likely to trip myself up during a short call. He answered his cellphone on the first ring.

"What's up, babe?"

"My mom's a little upset," I lied. "Sebastian started doing drugs again. He's in rehab but . . . She's been driving around France, looking at real estate in . . ." Okay, Normandy isn't even *near* Provence—that was a *bit* of a stretch. Much as I'd like to invoke the Calvados orchards and half-timbered barns in Mother's JPEGs, I probably shouldn't lie that much about my actual destination. I outlined, briefly, my mother's putative needs, leaving her Birkenstocked travel buddy out of my story, and keeping the regional flourishes vague. "I don't know. Should I go?"

"Of course you should, honey."

Did he say that a little too quickly?

"I don't know, though. It's like emotional blackmail!" I sighed. "And is it *my* fault Sebastian has a drug problem?"

"Of course not. That's his responsibility, but she probably feels like you're all she has right now. When Sebastian gets his act together, he can take a vacation with her. But right now, he can't be emotionally or even physically available. So you're It, you know?"

"I don't know!" I repeated, courting my husband's impatience.

"It's kind of sudden! And she's turning me into the babysitter again, the good child. It's a lot to live up to—"

"Let's—can we talk about this later?" He was making a sincere effort not to sound curt, and I felt a twinge of remorse for putting him through this particular ordeal. "I'll try to be home before nine. But I think you should probably tell her yes. You might regret it if you don't."

### Later

I suppose Liane has a point. Allie *could* get ideas about Milt if she comes to France, but Liane's out of the loop—despite having known Allie from day one, as a budding call girl. She knows nothing about the radical values (and friends!) Allie has acquired in the last three years.

"I don't have to stay in Barcelona for the whole conference," Allie told me, when I called her back. "If I go to France, I might go to Barcelona early and leave on the tenth. I was talking to Roxana—"

"Not about this, I hope! I don't want Roxana to know my business. If you're coming to Provence, this is just between *us*," I warned her.

"Wellll," Allie admitted. "I didn't say anything about YOU, but I told her I might have an opportunity to work in France. You see, Roxana and I—we're partners in a joint venture."

Uh-oh. Like most activist hookers, Roxana has talents that never much helped her in the sex industry. At this point, her looks owe more to activism than to hooking, so I'm not surprised she wants Allie as a partner in her new start-up.

"Customized Intimacy Coaching is going to change women's lives!" Allie told me. "Wives and girlfriends who are deprived of the sex worker's ancient intuitive understanding of men-relationships-and-sexuality will be empowered by one of our two packages."

What? Is she reading this off index cards?

"The Relationship Makeover is, like, six sessions," she explained. "It's a feminist approach to finding—and keeping—your inner courtesan. We're still working out the details of the other package. Roxana thinks too many women have been indoctrinated by The Rules and she wants to create some kind of detoxification plan. Anyway, I'm trying to pull together ten grand. Well, maybe just eight will do it, before the web launch in October."

"I see. Well, no wonder Roxana wants YOU to fund this. How would *she* ever raise that kind of money?"

Roxana's hooker cred consists of a few massage parlors where she briefly toiled in her early twenties—before she became a professional activist and workshop leader. Naturally, Roxana supplies the ideology and technique, while Allie supplies the funding—and the right look.

"We're splitting all the profits fifty-fifty!" Allie assured me. "And resisting a patriarchal value system that tramples all over our collective history!"

"You're what? How . . . so?"

"Well, this is a new career for me. But I don't have to renounce my sex work—I can build on the lessons of my past," she explained. "Under patriarchy, our history is always being completely stigmatized!"

I definitely think Liane is wrong about Allie trying to move in on my customer. In all our years of tricking together, Allie has never given her number to any of my guys. Doesn't seem like she'll be doing that *now*. I'm more worried about whether she can still have a normal conversation with a john.

"Okay," I told her, "but don't talk about all this with Milt. He might think you're lecturing him. Just keep it light!"

Customized Intimacy Coaching sounds cock-eyed (not in a good way), and a total waste of Allie's blondeness. I can't help wondering what Jasmine says about a business plan that offers our trade secrets to non-professionals, but at least they'll be paying.

Maybe Allie *should* start thinking about a new career. Still. Is fifty-fifty a fair split when Allie's providing all the seed money? Roxana's inner courtesan must have a great deal of hidden potential (if anyone can find it). Allie's the window dressing Roxana needs to attract women to her workshops. But I won't say anything critical about their feminist business model—that might give Allie an excuse to back out.

"Okay," I agreed. "But you have to promise. Not a word about me to Roxana. And don't tell her anything about Milt. She's way too indiscreet! We have to protect his privacy."

## Saturday, June 29, 2002

Here's something every wife should know: Cooking up a fresh explanation (and it's got to be fresh) for why you're going out is actually dangerous. It uses up valuable brain cells, and leads to harder stuff. It's easier and safer to explain your absence after you return to the apartment.

This morning, while Matt was sleeping, I tiptoed into the guest bathroom to avoid waking him and donned my exercise mufti— pale blue yoga pants, matching hoodie. I fixed my hair, brushed my teeth and flossed, anxious to be as fresh as possible for my meeting with Milt. When meeting a customer, even if it's just for coffee, and ridiculously early, I need to know that every part of me's groomed for intimate contact. Anything less would feel wrong.

I hopped into a cab on First, and had passed Fifty-seventh when I discovered I had forgotten my cellphone. Was I so anxious to escape without an explanation that I left it in my closet? Thank God the ringer's off.

But did I remember to clean up Call History last night? Not that Matt would snoop! But a girl must never underestimate her husband. I erase the history regularly, especially on weekends, when he has more time on his hands. (You just never know how people will behave when they have nothing pressing to do!) I was horrified by my oversight.

The logistics of this upcoming "mother-daughter vacation" haven't made it easy to maintain an orderly double life. But when I saw Milt, waiting in front of Agata Valentina, in his dark green Mercedes, I knew all was right with the world.

"Hop in, kiddo," he said. "You look cute in that get-up. I've never seen you at this hour, have I?"

"Well," I said wryly, "there's a first time for everything, but I won't be getting up this early in France. I wish we could go upstairs," I added. A white lie. Sex with a customer—even my favorite—is something I'm not sorry to avoid at seven-thirty A.M. "Charmaine would KILL me if I tried to throw her out of bed at this hour."

He handed me an envelope—the cash for our tickets, so that Allie and I can fly without telling Milt our real names. "And some expense money," he said. "A down payment on what we discussed. I didn't have time to get all your cash. Can you wait until I see you?"

"I'm not worried," I said, and meant it.

"Do you mind if I take care of the rest in euros?"

"Euros?" The possibility surprised me. "Do you—" *have a French bank account?* I almost said, but didn't "—prefer to give us euros?"

"It might be easier," he said with a shrug. "But if you prefer dollars, you'll have to tell me. Think about it and call me. You have all my numbers in France. I'll have everything for you when you arrive." He patted my knee, and started the engine. "This vacation," he said, "is just what the doctor ordered!"

It's not a real vacation for me, but perhaps it's what I need, too.

While I've never faked an orgasm with my husband, I definitely had to fake our last vacation. Sometimes you have to, if you want your marriage to work. Instead of providing the down time—I have a track record there—I was trying to be, well, more like my husband. A straight person on vacation. I'm not so good at that. I couldn't relax until Matt and I returned from Wyoming and got back to our respective jobs.

But this is different. Business as usual. I *am* the vacation.

## Monday, July 1, Air France, Flight 6230

Last night, while packing for the trip, I began to lose my nerve. When Matt's in the office, I feel safe in my own home: I can bolt the front door and have the apartment all to myself. But Matt's been home all weekend.

Packing for France was like walking on eggshells. How will I get out of our apartment on time? If I wake too early, I risk looking haggard when I disembark from the plane. But I need to stop at Seventy-ninth Street and pick up three boxes of condoms. Extra bottles of Astroglide. The satin apron Milt likes, my new crotchless panties, and the see-through teddy I picked out for my Provençal idyll. Not to mention four different pairs of heels to match all my bedroom outfits.

Suddenly, I had another reason to panic. *What happened to that new packet of birth control pills?* Of course, I'm using condoms with Milt—so birth control is beside the point. But my husband has no idea I've ever taken the pill, and I don't want him finding out now. When he thinks we're trying to conceive!

With an early morning departure and five-hour airport lines looming, I began to wonder. What if I end up flying to Nice and leaving Matt in the apartment with my pills?

The last time I went away—for Grandmummy's funeral—things went so horribly wrong that my house of cards almost fell to pieces. Have I been too eager to take this trip? Do I seem too much like a busy girl who can't wait to get out of town? Perhaps I've overplayed my hand here.

A feeling of dread began to take over. To make matters worse, Matt wandered into the bedroom, wearing a pair of boxer shorts and a T-shirt, carrying the latest *Wired*. He fell onto our bed, where he began to read in an absent-minded way while I tried to search discreetly for my new pills.

I gave up the search and bit the domestic bullet. "I—I don't know if I should really be doing this," I told him.

He looked up from his magazine. "France with your momz?" he said playfully. "Come on, you're doing the right thing, honey."

"Why is it so important to you that I go?"

He looked puzzled. "What are you talking about?"

"Why did you want me to do this? I feel like it's a mistake to leave you alone here for two and a half weeks!"

"I'm going to miss you, but I can take care of myself—"

"I'll BET you can."

"Honey." He still didn't know what was coming. "What are you talking about?"

"I'm talking about—" I steeled myself for a topic I haven't raised since last summer "—your other apartment. You hid that from me for a year! You let Gary fool around in your apartment!"

"Gary isn't me! We're two separate people," Matt protested. "What he did in that apartment has nothing to do with me! And what does it have to do with your trip to France?"

"How can you say that? He was having an affair! How can I ever trust you after that? You were his enabler!"

"Well, maybe I was but—" My husband put his magazine down.

"I can't undo my past, honey." Now he picked up his magazine and began reading. Or trying to.

"You never want to talk about our relationship."

"That's not true!" He sat up and threw the magazine onto the floor. "For Christ's sake, I gave up my other apartment, okay? I'm sorry I kept it from you, but it's wrong to keep throwing the past in my face! Gary's back together with his wife, and if she can forgive him for HAVING the affair, why can't you forgive me for knowing about it?" A good point, but I wasn't going to concede. "Besides," he added. "*I've* never had an affair."

"You have so! And she's working at your firm. I saw her at the barbeque. Your boss introduced us!"

He blinked and looked away. As soon as I had pulled Larissa out of my hat, I felt queasy. For bringing up something he did when we weren't even engaged—much less married. Still, I felt entitled to use it, because I haven't mentioned it since 1999. The material's fresh, and he can't say I'm nagging him.

"But that was a long time ago," he said. "And I don't even work with her. She's in a completely different part of the office. I promise you, we've both moved on. She doesn't even remember our—our—"

"Your summer affair? How do you know what a woman remembers or doesn't remember? Did she know we were dating when she slept with you?"

"Nancy, for God's sake, stop this. I have a past, okay. I haven't always been a fucking saint. But that was three years ago!"

I sat on the edge of the bed and said: "I need to pack! I have to be at the airport by six A.M.! You know what the lines are like."

While he held me, I felt my body wanting to relax, but I stayed tense. "Listen," he said. "I'm sorry about what I did, okay? I've grown a lot since that summer, and I'll never do anything like that again. I don't flirt with her. We don't hang out. We have a professional relationship, and she's happily engaged to a great guy. We're over each other, and I want you to get over it, too."

"I don't know if I can," I said. "Ever since you told me I should go to France, I've been wondering." I looked away from him. "Maybe it's a bad idea to leave you alone like this. But my mother would never understand if I canceled on her. I mean, now that Sebastian's doing drugs again, I'm all she has!"

"Honey." He was anxious to break free from our wrangling. "You'll feel better after you hook up with your mom. And so will she. I need to check my email. I'm gonna let you pack."

I locked the bedroom door and breathed a sigh of relief! As a general rule, it's best to hide jealousy when you're feeling it and pretend to be jealous when you're not. I thought I was playing by those rules, but when I found myself alone, with my open suitcase, I wasn't so sure anymore.

I located my birth control pills, and placed them in the pocket of some new jeans, which I placed at the bottom of the suitcase, underneath my polo shirts and my brand new $500 pony-skin flip-flops. It would take an act of the most willful unthinkable perversity for Matt to go *there*.

When I unlocked our bedroom door, I was packed—and finally ready to make up with him.

In bed with my husband, I felt less like a brilliant manipulator and more like the nervous girlfriend I was three summers ago. I was no longer in danger of becoming a smug passionless cheater. As I gave in to Matt's movements, I was hurtling back to that anguished moment when I discovered him playing around with a summer associate. Matt was more proprietary and in control than ever. He'll never admit this, but did he *like* being reminded of my jealousy? Was he thinking about that affair, and how it still enrages me, while we were coming? Or was he feeling hungrier because of my departure?

It was satisfying, but it was also hard to sleep. Was I turned on by my (real, after all) jealousy? Or by my own lies?

## Later

It's a shame to be sitting in business class yet forced to ignore that friendly man across the aisle. He's exactly the right age, weight, type for a working girl in her thirties! Though I'm surrounded by prospective customers, my face is covered with a thick mask—a ghostly looking cellular treatment that makes my skin tingle. How else can I emerge from this flight looking fresh? I've had almost no sleep, and when I close my eyes, my mind refuses to switch off.

After all the near-misses, the humiliations and rifts of the last four weeks—five grueling hours of enhanced security at JFK, and endless runway delays—I am finally in the air. En route to Nice Côte d'Azur, with condoms, lube and heels safely packed.

Will Provence be the antidote to my season in hell??

CHAPTER SIX

# France: State of the Tart

Being away from my usual bed in Manhattan presents a few challenges. Today, Milt proposed a rendezvous downstairs, in the library. Duncan was on his way to the garden center in Draguignan—a trip guaranteed to take at least two hours.

"The carpet's brand new," Milt said. "Spotless. We could practically have a picnic on it."

Sex on the floor.

It's never as good as it sounds, but I didn't want to be a kill-joy, having already said no to the solarium. You have to pick your battles and, since it's his house, not mine, I needn't worry about getting Astroglide on the rug.

"Okay, but . . ." I placed a large fluffy towel on one of the brocade armchairs, carefully slipping a condom into the corner. "Let's start here."

Leaning back on the towel, I opened my legs for him and pulled my panties to one side. Perhaps I'll turn this into two library visits?

*Finish him with a blow job, then come back tomorrow to execute the final deed.*

Of course, that means concocting another errand for Duncan. As I slid one finger into my opening, I closed my eyes. Milt was playing with my panties, pulling them toward my right thigh. But when I opened my eyes, he wasn't looking at my pussy or my fingers. He was staring at my face. That made me uncomfortable. He's usually so focused on some part of my body. Or his.

My pussy was naturally wet, and my mind kept traveling toward Duncan, sitting behind the wheel of his SUV. Does he know what we're doing? Does he wonder if we're fucking when he leaves the house? But he's not into girls, I remind myself. Still, I couldn't help wondering if, in some alternate reality—one in which Duncan IS (into girls)—he'd get hard thinking about me, half-naked in the library, masturbating in front of my customer . . . and masturbating for real, despite myself.

I never have orgasms with Milt. Sometimes with other clients, but never with Milt. I was getting too close. I had to stop. And Milt was playing with my bra, sliding his finger underneath the fabric of one soft cup, brushing against the nipple, a gesture that normally leaves me in neutral. When it's Milt.

I made a small sound, looked up, and said: "Stop." I pulled my legs together, and smiled. "I don't want to come yet. I'm saving it for your cock."

Then, I slid off the chair. Milt had to back away slightly while I got onto my knees. I threw him a slutty porn-star look, different from the way I look at a man I'm really into—more of a wanton gaze that says "I'll do this for anyone, anytime."

"Your cock's so hard," I murmured.

My hand reached backward and found the condom, which I opened and popped it into my mouth while he played with my hair. Then I rolled it onto the head of his cock with my lips. When it was securely anchored, I began sucking. My mouth moved up and down, while my right hand was bringing the condom firmly to the base. My left hand was pressed against my panties, feeling the outline of my lips.

For a second, I imagined Duncan, getting hard in the SUV at the thought of me using my mouth. I pressed harder against the outside of my panties.

I should take my hand away and do this later! I forced myself to stop, but my pussy was very swollen, twisting against my panties. As my mouth continued to work, an image from inside Duncan's SUV flickered through my head—me sitting in the front seat, fully clothed, leaning over to unzip his pants, touching the fabric around the zipper.

"Baby!" Milt sighed. "You are so hot right now. I can tell."

Well, I am, but he's not supposed to be able to tell! I forced my mouth lower and found that I couldn't stop myself from moaning a little. But I normally fake this. What's going on? I can't stop thinking about Duncan in the SUV, coolly contemplating my possibilities, trying to figure out whether he wants my mouth or—

"Get on your knees, and let me fuck you," Milt said.

*But not on the carpet! We'll do that some other time.* I turned around and climbed onto the armchair, allowing him to pull my panties down toward my knees. My bra was still on, a nice touch. I slid my finger against my lower lips and was shocked at how wet I was.

Where did I put the Astroglide? Oh God, it's on the table—and though I know I should get up, for safety's sake, just this once . . . I'm so wet, and this is soooooo unprofessional, everyone knows that condoms without lube are a major major no-no, but it's annoying to have to get up when you're already on your knees like this. And you don't want your customer to feel distracted.

And nobody else is looking. And I'm that wet. Just this once.

I slipped his cock into me and breathed carefully, quietly. If Duncan returns, I don't want him to hear me. Duncan . . . I really want Duncan to—

"Your pussy's nice and wet," Milt said, slamming into me. He was fucking me much too hard, and I was letting him. When I got really close, I pulled away suddenly. I can't come like this, not with Milt.

"I want to ride on top of you," I told him. He was more than happy to cooperate, and I moved the towel to the carpeted floor.

Now that Milt was lying on his back, I grabbed the bottle of Astroglide and massaged some lubricant onto his latex-covered erection—feeling guilty about that brief lubeless moment.

*Will this do something weird to Milt's lower back? Once, in my teens, I had sex on the floor, on my back—what agony the next morning! Maybe it's different for guys?* In any case, I didn't want to break the spell. I bit my lip and said nothing. Now I was back in control, ready to get my customer off, and my mind had slipped away from Duncan. I still felt swollen and my nipples were tingling, but I was focusing on Milt. As I rode harder, though, I realized that I wasn't. I couldn't stop thinking about Duncan. I closed my eyes and imagined his hands doing what *my* hands were doing—touching my breasts. I managed to unhook my bra and remove it, without missing a beat. Milt was getting closer, and so was I.

After I dismounted, he said, "I should take you out of your natural habitat more often."

I smiled mysteriously and mostly to myself. Thank God I didn't actually come. I can't let that happen with Milt. Not under his roof, when I have to see him every day. It would feel like a bizarre violation.

"I think I'll take a shower," I told him. "And a nap."

"Me too," he said. "I'll meet you down here at seven. We'll go to the convent for dinner. It's Duncan's night off."

In my bedroom, I locked the door, started running a shower, and threw myself onto the bed. My fingers didn't have to do very much. When I came, the sensation was so intense that I had to cover my mouth with a pillow. In the shower, I sprayed myself with warm water and found that my nerve endings were still tender.

OMG. Why Duncan? He's cute, sure, but it's so counter-intuitive. For one thing, I'm hardly a fag hag! I want to be desired.

Can we really be having dinner at . . . a convent? What should I wear?

## Tuesday night

The Hôtellerie du Couvent Royal, just down the road from Milt's house, turns out to be a converted Dominican monastery, owned by a hotel chain. There are no monks in evidence, but still, I'm glad I wore a long-sleeved, high-collared blouse and very loose pants. My only deviation: chunky revealing sandals and brightly painted toe nails.

We were seated in the outside gallery of the Cloister, sipping aperitifs under tall stone arches, and I couldn't help feeling that the ghosts of absent monks were padding silently through the garden in their robes, checking out my red toe nails. At the table next to us were two couples closer to Milt's age than my own, and it was impossible to avoid their curiosity. My outfit, at least, was blameless, might even (I hope) throw them off the scent. The last thing I want to do is make a spectacle of myself. Duncan's poolside meals don't generate gossip (or draw attention to Milt's interlude with a younger woman), but he has to have some nights off—and the monastery, according to Milt, is "the best joint in town."

I heard one of the silver-haired women laughing, speaking to the table in a Northern language—Swedish? I couldn't tell—and began to relax. Tourists don't gossip, not in any way that matters. When I heard my cellphone buzzing in my bag, I leaned forward and told Milt: "That might be Allison. She tried to call—" I paused coyly "—when we were getting busy. I don't want her to think we're ignoring her!"

I got up and looked for a discreet place to take the call, but soon discovered another kind of cloister, the modern electronic variety. A genteel but firm blocking mechanism that makes it impossible to use your phone outside the reception area.

"It's the hand of God," Milt said, when I returned to my Kir Royale. "We'll have to call back later. I'm looking forward to whatever you've arranged," he added. "But really, kiddo, you're more than enough company for one man."

With one raised eyebrow, I smiled discreetly, and picked up my menu. I can have two drinks max when I'm working. I need to be sober at all times. Thank God Milt likes to have sex before dinner, though! It would be a shame to order light from a menu like this.

"I'll have the fois gras with figs," I told him. "And . . . let's see . . . the duck?"

"A woman who eats real food!" he said with an approving beam. "You could pass for a vegetarian, though." In response to my quizzical look, he explained. "You're so thin, kiddo. Slim, not thin," he corrected himself. "There's just enough curve on you . . ." His salt and pepper eyebrows wiggled briefly. "Based on your figure, I thought you'd be one of these health food nuts."

"That would be Allison," I said. "She's very careful about what she eats."

"We'll have to warn Duncan! He'll do French provincial Atkins, if you ask him nicely. Unfortunately, my doctor put the kibosh on all the good stuff. But I can experience your fois gras vicariously. He didn't say anything about watching. Getting to know you . . . is a real treat."

"Is that so?" For a second, I felt as uncomfortable as I did in the library, when I realized that he was staring, not at my body, but at my face while I played with myself.

"Very much so," he replied.

A waitress approached with our bottle of Evian, saving us both from my awkwardness.

When I returned to my room, I discovered an excited voice-mail from Allie, heavily compromised by some sort of background music. A live band perhaps? "I'm facilitating the flamenco rehearsal, then I'm going into a meeting with Roxana and Lai Pook but I'll try to call you when we're done. I might have to stay an extra day!"

Flamenco rehearsal? I wonder who Lai Pook is. One of Allison's Cambodian sex worker friends?

While I was brushing my teeth, the phone began chiming. I threw my toothbrush into the sink and picked up immediately. To my surprise, it wasn't Allie's breathless hello but Etienne's surreptitious purr.

"Ah, finally, finally, petite mignonne, I am finally here! Comment ça va, chérie?"

"Here?" I covered the mouthpiece and rinsed some excess tooth-paste from my mouth. "Where . . . is here?"

"The Carlyle. Most eager to reconnect! I apologize for the short notice, cocotte, but since I return to Paris in two days, I was hoping that we might? Soon? Tonight is ideal."

"But—" If he knows I'm in France, he might try to fly me to Paris when he returns! I would rather not go into explanations. "I wish I could but—" I searched for a place that would sound truly remote to Etienne. "I'm in Alberta!" I told him.

"Where?" He was horrified and mystified, as if I had gone to Siberia or Saturn. "When do you return?" he asked hopefully.

"Well, I might be back next week, but it's hard to say. Family obligations. My mother . . ."

"I have all the luck," he said. "I will not try to compete with anybody's mother. Well, chérie, of course, you are not replaceable, and there is nobody quite as delectable as yourself, and the idea of visiting New York without a chance to undress your exquisite—"

"I think you have to meet Charmaine," I said quickly. "Wait. I need to call her first!"

After we hung up, I dialed Charmaine's cell and explained, "He's an easy five. He doesn't know I'm in France, though."

"Where—" she coughed politely "—are you? In case he asks."

"On vacation with my mother, of course! You have no idea where." The less detail you (or your confederates) provide, the more convincing. "He ends with a simple piano lesson." Our code for a hand job. But I hope she doesn't rush him the first time he goes down on her: "First, he wants to listen to a very long opera," I warned her.

Charmaine giggled. "Don't they all. But I can't see him until ten-thirty. Do you think I'll have a problem with security?"

It's almost ten-thirty *here*. Dark and cool, excruciatingly quiet. I'm very aware of not wanting to be overheard in this huge, silent house at this hour. Manhattan's still sunny, probably quite sticky, and there's that busy hum which doesn't stop until four A.M., if then. How could I forget? But I did—for a moment.

"Just wear something simple," I told her. "Put your heels in a bag. They won't stop you at the Carlyle."

Sometimes, I have doubts about Charmaine. Should I cut her some slack because she's new? Or treat her as a worthy contender for my business, deserving no mercy? But now, I feel released from those choices.

It's reassuring to know Etienne won't be left to his own devices while he's at the Carlyle, and strangely comforting to be connected, despite an ocean, to my business in Manhattan. To be in this remote private hideaway under a moonlit sky, away from my husband and his family, playing matchmaker with one of my oldest customers and one of the newest girls in town . . . on a sunny afternoon.

Oddly enough, this feels like home. Can you make a home out of familiar hotel rooms, long distance calls and sex acts in different time zones? If only.


### Wednesday, July 10

This morning, when Duncan drove into town, I decided to sit in the back. When we're alone, it seems natural to sit up front, but the fantasies I've been having make me want to keep my physical distance. I was carrying an out-of-print book, retrieved from Milt's library because the 1930s jacket, so expertly preserved, was irresistible.

"*Mont-Paon*," Duncan said. "Wonderful story. The previous owners knew the author. And I once met her niece."

"Really?" I was studying the back of his neck. "The owners knew the author of *Mount Peacock*? Did you read it in French?"

"Well, I *can*, if I work at it, but I'm lazy. No, I read it in English I'm afraid."

"So who did Milt buy the house from?"

"I'm not sure," he said carefully. "That's what her niece told me." I keep trying to place Duncan's accent, but his flat, evasive tone stopped me from asking such an obvious question.

I returned to *Mount Peacock, or Progress in Provence* and we were both silent—for about three minutes.

"The translator's obviously infatuated with the medieval heretics," he said. "The so-called Albigensians. Wonderful, isn't it?"

"Who exactly *were* they?"

"Provençal heretics," he told me. "A widespread rebellion against the Church. They converted entire towns. Eight hundred years ago, this region was a bit like Brazil—the locals had their own version of liberation theology, and the pope didn't like it. That restaurant where you had dinner—the monastery was at the center of some violent Church politics. There was considerable bloodshed." He looked at his side mirror. "How was the duck?"

"Just right," I said, closing my book. "The monastery? Violent? It seems so calm."

"Doesn't it. And duck is one of the hardest birds to get right."

"Yes, but chicken—" I mustn't reveal that I know how to cook a chicken or any other bird, in case Duncan—and, by extension, Milt—should get the idea I'm married.

Aside from what cooking does to my image—doesn't enhance my twenty-something look!—I worry that Milt will disappear if he finds out I'm a Wall Street wife. And what would Milt think of Matt? For some reason, that bothers me.

"Well," I added. "You're the expert. I can just barely boil an egg! And," I lied, "whenever I try to, it comes out too hard or too soft."

We were approaching the Avenue du 15eme Corps. "I'll meet you in the cibercafé," Duncan said, "I've got an appointment with the fishmonger." A part of me wants to follow him to the market, check out the food stalls, but I don't want my domestic self betraying me. Clearly, if Milt's chatting to Duncan about what I ordered for dinner last night, I have reason to be concerned about how chatty Duncan might be in return!

If either of these men thought for a moment he was being indiscreet, he would instantly clam up. But that's the problem with men—their idea of indiscreet isn't ours. I'll bet those two would never dream of discussing their sex lives, but food, far more than sex, is the not-so-innocent medium which could blow my cover.

When Duncan returned to the cibercafé, I was waiting outside—the only way to protect my hair from all the smoke! The back seat was surrounded by shopping bags. A perfect excuse for me to sit nearer to the driver. I reached for my seat belt, but Duncan beat me to it, and I felt like a captive in a love clinch with her prison guard. As he slid the belt tip into its buckle, the fabric brushed against my right breast. I made no effort to resist and he—oblivious, no doubt, to the susceptible qualities of a female nipple—made no apology.

As we turned onto the Boulevard Bonfils, I glanced out of the corner of my eye at his biceps and jaw line. I was thinking about my hands and his zipper. An insistent irrational tingle beneath my T-shirt, on the outside surface of each nipple, forced me to suppress a sharp breath. I looked resolutely out the window, and saw some dissolute men sitting around a table in the Cercle Philharmonique. Drinking, smoking, languishing, they weren't very appealing, but that only made me realize how difficult it is to silence a real attraction. I can't stop thinking about yesterday's session, the thoughts that crossed my mind when my mouth was on another man—and the way I came when I finally had a chance to be alone.

How could something so inappropriate happen to a sensible girl like me?

### Thursday, July 11

Today, while Duncan was in the kitchen, I tiptoed discreetly into Milt's bedroom wearing a frilly pink bikini top, Daisy Duke shorts and large heart-shaped sunglasses. As I straddled Milt's chest, I pulled my shades down so we could make eye contact.

"Now, that's different from what you had on this morning," he commented.

My poolside look—loose white pants, gauzy tops, expensive

straw hat—is designed to protect my legs from the sun, and my image from other kinds of exposure. But that's what I relish about this job—in bed, I get to wear things that I won't wear in public.

Milt unzipped my shorts slowly, as though unwrapping a candy bar. He reached up to tease my tiny triangle of hair with a fingertip. I leaned over his face to let him kiss it. My pussy, however, was out of range because my shorts could only be opened, not removed. Placing his hands on my hips, he said, "You'll have to turn over, so I can get these off."

"I know."

"A born schemer. I like that," he said, easing me onto my back. "You know all the moves."

"Just some of them." I removed my sunglasses and wriggled into position, feeling good about my size four tummy. Milt's additional girth—he could lose fifteen pounds—makes me feel even lighter.

I prepared to reposition myself, so Milt could lie back, but he held my hips firmly in place and buried his tongue between my lower lips. Is this a new and worrying trend? When he sees me at Seventy-ninth Street, he stays on his back, even while eating my pussy. Is Milt doing something different because we're on his turf? Because we're alone too much? Is our relationship going to change, or will he revert to normal patterns in New York? I must keep an eye on this!

But his tongue wasn't bothersome. It never has been, actually. Over the years, Milt has become my favorite because he never turns me on or off. It's so much easier to deal with a customer who doesn't arouse or disturb your nerve endings. My body can relax—and concentrate on him—because there's never a moment when I'll have to recoil. Still, I've always been able to tell that Milt has a good sex life at home. That COULD pose a problem, but I opened my legs wider to encourage him.

A faint sweet aroma was beginning to fill the entire house, the unmistakable fragrance of fresh red peppers roasting in olive oil. Duncan's cooking was slowly but surely wafting toward the second floor. Inhaling happily, I allowed my body to follow its own advice. As the sensation between my legs grew stronger, I was focusing . . . on Duncan . . . in jeans and a crisp T-shirt, taking a break from his work.

I was kneeling on the kitchen floor, completely naked, sent by Milt as an end-of-summer bonus. *Since I have no choice in the matter, it's easy enough to do whatever Duncan wants.* I unzipped him—magically, I did not have to deal with underwear—and began taking care of him with my mouth. I imagined him, the next day, coming to my room, sitting on the edge of my bed, while I did the same thing. I was following up with him on the sly, no longer doing Milt's bidding, because now I couldn't get enough.

If Milt had any idea I was capable of such unbusinesslike thoughts—!

When I came, I didn't have to smother my noise, because there was very little of it. I came quietly and carefully. Milt pulled his mouth away, and kissed the intersection where my outer lips meet. A gentle, accomplished kiss, as if to say, "I'm done."

I got up onto my knees, not too disoriented, found the condom, and took over. Milt was back in his usual position. I needed—he does too!—a break from that surprising intimacy. So I straddled his cock with my back facing him, and struck a slutty pose. When he finally came, it was a relief to know he was taken care of for the day.

"Hanging out like this is fun, kiddo!"

"But we don't have to tell Allison how much fun we've had without her," I said. It's okay to come with a customer *once* after— how long? Twelve years? Maybe more. But it's not okay to let it become a habit when you see him as much as I see Milt.

"No," he agreed. "We don't want her feeling left out."

And I WILL be glad when she arrives, because things will surely get back to normal when Milt has two girls keeping him entertained.

### Thursday night, July 11

Duncan has returned from Marseille, with Allie and her luggage—minus one item. "There's something I have to tell you," she whispered, as I showed her to her room.

How could Allie lose track of her Pyrex love baton? After getting it all the way from JFK to Barcelona? She has all these ideas and theories, yet she's so impractical! After telling me (and airport security, no doubt) that traveling with a large, vulgar—and very expensive—sex toy is a *human right enshrined in some UN document*, she then manages to . . . misplace a double dildo.

I'm really afraid to ask.

## CHAPTER SEVEN

# France: Part of the Solution

*Friday, July 12, 2002 2:00 A.M.*

So I helped Allie unpack. "Are you sure the dildo didn't, you know, roll into a corner of your luggage?" I asked. "How could you lose it?" Replacing Allie's $300 sex toy will be quite a challenge—in a town where the shops seem always to be closed, and the only good restaurant is in a converted monastery.

"I'm sorry!" she said. "The last time I saw it, I had it in my backpack. I was at the transgender rights flamenco recital! I put my backpack on a chair for a minute. When I came back, the backpack was open. It's the only thing they took. I should have told you before I left Barcelona, but I had my hands full trying to deal with Laypoot!"

"Laypoot? Not Laypook?"

"Pook?" Allie looked confused. "No. Laypoot!" she said, glancing around her spacious bedroom. "This is gorgeous, Nancy!"

"You have a view of the flower garden," I told her. "And don't forget to call me Suzy."

Allie was leaning out of the window at the other end of her bedroom, dressed only in her bra and a pair of tiny panties. She was opening all the shutters in the room, taking in the night air. "It smells so pretty. And it's sooo nice to have a room of my own. I've been sharing with Roxana for a week!" She took a deep breath. "Is that lavender?"

Allie turned to look at herself in the full-length mirror. "And the room didn't even have a real mirror! Do you know what that's like?" She pinched her abdomen cautiously. "All that conference food! Our hotel room had just one tiny teeny little mirror in the bathroom. When I can't see what's happening below my waist, I feel fat. Don't you? Come talk to me, while I shower!"

In bathrobe and slippers, I perched on the edge of the bidet, while Allie unpacked a large vanity bag.

"Gorgeous tiles!" she exclaimed. "So Milt had it all done when he moved in?"

"They're made in Salernes. The family's been in business since 1830. Tomorrow we have to—"

"This is my first visit to the south of France, did you know? So, anyway, our T-shirt was a hit! 'Sex workers are part of the solution.' But Laypoot tried to get Roxana thrown off two panels and almost succeeded. Those bossy sex workers from Montreal kept saying the Americans were dominating all the panels, and that was like ammunition for Laypoot . . ." Allie held the shower by its handle and looked up at the ceiling while she sprayed her soapy breasts.

"*Why* do they *hate us*?" She sighed unhappily. "Especially Laypoot!"

"Is she Vietnamese?"

"Is WHO Vietnamese?"

"Laypoot. Your trouble-maker at the shadow conference. Is she—"

"LAYPOOT? Laypoot is the sex workers' collective from Paris! There's six girls and a couple of trans—"

"You mean—" For days, I've been envisioning some enraged sloe-eyed Third World poster child, bearing down on Allie's American blondeness. Instead, it's a band of Parisian hookers accusing *Roxana and Allie* of dominating a conference in Barcelona? What theory will the French come up with next! "Do they really call themselves LES PUTES?" I asked. "Do you realize what *les putes* actually means?"

"Um. Yes, actually. I do!"

"It's like calling your group *The Whores*."

"It's not *like* that, it IS that. And they're anarchists! I'm totally psyched that they decided to embrace this stigmatizing term and redefine it for our collective good!" She sighed. "Even if more people in the world speak Spanish than French. But still. Their intentions are good! I just wish they weren't so difficult to work with. Is it MY FAULT that I'm American?"

"Omigod. Please do not say 'anarchist whores' in front of Milt! I don't want him to hear you talking like that. Milt thinks of you as a nice girl, Allie. We don't want him to get confused."

Allie turned off the water. "Who is we?" She stepped onto the dark blue tiles, and wrapped a large towel around her torso. "These patriarchal categories!"

"Milt has no idea what you were doing in Barcelona," I warned her.

"I thought you told him I was with a customer?"

"Sort of—but you can't tell him that either. Because if you WERE with another customer, you'd be discreet enough not to talk about it. So I let him think you were, but I never actually said it." Allie was sitting on the edge of the tub covering her damp legs with a honey-scented lotion, frowning as she listened. "As far as we're concerned, Milt's the only paying customer in the world, no other customers exist. Nice hookers don't talk about other customers. When we're with a customer. That's basic professionalism," I reminded her.

"Well, that's what those girls from Paris call putophobia! *Lahhh poo-toe-foe-bee*. Exploiting the false consciousness of the client."

"He's my client, not theirs," I pointed out. "At least I'm taking care of him. Your activist friends are always coming up with these totally unattractive ideas. I'd like to see how happy THEIR clients are. Anyway, these are the cranks who accused you of dominating the conference. I think I'll take their theories with a *grain*."

Allie was beginning to brood. "I wonder if one of THEM stole my love baton."

## Friday afternoon

My erotic fantasy life has completely dried up, now that I'm preoccupied with babysitting Allison and locating a new dildo. Having to pay attention to a friend as high maintenance as Allie can really put your own issues in perspective. And I have to make sure she doesn't slip up, by saying the wrong thing in front of Milt—or Duncan.

This morning, I took a discreet walk through the side streets of St-Maximin, while Duncan drove Milt to the golf course. On the Rue Colbert, I discovered a boutique stocked with miniature unicorns, gowned damsels in conical hats and flesh-tone elves. A sword, embedded in a plastic rock, rotating on a turntable, gave me hope. What CAN'T you sell in this neighborhood?

Around the corner, in the Rue du Général de Gaulle, I found a cavernous dusty *quincaillerie* with some kitchen appliances and power tools in the window, next to a narrow shop with promising signage: "Fantaisie de Femme." Might there be bedroom appliances? But all they have on offer are piercings ("de 10H00 à 12H30"), a small selection of animal-print lingerie, and a rack of New Age crystals.

If they have sex toys under the counter, my French isn't advanced enough to find out.

What drew Milt to this odd little town? When I called Isabel from New York, to tell her where I'd be staying, she'd never heard of St-Maximin. Still, it's not remote enough to be labeled a bucolic getaway. Nor is it chic. The house must have been a steal.

I waited for Duncan outside the No Smoking café. When he picked me up, Allie was sitting in the front seat of his SUV. She lowered her window. "Well?" she asked eagerly.

"We'll talk about it later," I said.

As I climbed into the back, Duncan met my eye with a searching but cautious look. "If there's something in particular?"

"Oh! Not really," I told him. "I was just checking out some hair salons." I was anxious to change the subject. "I wonder if St-Maximin's the next big thing," I said briskly.

"How so?" Duncan asked, more than happy to play along.

"Well, a town on the verge of a property boom. It's a very unusual place to build your hideaway, isn't it." I don't want to sound critical of Milt. Or nosy. Is he speculating? Privy to something nobody else knows?

"I think the boom has come and gone," Duncan told me "St-Max was thriving eight hundred years ago, when it was a pilgrim hang-out. It's more like the *late* big thing, if you see what I mean. The basilique in the center of town—"

"Let's go to Sunday Mass!" Allie interrupted. "What do you think, Nnnn-um-Suzy?"

"Not if it's early!" OMG. She almost called me Nancy.

"They have one at eleven," she said. "That's not too early is it?"

"Not at all," Duncan said with a bemused chuckle. "We might even get Milt up for the occasion."

"That's a WONderful idea!" Allie said. "I think he'll enjoy that a *lot!*"

*Milt is not getting it up for Sunday Mass!* I felt like saying, but didn't. This is a guy who avoids going to his own *temple*. Allie is sometimes woefully off the mark about who guys really are. Which might also explain the looks she keeps throwing at Duncan, and her fondness for sitting up front with him.

Does she really not get it?

## Friday, later

This afternoon, Allie and I occupied one of the guest rooms on the second floor. Milt's sexual ambitions—"every room in the house"—and Duncan's unavoidable proximity were pushing me toward a large sunny bedroom in a corner of the west wing, far from the kitchen and pool. Where Allie's giggles and Milt's groans aren't audible.

We waited in our matching undies for Milt to complete his afternoon swim. He's up to forty laps a day.

"I can't help wondering . . ." Allie stretched her legs out on the huge bed and pointed her toes at the ceiling. "I know this sounds sexist, but I don't think a *girl* stole my dildo. I'm pretty sure one of the boys took it."

"One of the boys?" I echoed.

"There's an international hustlers' caucus, all boys, and they tried to pass a resolution for Bad Girls Without Borders to change its name!" Allie sighed. "Roxana took their side and said the name isn't inclusive enough. Les Putes, which has a lot of clout, said it's a principle of *theirs* to use the political feminine for *all* sex workers. So *I* said maybe we SHOULD change the name, but . . . Bad People Without Borders just sounds wrong! And this is a *shadow* conference—we don't want the people at the *official* conference to find out we're having internal disagreements! Changing the name in the middle of the conference would actually be *divisive*."

If only Allie would think this strategically about her actual job.

"So," she continued, "the members of Les Putes are mad at

Roxana for supporting the hustler caucus because the boys are mostly Americans and Germans! And the boys were mad at *me* for calling them divisive! I know this sounds paranoid, but *do you think someone stole my love baton to make a point*? Or maybe it was someone who needs it more than I do."

"But why," I had to ask, "are you walking around with a dildo in your backpack? Why didn't you leave it in your room?"

"I was coming from the Safe Sex Breakfast. The Cambodians insisted I bring it for the condom demo, and they asked how much a sex toy like that costs. So everyone KNEW I was carrying this beautiful expensive Pyrex dildo."

Was that a little ostentatious of Allie?

"After that, I went to the transgender flamenco recital which was a fundraiser for BGWB. The boys from Berlin are very upset with the transsexuals for supporting BGWB," she explained. "This wasn't stolen for personal use! *I* think whoever took it was trying to send a political message! About MY RELATIONSHIP with the transsexuals—"

Allie stopped suddenly and covered her mouth. The bedroom door swung open. "Don't stop on account of me!" Milt said, cheerfully. "Pardon my lateness, ladies. And my sarong." He was wearing nothing but a towel around his middle. "I just took a shower."

Allie reached out to remove the towel, while I slithered down to the foot of the bed, so I could give Milt some much needed girl-on-girl action. Allie focused exclusively on Milt's cock, while I made a point of seeming to ravish my long-lost girlfriend. She stayed on her knees and opened her legs. I kneeled behind and buried my face between her thighs.

"Oh!" she gasped. "I've been thinking about Suzy *all week*! Her tongue feels like velvet!"

I rolled onto my back, and slid beneath her, holding her hips lightly, pulling her down so my mouth could meet her pussy. She hovered there, politely, and I wondered if she was close enough to my mouth. But Milt, standing at the edge of the bed, wasn't close enough to check. I moaned loudly, rubbed my nose against her blonde fuzz, and hoped for the best. Velvet, indeed.

The session went better and faster than I expected. Allie disappeared into her bedroom to shower for dinner, leaving me to tidy him up. Without having to be asked, Allie keeps a polite distance from Milt now that we're in his house, emphasizing her connection to "Suzy." A turn-on for Milt—even if we mostly fake it—and a reassuring business practice for me. She does this by instinct because, I think, she can tell I'm rather attached to Milt. Liane might disagree, but I think I made the right decision. And, with Allie in the house, even when I have to monitor her every move, I feel more . . . at home.

As I wrapped a hot washcloth around Milt, he confessed, "It's never been in my nature to listen at keyholes." Uh-oh! "But I couldn't help overhearing. So—" He wriggled his eyebrows. "—Allison's got a transsexual friend? In Barcelona? Is she pre-op?"

"A trans—" I backtracked for a second. "Why do you ask?"

"I just wondered." He smiled and patted my hip. "It's food for thought, kiddo. We haven't done that in awhile." He's alluding to his annual birthday treat, which isn't always easy to arrange, because his favorite pre-op tranny keeps changing her number.

"I don't know how much you heard—"

"Not much," Milt said. "But you know I've always had a weakness for a chick with a dick. Sounds like Allison does too." *No wonder he came so fast!*

"Well," I told him. "Great minds think alike. But right now, Allison and I have a mini-crisis. Allie has—she *had* this beautiful state-of-the-art double dildo, designed by that famous porn star, Tiffany Millions. While she was in Barcelona, it got stolen from her bag! Maybe you could drive us to Nice? Or someplace where there's a sex shop? With a good selection? Tomorrow?"

"Kiddo, I'm all for helping you out here, but tomorrow's out of the question. I have an important golf date. It's business, and I'll be in Aix all day. In fact, I won't be back until very late. Otherwise, I'd be happy to drive you girls to Nice! It would be my distinct privilege. But I wouldn't even know where to begin—I'm kind of new around here."

"Why don't you ask Duncan? He MUST know where the sex shops are. *I* can't ask him."

Catching the worried look on my face as I contemplated all the closed shops on Sundays and Mondays, he said, "Tell you what, I'll give you girls a thousand euros. I'll find out from Duncan where you should go. You can have the keys to the BMW. Duncan will take me to Aix. That way you'll be able to shop in comfort and privacy, no questions asked. Have a nice lunch, get your nails done. And we'll try out your new toys on Sunday!"

Milt beamed at me like a beatified manager, but I returned a look of dismay.

"There's only one thing wrong with your game plan," I said.

"What's that?"

"Neither of us can drive."

Milt was stunned. "Are you sure? For some reason, I'm not surprised about Allison but—you really can't drive, Suzy?"

It's the other way around, of course—Allie should be able to, because she grew up in Connecticut. "I never had to." I shrugged. "I live in Manhattan, remember?"

"You never took driving lessons?"

"Uh—no, actually."

"Would you like to?" I could see wheels of benevolence churning in Milt's head. Allie took two driving lessons when she was sixteen, but found it so terrifying that she preferred to rely on her high school boyfriends. For me, the mere *idea* of driving lessons is terrifying. What if Milt offers to pay for lessons when I get back to New York?

"I don't actually WANT to, Milt." Probably the first time I've had to say something that blunt in his presence. "I've survived this long without it, and besides . . ." I smiled at the hair on his chest. "I like it when the man drives."

It would never occur to him, I guess, that girls like me don't drive. He works in Manhattan but lives in New Jersey where everyone *has* to. Half the cars in Manhattan must be from Jersey.

"It makes you stop and think." Milt was staring at the ceiling. "You can have sex with the same woman twice, maybe three times, a month. You know her for more than a decade! Without ever knowing she can't drive. The bottom line, kiddo—" he sat up and gave my waist a comradely squeeze "—is that men really don't know a thing about women at all. And the longer we know you, the less we know."

Oddly enough, this is only a source of comfort for him. He sat up and rumpled my hair gently with his fingers.

"But we'll figure something out. Don't worry. You can tell Allison that I feel her loss, and I'm on the case. We'll get her some new toys," he said decisively. "I wonder what kind of freak goes around stealing designer dildos out of ladies' purses!"

## Later

Whatever her shortcomings, Allison's the buffer who keeps things normal and commercial. Now that she's here, Milt has no reason to make comparisons between the unmistakable hotness of our one-on-one sessions and the more industrial sex we had this afternoon. It's a pleasant seamless transition, and there's no longer any danger of Milt getting to know me too well.

### Saturday, July 13, 2002 9:00 A.M.

Last night, while Allison was giving herself a mini-facial in her bedroom, I went downstairs to confer with Duncan. He was in the library, straightening out the local history shelf.

I decided to go for it: "Did Milt get a chance—?" This can't be any different from discussing pubic hair with Lorenzo, my hairdresser. For a call girl, gay men are Sexual Switzerland, or—on a good day—the Allies. "We were thinking you might be able to drive us to Nice because, ummm." *We're just two girls from New York shopping for tasteful dildos?* "We're looking for a certain kind of shop, you see." I felt rather sheepish about losing my nerve.

"Yes," Duncan assured me, with a playful half-smile. "Milt's driving himself to Aix tomorrow, he'll be fine. But I have a better idea. Nice is rather a long way to drive for a day of shopping." The lightness of his verbal touch! I felt my embarrassment receding. It made me want to throw my arms around him—a brother-sister sort of hug.

He seemed to read my thoughts. "Don't worry," he said. "We'll go to Draguignan instead. In fact, I've been wanting to visit the plant nursery and take another look at some hedges for one of my English clients. There's a man nearby who breeds free-range rabbits. I might pick up—What's wrong?"

I was examining the carpet—discreetly—for any telltale evidence of Astroglide spillage. And I was looking at the chair. The chair where I was sitting the other day, mostly naked, with my legs open, when I realized that I was curious about . . . Duncan. The chair where I was kneeling and thinking about him while Milt—

I turned away, toward the bookshelf. "Nothing," I said. "I was just wondering who lived here before. It's a wonderful collection. And perhaps a little unusual to sell your house with the library intact. But not unheard of, I guess." There are as many out of print books in English as in French. *Laughter In Provence. Long Ago in France. Trampled Lilies.*

My heart started beating faster when I remembered myself sprawling on the chair. I remembered touching my panties, teasing my breasts, and—in my own way—using Duncan to entertain Milt.

The sensation was unforgettable.

He was staring at me with something like solicitude. His hand reached out to touch my arm, then pulled back. "Suzy? Are you—"

"I'm fine!"

"You look—"

"I've had some strange news from New York, that's all. I'm okay. It's nothing serious. Just—" My inane story was falling apart before it even came together. "Everything's going to be fine."

He gave me that searching but polite look—one he specializes in because, like me, he has a very specific job to do, and it involves protecting other people's privacy. It made me feel strangely close to him. We're both here to earn some money but, in my case, it's covert. He can never refer to what I do as a job. His diplomacy about shopping for sex toys is part of that. Only a gay man can really understand these things and handle them so well.

But I had an irrational urge to grab his upper arms, pull him into me, and kiss him—really kiss him, for a long time, on the mouth. I've thought about doing other things—but not kissing, until now. Yes, it really is a shameful waste!

"Is there something on your mind?" he asked.

Finally, I came to my senses. "I've been trying to place your accent," I said. "I keep wondering if you're from New Zealand. But I don't like to ask nosy questions. I'm sure you understand?"

"I do," he said. "And you have a good ear. I spent two years in Auckland and four years in a town called Aylesbury. But I was born in Halifax. And I won't try to place yours," he added. "It suits you to have a few secrets."

### Saturday, later

Just back from Draguignan.

Manhattanites think they're more European than other Americans, but I guess that's a delusion. The fact is, Europe *drives*. Allie and myself—modern women who expect a *man* to do the driving—are only modern by Manhattan standards.

"A perplexing anachronism," said Duncan, as I followed him to the SUV. "So it's a New York thing, is it?"

"A badge of honor," I told him.

Allie was already strapped into the front seat. Thank God, because I might be tempted to sit there myself. Before setting out for Draguignan, she insisted on a visit to the Ste. Maxiphony cibercafé to check on her email. "I won't be long," she promised. "I just have to check in with Roxana." When I followed her in, she looked surprised. Did she think I was spying on her? Or was I imagining that?

"I have to stay in touch with Matt!" I explained. "He thinks I'm on a road trip with my mother!"

I composed a harried-sounding message to my husband, re-inforcing the impression that I've stayed in six different *hôtelleries* in seven days:

> *This is the most exhausting thing I have ever done! Wish I could get my phone to work here! Lots of dead zones on these autoroutes. And, whenever we get to an internet café, it's closed. These cute little French towns are impossible—if they're not closed for lunch, they're taking their siesta. Every town seems to have a different system. Result being—nothing's ever open!*

A slight exaggeration, I suppose, but true enough by New York standards. I began a colorful description of the Var real estate Mother has supposedly been contemplating, then deleted my handiwork. The less said about this nonexistent experience, the better.

*I am cross-eyed from looking at one charming converted mas too many. Will write again soon, when we are in one place for more than two days. So far, Mother has not been tempted to sign on the dotted line. She sends her best.*

When we returned to the SUV, Duncan was talking on his phone. "She's right here," he said, as Allie climbed into the front, and I settled into my safe spot in the back. Handing his phone to me, he showed no expression when my fingers brushed against his. Milt was calling from a gas station on the N7. My eyes were trained on the back of Duncan's neck, as I listened.

"I'm on my way to Aix!" Milt was almost shouting. "And then I'm having dinner in Avignon. I won't be back till midnight, so don't wait up for me." I wonder what he's doing in Avignon, of all places, but asking would not be cool. Still. I had no idea Milt was so familiar with this region. "Why don't you go out for dinner? Ask Duncan to recommend someplace nice. Or you could go to the convent. It's on me. But that's not why I called," he said with a sly chuckle. "Can you talk?"

I reached for the door, and stepped onto the sidewalk. "I've been fantasizing all morning. That chick in Barcelona. The chick with a—with something extra. Can you ask Allison—"

"One thing at a time. When we're finished shopping for our toys, I'll put in a few calls on your behalf. Have I told you about my friend Isabel?"

"Baby! No! Who's Isabel? Have I told you that you're the perfect houseguest?"

"She just moved to St-Tropez, and she might have someone for us." I spoke very deliberately now. "She has a brand new collection, very exotic. And a driver. There's a travel charge, unless you visit her apartment in St-Tropez. Now, if she can't find someone who meets your exact specifications . . ."

"The more the merrier," Milt said. "Make the arrangements for us, and I'll be there with bells on. St-Tropez is a lot of fun."

He's not seriously considering a day trip to St-Tropez just to get laid—is he? I'm not sure I want Milt wandering into someone else's lair—especially a madam with girls from all over the map, some perhaps being far more exotic than myself.

I got off the phone quickly, making a mental note to watch what I say. Keep Milt focused on Isabel's outcalls, instead!

As for Draguignan, it's as wide-avenued, alive and bustling as St-Maximin isn't.

"And," said Duncan, "it's relevant in ways that St-Max never will be again."

This piqued Allie's curiosity. "Are you sure?" she asked in a surprisingly pointed way.

"Yes. It's got *military* relevance. You see that?" He pointed to a large white sign. "The Rhône cemetery's filled with Americans who liberated southern France from the Germans in 1944. Battles make a place relevant. That's why," he said, looking sideways at Allie, "there are two of those boutiques in Draguignan and you can't even find one in St-Max. Its economy is gathering dust now. St-Max used to be relevant because of its Church connections, but nobody cares what the Church establishment does anymore."

"Nobody?" Allie said.

"Well, nobody who—not in France and not enough to fight over it. What are you getting at?" Duncan said.

"Nothing." Allie, blushing nervously, looked away. "I guess you're right." Allie began to fiddle with her backpack. "Tell us about the two shops! Which one do you think we should go to first? Did Nnnnn-Suzy tell you about the item I'm trying to replace? We're looking for something that—"

"Something tasteful!" I said a little too loudly. "I'd love to know more about the American cemetery. Has Milt been?"

We were pulling up in front of the Ero Shop on the Boulevard de la Liberté. In the window, a neon sign, punctuated with a big X and a red heart, announced on one side: "Prêt à Porter. Cabine." On the other: "Fermé dimanche et jours fériés. Ouvert nonstop."

A French business that doesn't close for lunch?

"Couples come here," said Duncan. "The Pink Market on Clemenceau's more down market. I'll be back in a jiffy. I'm going to pick up some rabbits for Sunday dinner. Best rabbits in the region!"

In the Ero Shop, I pulled Allie aside. "The last thing I want to discuss with him is the specifics of your double dildo!" I told her. We were standing in front of a glass case containing some of the largest butt plugs I've ever seen. I looked away in horror and took comfort in the sight of some silly purple handcuffs. "It's enough that he's taking us here—he doesn't have to hear about what we're buying."

"He seems so open-minded," she protested. "It's not as if he doesn't KNOW that we work!"

"Of course he knows. But he's Milt's staff. You have to walk the line in a situation like this. He's respectful of our privacy. He's—he's a gentleman. We want him to stay that way."

Should we buy the Passionate Purple Twin Twister for fifty-nine euros? Why not. I pulled it carefully off the wall. As we wandered through the aisles, I saw the usual party gags—a German jock strap with a donkey face ("mit sound")—and lots of flexible jelly dildos with names like Toy Joy and G-Stick, in vibrant tropical colors. But no tasteful high-end Pyrex.

"We'll just have to make do with something bouncy and pedestrian," I sighed.

"Did Duncan say something about—" Allie wrinkled her brow. "*Rabbits?* For Sunday dinner?"

Milt and I have really been looking forward to Duncan's *lapin dijonnaise*. "They're free range!" I told her. "Don't you want to try something new?"

Her eyes popped open in distress.

Oh dear. It's bad enough that my best friend is a former cheerleader. For the first time since my arrival in France, I actively wish I hadn't stopped speaking to my *other* best friend. Jasmine would NEVER have qualms about a good rabbit dish. As long as it's on Atkins.

"Don't tell me you had a fucking pet rabbit!" I hissed.

Allie wrinkled her brow again. "As a matter of fact, I did. She died when I was eight, of natural causes. And her name was Nancy."

I almost dropped our brand new dildos onto the shop floor.

"Duncan will be very happy to make you a niçoise salad. I'll talk to him when we get back to the house," I promised, trying not to show my discomfort. "Just—just—don't forget to call me Suzy!"

CHAPTER EIGHT

# France: Noli Me Tangere

*Sunday morning*

An early breakfast with Milt, just the two of us, poolside, while Allie had coffee in her bedroom.

"Yesterday was a success!" I told him. "We had dinner in Villecroze. And Allison found some toys she wants to try out. At the Ero Shop in Draguignan. You were missed."

"That little auberge in Villecroze? Good choice." Milt cocked his head in the direction of Allison's window on the second floor. "Rapunzel's not bored I hope?"

"Not at all! Allie and I were thinking . . ." I waited for Milt's inevitable response, a mischievous, hopeful leer. "Maybe," I offered, "you'd like to watch us playing with our new toys in the nursery."

"Later this morning?"

"Can you wait until Allison gets back from church?"

"Allison's a churchgoer?" Milt looked surprised, avuncular and highly titillated—all at once.

"Well, I don't know if it's a habit with her, but her heart's set on attending Sunday Mass at this *particular* church, and I think she wants me to go with her. She got really intrigued when Duncan

107

talked about the basilique. She's very curious about the history of St-Maximin. She might want to look at the monastery."

"If you ask me, the monastery's cozier. And the service is better! But the church has quite a reputation," he said. "I think you should keep her company. This town's not exactly a shopping mecca, and I don't want you ladies getting bored."

It would never occur to me to attend Sunday Mass—but I'm glad if Allie wants to play religious tourist. It gets Milt out of my hair for a few hours, lets me off the hook (because it's HER idea), and reinforces the idea that we're two nicely brought up girls with wholesome cultural interests—who just happen to turn tricks for a living. Together.

It's the kind of thing every decent customer likes to think, and makes our bedroom activities seem ever more piquant.

### Sunday, later

When we entered the *basilique*, Allie looked around eagerly. "Where's the holy water?" she asked me. She was carrying a guide-book: *Christianity's third most important tomb*.

Has she ever been in a Catholic church before? Well, she's making up for lost time. I pointed to the font, but the disposable camera she pulled from her brand new Vuitton backpack had me worried.

"What are you doing? Didn't you see the sign?" The camera with the line through it? Over the large wooden door? Cameras, phones, dogs, junk food—taboos all. I guiltily remembered my phone and switched it to vibrate.

I'm waiting to find out whether Tini, the exotic star of Izzy's stable will honor Milt with her presence tomorrow. Malaysian, trilingual, pre-op, she's a bit of a triple threat. Let's hope Isabel calls soon. It will be a nice coda, something Milt can remember me for when this vacation (his) ends.

We were early for Mass, and people were milling around, looking at historical displays, lighting candles, visiting the gift shop. Milt's right. There's a buzz about this church, even if Duncan says it peaked in the fifteenth century. And now, it's hard to sort out the worshipers from the tourists.

"I'm here to *document* something," Allie said. She slipped the camera under her guidebook and held it tight. "I can't believe NONE of those people are taking pictures. Do you realize where we are?"

"Don't try to take pictures during Mass," I warned her. "They might throw us out. What do you mean? Of course I know where we are."

"I'm taking these pictures for a reason! Anyway, I'm going down there." She pointed to a gate at the top of a stone staircase. A little girl, with a long pale face and straight brown hair, was standing next to the gate wearing a linen alb. She leaned over and watched, with a serious intensity, as Allie descended. It would be just like Allie not to realize that she's about to get busted by an eight-year-old. I followed Allie and made my way downstairs, nodding politely at the juvenile gatekeeper.

"*Madame.*" I looked back. The altar girl was tapping her wrist. "*Cinq minutes,*" she told me.

When I got downstairs, I found Allie standing before a stone archway. She was peering into a glass window at a copper reliquary the height of a toddler, with elongated pointy wings, and thick wavy hair surrounding the face of a human skull.

Two pot-bellied men in travel vests were competing with each other for a closer view of the blackened skull. Allie was completely blocking them. She was oblivious, concentrating hard, fiddling with the forbidden camera beneath her guidebook.

"Hey!" I whispered loudly. She jumped and turned around. "They're about to close this shrine for the Mass, and that kid *works for the church*. She's coming downstairs to get you."

"You have to see this!" Allie beckoned to me. "This is Mary Magdalen's skull! Christianity's Third Most Important Tomb."

OMG. Well, the presentation's both garish and ghoulish, but there's something compelling going on here. Pilgrims, kings, Dominican priests, hotel chains. They've been making a huge fuss over these relics for eight hundred years. I peered into the shrine and studied the face of the skeleton.

"You can't possibly know if it's her, Allie. And what is that?" I pointed at a glass tube, encased in a gold seal.

"That's the noli—noli—" Allie touched her forehead with her index finger. "Something Christ said to Mary Magdalen because she thought he was the gardener. He could touch her, but she couldn't touch him."

A curious deal—if Mary Magdalen was, indeed, a hooker.

"It's a little bit of skin or something from Mary Magdalen's forehead that got preserved," Allie said.

"It can't *really* be." I shook my head, sighed deeply, and looked at the ceiling of the crypt. Is this Allie's latest hobby?

"Noli me tangere," said one of the men in a low, jovial tone. *Do not touch me.* He turned to his friend and smiled wryly in my direction. "Elle ne croit pas."

No longer vying for a glimpse of the unattainable relic, they were appraising the real live blonde before them and her skeptical Asian friend. They probably can't afford us, but that never stops anyone from looking. And we do look rather good together. Something about our bodies being almost the same but slightly different. A man just knows he won't have to worry about favoring one over the other—because we're equally pretty.

The altar girl, in her severe linen robe, appeared in the doorway. Her precocious aplomb must have put a damper on whatever fantasies those two were having. They scurried upstairs.

During the service, the little gatekeeper tag-teamed with an

African altar boy whose face is as round as hers is long. "Isn't that sweet!" Allie whispered, when the two children stood before the priest. The boy holding an open bible with both hands; the girl holding aloft a cordless mic in hers.

You shouldn't need a mic in here! Wasn't this church built for sound? But microphones are to priests as the internet is to call girls. A done deal. The priest who works unmiked. The hooker without a website, who still believes in getting new business the old-fashioned way. We're all becoming relics.

Though relics, if that crypt is any indication, can have staying power. Thank God for old school madams like Isabel and Liane, then.

## Monday, July 15

Tini arrived at noon, in a black Lexus, driven by a tall, muscular man with a permanent suntan, as the French sometimes say. You wouldn't want to mess with Serge—he's got bouncer cred—but his manner, with me, was both gentle and cordial.

Serge offered to wait in his car, but Duncan urged him to hang out on the chaise longue in Milt's media hut. The converted dairy shed (!) has air conditioning, a small bar, and a plasma TV that fills an entire wall. "Or the pool, if you prefer?"

They chattered quietly about road work on the A8 and municipal politics in St-Tropez—Serge, practicing his English; Duncan, putting his French to work.

I whisked Tini upstairs to her designated bedroom, where I handed her an envelope—2000 euros for an hour of pleasure and God knows how much travel time. I wonder what the split is, with Isabel.

"I woke up at seven to get here on time!" She moaned in a good-natured way, opened the envelope, and counted the money carefully. "I hope this man of yours is not going to be difficult. I'm not used to these early mornings."

Who, among us, is? And I'm not used to girls I work with counting the money in front of me. Then I remembered: it's been many years since I did business with someone—whether madam, client or call girl—who is almost, well, actually, a total stranger. I felt rebuked, but couldn't really blame her. Maybe she hasn't known Izzy as long as I've known Liane. In which case, my connection to Izzy through Liane would mean nothing to her.

"You're very beautiful," I told her. "Even more beautiful than Isabel suggested."

Tini smiled—a glittering, happy, feline smile, the smile of a working girl who has invested many tens of thousands in her body and her face. Far more than Charmaine, since her work is more intricate. She knows the value of praise. Her skin is flawless and creamy-smooth. Her eyes may have been done—but they're gorgeous almonds, not round and childlike, the way some cosmetically altered eyes end up. If Charmaine could see the work on Tini, she would be floored.

There's a shiny elegance about her. If she used to be—still has some of the attributes of—a man or a boy, you would never know it. With her clothes on—she was wearing a trim white pantsuit, beige patent leather sling backs—Tini looks thoroughly post-op. She's taut-limbed, with precise cheekbones—you can't buy those—and must have been a tiny male. Now she looks like a beautiful girl, period, and knows it.

"Do you mind if I ask? Is that your hair? If it's a wig, I should be careful not to touch it in bed."

It's supernaturally long and thick, almost black. She ran her fingers through it, flipped it over her shoulders and said, "All mine." Wow. Is that from all the hormones she's taking? But I don't know her well enough to ask. "Don't worry about my hair," she laughed. "You can touch it. But I don't do girls. Don't touch anything else!"

"He might ask you to, you know, do stuff with one of us—and there's another girl staying here."

"I'm not worried."

I suppose, with all Tini has going for her, she doesn't worry too much about the consequences of saying no. I felt a twinge of envy for this gorgeous Asian call girl who has that extra something I lack. Maybe it's because I've never worked with an Asian tranny before. Sandra, in New York, is Brazilian—or says she is. Will Milt be making comparisons? Could Tini be some sort of idealized version of the call girl he sees twice a month, sometimes three times, in New York?

I wanted to ask how recently she had the work done, whether she plans on staying pre-op for life. But I didn't. She, however, surprised me by asking: "Where are you from?"

"New York," I told her. "By way of London."

"No, I mean—where are you really from?"

"Well, I was born in Trinidad, but I left when I was a baby, then I grew up in Ottawa." Why was I telling Tini so much about myself? Was I maybe trying to please her? Keep her in a happy mood, so nothing would go wrong in the bedroom? Get her to trust me more?

"But you look—what about your family?"

"My mother's Chinese," I said. "Is that what you mean?"

She nodded. "I'm going to take a quick shower, no problem?"

There was something unnerving about the whole exchange, the closed look on her face when I said Chinese. Is this a Malaysian thing? Then I remembered that I once told a guy—my first customer—that *I* was Malaysian. I couldn't think of anything else to be, for some reason. I wanted one word to describe myself, not ten or twenty. Whatever Tini's background, she's come a long way from somewhere—maybe it's not really Malaysia—and she's got something against the Chinese. Should I have said something else?

In the bedroom, when all three of us ooohed and ahhhed over her unusual beauty, Tini warmed up. She allowed Milt, but not Allison or Suzy, to touch her high, perfect breasts. I felt like keeping my bra on, just to keep up, so to speak. That was easy enough— Milt was focusing on Tini.

Allie and I became administrative assistants, taking care of Milt's lower body, while she monopolized his eyes and his mouth.

"You are one gorgeous incredible hot piece of, ahhhh, well, work of art," Milt sighed, reaching up to play with her nipples. "Suzy's been telling me how much she wants to suck your cock!"

Tini threw me a dirty look. Well, what else was I supposed to tell him? Sure, I'd like to, just to be able to say I've tried it, like a new restaurant. But mostly, it's the polite thing to say. At all times. About ANY other hooker who's sharing your customer's bed. That you're hot for her. So why the prima donna scowl? Maybe something to do with where I'm "really" from?

"Mmmmmm. So do I!" Allison said. "Want to, I mean."

Tini was kneeling over Milt, rubbing her cock on his chest and his face. She tossed her long hair over her shoulder. "I'm not into women," she said. "I don't do anything with girls."

Allie looked crestfallen. However, Tini's bitchiness wasn't bothering Milt. His cock was growing harder, and I sensed that a little more pleading on our part might do the trick.

"Are you sure?" I asked her. "Just once?"

Allie was rolling a condom onto Milt with her mouth. Without missing a beat, with Milt's cock still in her mouth, she handed a condom to Tini.

"Don't put that on yet," Milt gasped. He intercepted Tini's condom. Would she or wouldn't she? Let Milt perform some bareback oral sex?

Allie and I were kneeling on the bed across from each other, with Tini's tight, yet not too muscular, back hiding our faces. Allie gave me a shocked "Now what?" stare.

Like most girls, I think it's fine for a customer to go down on *me* without a barrier—and so does Allie, despite all the NYCOT rhetoric about dental dams—but I always use a condom to go down on HIM. I thought our double standard was based on a hierarchy of sex organs—a cock is always held to account, a pussy gets away with more. Tini's double standard seems to be purely about *herself*. Like mine.

She dipped forward, placing her uncovered cock between Milt's lips. You can't argue with success. Milt came so fast that, if I hadn't known him this long, I'd be tempted to develop a complex.

Ten minutes later, I was surprised to find Allison in Tini's room. As I entered, I heard Allie saying "down some stairs"—or maybe not. They both fell silent. Allie was still in her underwear, trying to hide her camera, but she had nowhere to put it.

Pretending not to notice all this, I handed our guest a roll of post-orgasmic euros, hastily organized by Milt. "Thanks for taking him off our hands. He's taking a nap now! But he asked me to give you something extra. It's just between us. Nothing to do with Isabel."

Allie slipped out of the room, looking like a child who's been caught raiding the cookie jar. Tini gave her a cool wave and began changing into her equally cool travel gear.

When I returned to my room, I noticed that my phone was vibrating noisily—signaling a voicemail. What a joy it's been, alone with my phone for the last eleven days! I never have to erase Call History—and I've actually begun to feel more relaxed—because I'm not constantly looking over my shoulder.

Matt's message was an almost dutiful "just checking in" voice-mail. Occasionally, I get a late-night email that's a little sentimental,

115

a little casual. The emotional routines of a happy husband, a successful marriage!

I'll be sad to leave this oasis of extramarital calm to return to New York, but all good things must come to a gentle (not screeching) halt. If you want the best of both worlds, you have to quit while you're ahead. And who knows, perhaps Milt wants me to come back to Villa Gambetta next year.

He's clearly impressed with my international connections and, more to the point, doesn't have direct access to Isabel. But . . .

What was Allie doing? Taking pictures of Tini for her scrap-book? I really have to talk to her about this camera when she gets back from the cibercafé. And make sure she hasn't done something to gum up my relationship with Isabel.

## Monday evening

When Milt knocked on my bedroom door, late in the day, I was sprawled on my bed wearing nothing, save a thick layer of grey cream on my face and neck.

What's up? He never does that!

"Ummmmm. Ummmmm. One sec," I called out. The mask was making it hard to move my lips.

"It's all right, kiddo, I'm going for my swim. I'll meet you by the pool. We need to talk."

I rinsed my face quickly and, just this once, since nobody else was home, appeared poolside wearing nothing but a bright pink polo shirt, bikini panties, and my pony-skin flip-flops. I settled into a long pool chair next to the deep end and listened, with my eyes closed, to the sound of Milt swimming.

He stopped near my chair, grabbed the side of the pool and began to kick the water vigorously.

"It's good we can talk alone," he said, panting slightly.

"What's wrong?" I turned a little so I could see his face. "Did something happen?"

"I have to go to Luxembourg. There's something I need to deal with there. I'm sorry to leave you alone like this, but I'm leaving tonight. Duncan's driving me to Marseille." He stopped kicking the water. His hands were resting on the side of the pool and he looked up at me. Our eyes met. In the more than ten years we've been doing business, has he ever looked at me quite like that? He was more direct and businesslike than usual, none of the usual kidding or lechery in his gaze.

"Nobody else has to know where I am. Don't answer the phone—it goes straight to voicemail. You'll have a way to contact me at all times. If there's a problem, I don't want you to be stranded here. But Allison and Duncan don't have to know where I am. It's just between us. If Allison asks—you can tell her I went to Paris. But Duncan won't ask . . . Come here." He reached up with one hand. "Don't worry," he laughed. "I'm not going to pull you in. That ain't my style. I like knowing you're safe and dry."

Extending my hand cautiously, I allowed him to hold it lightly. An unusual gesture for a customer, even one as familiar as Milt. He was careful not to enclose my hand, but found a way to keep it there.

"I really enjoy your company, kiddo."

"And mine enjoys yours," I said. "Will you be back in time to kiss me goodbye?"

"Oh, I'm just going for the day," he said. "Sure. But where do I get to kiss you?"

"Any place below my neck," I told him.

"You're a nice girl, but you're nobody's fool. That's a pretty outfit. I've never seen that particular combination before. Your breasts are just right. Natural."

"Oh?" I smiled. Three hours ago, he was fondling Tini's silicone splendor! Men are such inconsistent freaks. "Flattery will . . . get you somewhere, I guess."

"I guess it will," Milt said, laughing. "If we had both been single and I were just a bit younger, we'd be a couple. I would have made it my business to court you."

That again! I like hearing it—once a year—but he's so wrong about us.

"You're saying all these things because I'm leaving soon." But I said it in a warm, teasing way. "You guys are all the same."

"No, kiddo. It's actually my way of asking you to stay an extra week. I realize I'm not the most interesting company—maybe you can persuade Allison to stay, too, if she's not all booked up in New York. I know how busy that girl gets." *No, you don't quite know how, but that's okay.* "Whaddaya think?"

He let go of my hand and ran his fingers along the tiled lip of the pool, while I thought.

"I need to . . . figure some things out." And, if I stay another week, get a pedicure!

"Okay! So let me finish my laps, pack, get my butt to the airport. I'll call you when I land, and we'll take it from there."

"But," I warned him. "I can't guarantee Allison. You know how busy she gets." She probably needs to lead her first Intimacy Coaching workshop! Or chair the next NYCOT meeting.

I raced upstairs to call Isabel, to see who else she might have for us.

Though I haven't officially made a decision—I'd like to keep Milt dangling, for some reason. Could that mean I'm developing real feelings for the man?—I want to get all (or at least most) of my ducks in a row.

What should I tell Matt? And, more to the point, should I deliver my alibi via phone? Or email?

CHAPTER NINE

# France: There's Something About Marie

*Monday, much later*

On his way out the door, Milt left a small envelope in my bedroom: "In case you want to go shopping," he told me. "It's on the dresser. Do some sight-seeing with Allison, Duncan will take you girls anywhere you want. I'll be back soon." He winked at me. "You get cuter every summer." And then, he hopped into Duncan's SUV.

Allison was sitting at one of the outdoor tables near the pool, with a bottle of rosé, contemplating the setting sun. Now that Milt's on his way to Luxembourg, we can drink as much as we want! I found a glass in the kitchen and sat across from her, slipping out of my flip-flops.

"It's soooo pretty and still!" she said with a wistful sigh. She topped up my glass. "When does Milt come back from Paris? Can we—can you ask Duncan to drive us to the mountain? There's something I really need to see. And—" her tone was strangely urgent "—I should really see it *tomorrow*."

"Which mountain? Sure, I guess, why not? What do you need to see?" Allie is unnaturally well-informed about this town. Is she doing this to curry favor? With who though? Milt? Duncan? Certainly not with me.

"The interior of Mary Magdalen's cave," she informed me. "It's an important part of my camera project."

*Oh. That reminds me.* "Have you been taking pictures of this house?"

Allison looked shocked. "No! Why would I?"

"I don't know. You said you were documenting your visit. Milt's very flattered by the way—he likes it that you're interested in the local history. But you have to realize that we're here on business. Milt needs to have his privacy protected. You know he's married, and he's a partner in his firm."

And, I didn't tell her, he's obviously worried about something. Something that occasions a day trip—to Luxembourg, of all places. He's also delaying his return to New York. Business? Or something marital? No, it wouldn't be marital. But I can feel it when he's got something on his mind. And I remember how, three summers ago, that scary girl from California tried to blackmail him. If Milt sees Allie walking around with a camera, he might—in his current frame of mind—be reminded of that.

"I mean, Milt has a very nice house," I said, "but I don't want you going back to New York with identifying shots." I'm responsible for what Allie does while she's here. God! It's really like babysitting.

"The Document I'm Creating," Allie intoned, paused, had some more wine, "has-nothing-whatsoever-to-do-with-Milt-or-this-house." She set down her glass. "This IS a nice house, but wait'll you see this cave! Mary Magdalen's final dwelling. I've heard that it's the size of—the size of a small townhouse! Like a duplex! Have you seen the pictures on the web?"

"No," I admitted—impressed, despite myself. "This is all news to me." *That's a lot of real estate for a single woman!* "But . . . didn't you take a picture of Tini today? Inside *this* house?"

"No! I was just showing her . . ."Allie sipped some more rosé, avoiding my gaze.

"What were you showing her?"

"How many pictures I had left on the camera."

Strange.

"But you hardly know her."

Allie looked confused and uncomfortable. "I—I *know* I hardly know her!"

"What were you doing in there?"

"I told you! I was showing her . . . I was just showing her how the camera works. I don't know. It seemed like a good idea at the time," Allie said in a high voice. "She seems like such an interesting person! Is there some reason why I can't befriend another sex worker when I'm in a foreign country? Is it a crime for two sex workers to fraternize? Sex workers all over the world are divided by borders and laws, but we still have the right—-"

"Allie, please, this isn't a press conference! Sometimes, it's not a *good idea* to 'fraternize.'" I poured some more wine. "Did you two exchange numbers?"

"Of course not!" Allie said. "Why would I do that?"

"You looked awfully chummy, and you were just ranting about your right to befriend someone five seconds ago! Why WOULDN'T you exchange numbers? I need to make sure you don't do something that will create a problem for me. Or Milt."

"How would I do THAT?"

"Well, you just never know. There are too many variables. Do you understand?"

"I *guess* so." Allie looked lost now.

"Okay, look, if Isabel hears that you and Tini exchanged numbers, she might get the wrong idea and think it's all about me going over her head. If she thinks I'm trying to cut her out by dealing directly with Tini, that's a huge problem for ME. Look,"

I pleaded with her. "I don't want Isabel to stop taking my calls! I just started doing business with her, and she's an important contact. I've had some bad experiences, okay?"

That meltdown with Trish—I still haven't recovered from it, but I don't want to go there with Allie. It's too embarrassing. I allowed her to think I was remembering some hellish incident from the long ago past when I was a junior call girl.

"Well," Allie said, in a shaky voice. "I can promise you that Tini and I weren't exchanging numbers—and if we did, it wouldn't be for business! I wouldn't lie to you about that!"

Then why is Allie so jittery?

OMG. How could I be such an insensitive, sexually naive, clod??

Allie has a *crush* on Tini. I've never known Allie to be hung up on a girl, but I suppose there's a first time for everything. And perhaps, well, she feels shy about telling me something so . . . unconventional? Yes, this might be a little more than Allie was prepared for emotionally. Despite all her radical posturing.

Anyway, Tini made it very clear that she's not into girls.

Oh no. Is there something in the Provençal breeze? My unrequited hots for Duncan. Allie's sudden infatuation with a pre-op tranny who won't give her the time of day.

Well. These inappropriate longings are like hundred dollar bills in the hands of a runaway teenager. They come, they excite you, they're gone within a week. Or a day, if you're lucky.

It's nothing another glass of rosé can't fix. We both needed a day off from Milt!

### Tuesday morning, July 16, 2002

. . . But perhaps did not need this hangover. Where did I put the Prontalgine?

Still, I'm glad that Allie and I have decided we can stay for another week. We work well together, she uses condoms the same way I do, and I know all her faults and her quirks.

A visit to the retirement-grotto of Marie-Madeleine! Perhaps the mountain air will do us both some good.

And Duncan has promised to stop at the cibercafé before we head out for the *massif de la Sainte-Baume.*

## Tuesday, later

I didn't expect the road from Nans-les-Pins to Plan d'Aups to be quite so challenging—and I wasn't even driving! Duncan, of course, was equal to the challenge. I, in the back seat, tried to reduce my anxiety by making light of it.

"I can see why people might prefer to travel this road by donkey—if they had a choice," I told him.

"Yes," Duncan agreed. Once again, I was staring at the back of his neck admiring his neat hairline—but this time, it was to avoid looking out the window. "Imagine what it must have been like during the transition from mule to motorcar," he said. "Sort of like being able to choose between DOS and Windows, when both platforms were in use."

"Omigosh!" said Allie. "It's really steep!" She lowered her window, and faced the breeze. Gazing out at the sky she pointed toward a pale building on a distant windswept plain. "Do you think we can stop at that Benedictine hostel?" The building she was pointing to was about the size of a thimble. "It's soooo inspiring! To be so high up! I wonder why there's no railing, though. Shouldn't there maybe be a fence here? I mean, look how close we are to . . ."

I looked away from the sky, wishing she would shut up, yet hoping to sound magnanimous. "It's really amazing," I said, "how much you know about this area. I mean it's your first trip to the south of France."

"Oh!" Allie simpered. "It's not so amazing. And Mary Magdalen *is* our patron saint, after all."

"You're sure about that?" Duncan spoke in a flat, noncommittal voice.

"Sure about what?"

"Your patron saint."

"What do you mean?" Allie turned to face him but he—to my relief—didn't reciprocate. He was focusing on the road.

"She's also a patron saint to hairdressers," he pointed out. "There's a lot of debate about the Magdalen's identity. The details of her life are unclear."

"*Are you saying* that Mary Magdalen needs to be *rehabilitated*?"

"No," said Duncan. "I'm not."

"Well, that's what it sounds like."

Why is Allie taking this shrill tone?

I, staring down the side of the hill, didn't feel this was appropriate. There was a sheer drop and Duncan was about to make another sharp left. Now is the time to agree with every opinion the driver's ever had in his life, about everything. On the other hand, Duncan's quite socially skillful—he didn't actually express an opinion just now!

I cleared my throat and tried to change the subject. "These things are highly subjective, aren't they?" I said.

"Subjective?" said Allie. "Well, in my opinion, Mary Magdalen having a bad reputation is a GOOD thing. For everybody! Whether they realize it or not!"

She's being unnecessarily querulous, and needs to remember that Duncan is performing a valuable service here. Getting us up this winding mountain road! As he came to a sharp bend, we heard a horn. I looked behind, saw nothing and held my breath. The vehicle coming toward us. *Let it be a small bicycle or at least not the size of a tow truck.* A mid-size Citroën. It seemed to take forever for us to pass. When I opened my eyes, we were making another sharp turn.

I tried, again, to get Allison out of this argumentative mode. "You seem very interested in the saints," I said. "You're not thinking about conversion, are you?"

"Conversion?" Allie said. "What do you mean?" Best not to go there—don't want to give her any new ideas! She turned to Duncan. "Maybe the monks at the hostel will let me take some pictures?"

"The hostel is actually run by nuns," said Duncan. "Benedictine monks took care of the cave for two centuries, but Dominicans took over the Magdalen enterprise in 1295. The Benedictines were chased out—evicted by Charles of Anjou."

"That's terrible! Where did they go?"

"Nobody seems to know or care," said Duncan. "History is written by the sitting tenants. Dominicans were the next big thing."

"People were just—thrown out?" Allie looked horrified. "After taking care of her cave? For two hundred years?"

"Mmmm." Duncan was expressionless. "Supposedly, they left without a fight. Dominicans in, Benedictines out. That's how it goes."

"The poor things! I wonder if they starved to death!"

"A hundred years ago, some Benedictine nuns came back when that hostel was built, but the Dominicans control the cave and they keep the Benedictines in their place—at the foot of the mountain."

"Is this really true?" she asked. "Why are you saying these things about the caretakers of Mary Magdalen's home?"

"I have a feeling—" Duncan spoke very carefully "—that the history of Magdalen-worship isn't as pretty as you might like it to be."

Allison became rather subdued, and didn't speak to Duncan again, until we reached the parking lot of the Plan d'Aups snack bar, next to the Benedictine hostel.

"So, ummmm, do you think any of the Benedictines will be able to, um, speak English?" Allie asked him.

"I wouldn't count on it," he said. "Why don't you let me translate?"

*Quel* relief to be on flat ground again! The *hôtellerie*—no longer a thimble—is a big boxy affair, bright yellow brick with a red sloping roof. I watched Allie and Duncan disappearing through an archway, and found a corner table in the snack bar, where I could recover from the unsettling car trip and the remains of my hangover.

A banal accordion tune—French folk Muzak—was coming from the overhead sound system. The perfect accompaniment for my thoroughly mediocre cup of tea. The cure for a hangover isn't mountain air so much as mountain fear, followed by some stale tea and even staler music. The combo was strangely refreshing.

After a second cup, I was ready for the trek to Marie-Madeleine's mountaintop "maisonette."

But first: a voicemail from Isabel with scheduling possibilities for Katya—young, tall, Hungarian, "and very refined, like a 1950s supermodel." And a message from Milt, happy to receive my news: "Excellent, kiddo! Glad you ladies can honor me with your presence. But things got a little screwed up here, and I have to stay another night. Tell Duncan I'll be coming back in the A.M., will you? "

Allie appeared at my table, carrying a stack of brochures—*Pèlerinage à la Grotte, Fête de Sainte Marie-Madeleine*—but wearing a sad frown.

"They closed the footpath to her cave! For security reasons!"

"Where's Duncan?"

"He's making some phone calls for me. And talking to the nuns about—um—about the footpath."

That strange look again! Or did I just imagine it? She seems to be worried about something.

On our way back to St-Max, Allie sat in the front of Duncan's SUV, staring mutely at the pine forest alongside the N560, sighing occasionally as she fiddled with her cellphone. I closed my eyes and drifted off, grateful for silence. When I opened them, we were pulling into town, and Duncan was negotiating (with his usual deftness and civility) a minor knot of cars, pedestrians and mopeds around the Restoration fountain in the Place Malherbe.

After driving up that treacherous road, to the tune of Allison's whims, Duncan surely deserves a break. And a good meal. I've suggested taking us all to dinner at the monastery because it's almost around the corner, a three-minute drive. He thinks we'll have a better time in Entrecasteaux where his friends run a small restaurant called, what else, Lavande.

"The roasted gambas—" he smiled when my eyes lit up "—are locally famous. If we leave early enough, you can visit the castle. Check out the local architecture. It's very eleventh century," he added. "And Allison's curious to see the old church."

## Later

Dinner with Allie and Duncan, in a well-preserved, relatively unhyped, medieval village . . . seemed like the best idea I've heard all day.

As we sat in the SUV, waiting for Allie, Duncan filled me in on recent history. "When the castle was auctioned off last year, the new owners agreed to allow daytime visits." He glanced at his watch. "We might have to settle for an exterior view." He looked at his watch again, with as little expression as possible, and raised his left eyebrow.

"I'll go upstairs and find Allison," I said.

When I knocked on her bedroom door, there was no response. Turning the handle gently, I listened for Allie's blow-dryer. The room was silent, and the bathroom door wide open. No sign of Allison herself, but her suitcase—a kind of window to her soul—was lying on the floor, wide open. I spotted some *Queer Diaspora* T-shirts, two boxes of Trojans, and a battered paperback—*A Vindication of the Rights of Whores*—before I noticed the brochures and maps on her bed, her disposable camera on top of a half-open map. Feeling somewhat uncertain about my behavior, I stole a quick look at the open map before exiting my best friend's temporary sanctum. It's a very detailed street map, with purple arrows added, perhaps by Allison, and some unfamiliar, red handwriting—not hers. A map of St-Max? Or somewhere else?

Downstairs, I heard Allie's breathless voice. It was coming from behind the library door. "It's a *really* steep road!" she was saying. "I don't know. I'll find out. No, I can't ask him. I just can't!"

Who on earth is she talking to? I felt embarrassed about listening, and tried to compensate by rattling the door before I entered. The guilty look on her face surprised me.

"I—I was just taking a quick look at something in here." *Here* being a book on her lap, a glossy edition of *The Golden Legend.* "And then my phone rang!"

I took a quick look at the carpet. My inner housewife feels almost guilty about spilling Astroglide while fucking Milt on that chair—though I'm the only one who can see the spot. As for *The Golden Legend,* I was mystified.

"If we don't leave soon, we won't be able to see much," I warned her. "Don't you want to visit the church before it gets dark out?"

"Yes!" she exclaimed, bouncing out of the armchair. "Let's!"

During our meal at Lavande, Allie's interest in *The Golden Legend* became much clearer halfway through her first glass of rosé. I listened with half an ear, savoring the texture of the gambas.

"Don't you think it's kind of a neat coincidence?" she said.

"How Mary Magdalen landed at Marseille? *So did I!* And so will—" She paused, frowned, turned to Duncan. "Are you *sure* you don't want some wine?"

"I'll just nurse my Evian, thanks."

"I had no idea Mary Magdalen was ever in Marseille," I confessed. "Where'd you hear that?"

"Mary Magdalen was in a boat with Maximinus and a few other people." She picked up her wine glass. "Maximinus was one of the original seventy-two disciples—and the original Saint Maximin who settled here." Amazing. Almost overnight, Allie has latched onto some quite specialized Catholic folklore. "They all landed at Marseille. According to *The Golden Legend*."

"The golden *agenda*," Duncan pointed out. "Written by a high-ranking Dominican."

A cloud passed over Allie's face. "Do you think you might be a little prejudiced? About Dominicans?"

"I don't have a dog in this fight." Duncan refilled my wine glass, then Allie's. "The Dominicans made themselves useful to Charles of Anjou. They suppressed local heretics, helped out during the Inquisition and squashed a social movement, but it wasn't enough. *The Golden Legend* gave them a prestige that wasn't purely military."

"They squashed . . . a social movement?" The look on Allie's face—sheer terror—made me recall my own feelings on that precarious mountain road. "Could they do something like that *now*?" Allie was gazing directly into his eyes, causing me to look away—embarrassed, yet grateful that she wasn't bored.

"The Inquisitions are over," Duncan told her. "I recommend the linden soufflé. It's Nora's special recipe."

"Perfect," I said, as Duncan looked around for the owner. "Let's have three. I never share dessert."

All seemed normal during our return trip.

As Duncan turned right, onto the N7, Allie piped up: "Let's all have brandy by the pool!"

Our last chance to drink freely before Milt, like Magdalen, alights at Marseille. At which point, Allie and I revert to our two-drink rule. "Excellent idea," I agreed. "Duncan?"

I was wide awake as we made our way back to the house, but must have had blinders on. I dashed upstairs to brush my teeth, checked my voicemail, then wandered downstairs to set up our after-dinner drinks in the kitchen. I switched on the pool lights, and noticed that the house was much too quiet. I found a bright orange napkin, large enough to function as table cover, and organized three glasses of Armagnac on one of the low poolside tables. My first domestic gesture in days. It felt good to be playing house again.

I sipped some Armagnac and stretched out, under the black sky, on a sun chair. Could Allison be in the library? Double-checking the virtues of *The Golden Legend*? A familiar sound—hard to describe—made me get up. Cradling my glass, I walked past the rose garden, through the olive trees, breathing in thyme and lavender, remarking silently on all the competing scents.

The SUV was parked in its usual place and Allison's window was rolled down. What I saw was so shocking—yet normal—that my entire body felt betrayed. Allison, with her seatbelt still fastened, was holding onto the back of Duncan's head with one hand. His face was buried in her neck—thank God he didn't see me. I could tell, from the way he handled her, the things she said, that his fingers had slipped between her legs. She gasped loudly, moaned in a way that she *never* does when it's business, and began kissing him, hard, on the mouth. He wasn't resisting. He wasn't teasing her. He was too hungry for that. *How could you*, I wanted to scream—but didn't. And that's when Allie opened her eyes.

I covered my mouth, turned around, and disappeared into the garden with my glass of brandy. When I returned to my pool chair, I realized I was shaking. Not crying, just shaking. Uncontrollably. I downed the rest of my drink, then picked up another glass of brandy.

"How could you?" I whispered. But who was I saying it to?

CHAPTER TEN

# France: Access to Evil

*Wednesday, July 17, 2002. The Morning After*

Milt returns in a few hours, and I need to be ON. Cheerful. Sexy. No make-up. Glowing with confidence. Witty. Though I feel, at this moment, socially retarded, sexually inept, an exile from All Things Call Girl.

Last night, after consuming that third Armagnac in bed, I was numb. When I woke, my pillow had fallen to the floor, the phone was buzzing, and I was in desperate need of a Prontalgine. *How fucking thoughtful* of Duncan to provide me, in advance, with the answer to this morning's headache. The perfect . . . concierge, I thought bitterly.

I waited for the sound of his SUV pulling out of the driveway. *Okay, he's on his way to Marseille, and the codeine is kicking in.* I opened my window. Another beautiful morning in Provence!

Allie was sitting at the edge of the pool, wearing a sleek white one-piece with a diamond-shaped cut out that shows off her back, and a white sun hat, splashing her feet like a carefree child. I watched as she threw her hat onto a chair. She jumped into the water and began floating, in a rather aimless way, on her back, then switched to a butterfly stroke.

I emerged from my sad cocoon, and tiptoed into Allison's bedroom. Her suitcase was still on the floor with most of its contents untouched, except for one box of Trojans. I couldn't bear to look, but I did. I covered the ripped box with a T-shirt. Then I removed the T-shirt and forced myself to count. She took FOUR condoms to Duncan's room? The pile on her unused bed—maps, camera, books—was exactly as I left it before dinner.

Just as I suspected.

She fell asleep in his bed. In his arms. I felt a knot in my chest. That day in the library when I wanted to grab Duncan and pull him very close. Why did I think he was off-limits to girls? What's his deal? Is he bi?

But wait. Allie never thought he was gay. Milt doesn't either.

What made *me* think it? Am I the last person in this house to figure out that Milt's cook, object of all my lurid unprofessional fantasies, isn't into guys at all? Let's face it. When it comes to males under thirty, my gaydar's a pathetic mess. I've spent too many years dealing with guys like Milt. Straight boys seem gay, and gay guys seem too masculine.

I rushed out of Allie's bedroom into my own, filled with an awful kind of hatred. Hating myself. For hating my best friend. No. I hate myself for HAVING a best friend. A friend who could make such a fool of me.

My phone was buzzing again, reminding me that—omigod— while I was inspecting another girl's recreational condom stash (arguably none of my business), I was supposed to be taking care of business. When I picked up, Izzy was terse.

"Are you all right? This is my third attempt to return your call."

"Sorry!" I gasped. "It's been a busy morning. I, um, had some other calls to make. Mil—My friend's coming back from Lux—from Paris—in a few hours. I've been meaning to call!"

"Yes, yes, I know all that. Please don't babble. I'm trying to sort this out." The impatience of a madam who could write the Call Girl's Encyclopedia of Excuses. If she only had time. "Katya won't be arriving until fourteen-thirty. Is that going to be a problem? I have Natalia—she could be there earlier. Blonde. Like Katya. Quite similar."

The more players in Milt's bed, the more distracted *I'll* be. The orgy was surely invented, by some heartbroken hooker, a million years ago, as a form of occupational therapy. Perhaps he'd like four girls? No. Better to dish out the supplementary girls one at a time. For a guy like Milt, three is plenty.

"Who's younger?" I asked. "Katya? Or Natalia?"

"If *that's* the issue . . ."

"Well, it's not really, but it might be nice to have someone super-young. Just for a change of pace, you know?"

"Katya's nineteen," Isabel told me. "She's what you have in mind."

Nineteen. That's about twenty-five in hooker years. But still, younger than Allie. And, if blondes are anything like Orientals, they're fundamentally a lot more jealous of *each other*. It's no coincidence that Allie's closest friends (that would include me!) aren't blonde.

What if I bring in a succession of MUCH younger blondes, just to needle Allison? And what if Duncan develops an interest in Katya? Hit her where she lives.

Can I really engineer that?

The trouble with jealousy-rejection-betrayal is the outsized mega-lomania. In your waking dreams, you have unlimited access to evil and you're everyone's worst nightmare. But your ego's all dressed up with no place to go. Then you start to implode. The pain you'd like to inflict on others starts chewing up what's left of your soul.

"Katya today," I told Izzy. "And let's book Natalia for Friday. Is she pretty?"

"She's actually, to be blunt, more beautiful than Katya. And takes care of her body. But she's older than Katya."

"Then it's perfect. If he sees them in the right order, he'll appreciate what he's getting. And they'll both look totally gorgeous."

"Exactly," said Izzy, and I could tell she was warming up to me. "I never book them together."

"No," I agreed. "That would be . . . a total waste of blondeness, wouldn't it?"

### Later

The Lexus, bearing Katya, was prompt. Serge arrived while Milt was taking his post-swim shower. Duncan—best laid plans!—wasn't here to greet them after all, so I did the honors.

As Katya climbed out of the back seat, flashing her long delicate legs, Serge held out his hand to help her. I see what Izzy means: she's plain yet ethereal, with a dreamy expression that makes her pretty. Katya straightened her dress, and smiled shyly as she took his hand. For a split second, their eyes locked. There is definitely something—something between them.

With Tini, the other day, there was none of this courtly tenderness. They treated each other like mates—though Tini also seemed to regard him as a kind of functionary cum errand boy.

Not so with Katya. She was carrying a large square tote bag, and wearing a simple summer dress, sleeveless, with expensive black and white sandals, very flat. Her limbs are long and soft—this isn't what twenty-something passing for nineteen looks like. She's slim, smooth, has probably never exercised, yet has a gorgeous body.

Upstairs, my suspicions were confirmed when she undressed—

she's really nineteen! A Pilates virgin without even the embryonic hint of a six-pack. Just a very girlish accidental flatness. As I went through the obligatory motions, I noticed that, lower down, her natural golden hair—much fuller than New Yorkers are used to—showcases her innocence. And perfectly matches the soft waves on her head.

But something began to worry me.

Could her mind be as new to this game as her body looks? Then what's with Serge? He's obviously been around this business for awhile. Is he playing her? Getting money from her? Why am I thinking this way? Could his tenderness be genuine? What I saw between them in that brief second felt so real, but you'd have to be a romantic fool not to wonder what he's up to.

And maybe that's what she is.

Katya seemed to be meditating on her back, almost bored, while we gave Milt a three-girl show. But when it was her turn to straddle his cock, she woke right up. Her movements became more efficient and focused. She said very little—"Your cock, it's too big for me"—but said it with just enough of an accent, and just enough volume, to keep Milt hard. Something about the economy in her movements, her withdrawn manner, tells a story. Katya's been coached by someone who doesn't want her getting too close to the johns or the other girls. Before she met Isabel, she probably worked in a house with a very high turnover. Girls like that feel no obligation to make small talk—their obligations lie elsewhere.

As for Allison, I should have realized—she's way too self-absorbed to see Katya as any kind of threat to her visual franchise.

Downstairs, Serge was sitting by the pool, reading Milt's copy of the *Herald Tribune*. Improving his English. Could that be a pimp thing in France? Or am I being . . . unfair? *Someone* has to convey Izzy's girls from St-Tropez to St-Max, but why does that someone have to look like Serge? He's too good-looking and doesn't even pretend to keep his distance from Katya.

As he looked up from the paper, she gave him a deliberate nod. And this time, when he held the car door, there was playful adoration in her gaze. Those eyes which had been so expressionless for the last hour revealed a lot in that brief exchange. He stood very close to her for a moment, responding to her flickering look with something deeper and less playful.

If I hadn't been standing there, watching? And what the hell did I just see? Why do I care what they do? It's none of my business but—I care because . . . because my heart was responding to their flirtation, beating a little faster. And the sensation made me understand why Katya can't be saved from whatever she's doing with Serge.

This routine of theirs, driving her to a date, waiting while she (cold, quiet, in control) makes another man come, must be a huge turn-on. And it must be addictive. As addictive for them as lying to my husband is for me.

I never wanted a man like Serge in my life. The time for that is when you're starting out. Even then, I was doing it so one man could never own me. Turning tricks made me feel unfaithful, and I was shocked when I found out that some girls do it because they're being faithful—to a man. But which way is really better? Lying to a straight guy like Matt? Or being truthful with a man you can't bring home to Mother? The hardest part of being with a pimp would have been the loyalty factor—reporting the truth about my earnings.

I returned to the house, in a state of muddled emotion.

"Nancy!?" Allison's panicky whisper startled me when I reached the door of the library. She was standing inside, waiting for me to saunter past. "Are they gone? Can you talk?"

"What are you doing?" I said. Allie was peeking through a crack in the doorway, wearing just her bra and panties. "Why are you walking around like that!"

"I had to come in here to take a phone call," she said. I shut the door behind me. The small table next to the armchair was covered with books. Her phone was sitting on top of a large atlas. What's going on in here? "I need to talk to you!"

"Listen to me," I hissed. "You cannot walk around dressed like— I don't care what you do with Duncan when Milt's not here, but this is totally inappropriate! And—and you have to observe protocol! If Duncan sees you like this when Milt's here—if Milt sees you parading around in front of Duncan in your panties—"

"Duncan's in Tanneron!" she protested. "He's taking the night off, and he's not coming back till tomorrow."

"He's not?"

"Why are you mad at me? What's wrong?"

"Nobody tells me what's going on around here! Why didn't someone tell me?"

Allie blinked nervously. "I thought you knew! Where's Milt? Is he taking his nap?"

"Out like a light." He did forty-five laps today, followed by a foursome—he's entitled to some rest. "Who were you talking to on the phone?"

Did Duncan call her from the road? I feel sick just thinking about it.

"Why are you looking at me like that?" She has no idea what she did to me. Thank God. If she knew, I would never hear the end of her efforts to discuss my feelings! And it's best for all concerned if I keep those to myself. "I—I'm worried about something," she told me.

"Oh?"

"Well, um, last night?"

"If Milt finds out . . ." I warned her.

"Duncan doesn't want him to know either! Anyway, that's not the issue!"

"Well, you'd better not repeat the experiment. It will totally screw up Milt's vacation if he finds you in bed with his cook. I brought you here and I'm responsible for what you do." It gives me some satisfaction to know she has to refrain from fucking him again, but Duncan's reaction is hard to predict. Guys get far more interested when they can't have a second helping of something they like. Will this hands-off situation create a Romeo and Juliet effect?

But Allie was worried about something else entirely.

"I'm not sure what to tell Lucho."

"About what?" Is she thinking of leaving Lucho for Milt's cook? That's madness. He lives in France and she lives in New York!

"I just remembered that I promised Lucho I won't sleep with— I mean, only with customers, you know?"

"You just remembered? How could you forget something like that?"

"I mean—for the last few days, it sort of slipped my mind! Don't you understand? How that could happen?"

"No, I don't. I really don't." I understand having sex with someone and keeping it a secret because you broke an agreement. But I can't understand how you forget an agreement when you're about to break it! What is she thinking? And how can you manage your secrets when you're this scatterbrained? Didn't Jasmine once call Allie a moral idiot? I'm beginning to wonder. "When did you remember that you're not supposed to be having affairs?"

"This morning! When I . . . when I woke up in Duncan's bed." She looked at the carpet. "I told Lucho I don't do overnights. I won't sleep in the same bed as a customer. Lucho's the only guy I sleep with now. I mean, sleep. Like falling asleep. I actually *fell asleep* with Duncan."

"I get it. You don't have to explain."

"I thought we would just make love and then I'd . . . Anyway, I don't know what to tell Lucho. I broke our agreement! And the worst thing is—it's an agreement I pushed for! Because I couldn't stand the thought of HIM falling asleep in another woman's—"

"Look," I told her. "I hope you don't intend to discuss this little slip-up with Lucho."

"I was thinking that maybe I—we—he deserves . . ."

"Well, don't. Just don't. If that's what you agreed to, leave it alone."

"But I broke my agreement!"

"Exactly! And you have to be willing to pay the price. You have to be able to live with your secret," I told her. "If you tell Lucho about this, you're making *him* share the cost. Why should he? It's not *his* fault you cheated. This is one bill a girl has to pick up on her own."

"Did I—did I really *cheat* though? I fell asleep because I had too much wine."

Why did I bring Allison to Provence? Stop speaking to Jasmine? Because she's tactless and self-centered? *What was I thinking?* Jasmine would never do something so unprofessional.

"It doesn't matter," I said. "You'll never see Duncan again. I mean, after you leave France."

"But I gave him my phone number. I watched him enter it into his phone. What if he calls when I get back to New York? You think he *won't*?"

"Does he know about Lucho?"

"Um, no."

"I see." I couldn't hide my sarcasm now. "You just forgot, did you? Well, that puts another—"

"How can you talk that way? You don't tell your customers you have a husband!"

140

"But they're customers. That's business. And they don't want to know." Anyway, I'm doing that to protect my husband's reputation, but Allie wouldn't understand. "If you have an affair, you have to let the other guy know you have a boyfriend. Or a husband."

"Have *you* ever had—" Allie paused "—an affair? While you've been with Matt?"

"Once," I admitted. "When we were still dating. But not since we got engaged. Where would I find the time?"

CHAPTER ELEVEN

# France: Postcards from the Edge

### Wednesday, very late

I was sitting by the pool, catching up on back issues of the *Herald Tribune*. Milt appeared, looking rested from his post-coital nap, in a boxy linen shirt, khakis and his favorite safari sandals. Allie, lost in her copy of *Revue de la Basilique Marie-Madeleine,* barely looked up. Though she knows only one word of French—and a trendy one at that: *la putophobie*—the *Revue* is full of old photos, floor plans of the basilica and maps of the *vieille ville.* When Milt offered to drive into town, Allie stopped reading and sprang to attention. "If we get there before six," she said, "I can take, um, a closer look at the reliquary. Just wait!" She ran upstairs to get her camera.

Unfortunately, the gate to Marie-Madeleine's tomb was already locked. In the gift shop, a cheerful gawky boy sat behind the register, mesmerized by Allie and eager to do her bidding—if only he could. "Je suis désolé," he said. "I have not the key."

"You can't always get what you want," Milt told us. He winked at the boy in a collegial way, and ushered us out of church. "Okay, ladies. Let's get you some refreshments."

As we strolled past the fountain in the Place Malherbe, toward the outdoor tables of the Café Renaissance, Allie was still pouting. "I really need to get that Before shot."

"Duncan will drive you to church tomorrow afternoon," Milt offered. "You're taking Before and After pictures? Of what?"

"It's just for my scrapbook," she said nervously. "I'm taking pictures of the relics before the procession. And maybe after."

"That crazy parade?" Milt chuckled. "It's for serious participants only," he warned her. "You really have to be some kind of fanatic to walk up that hill."

"You mean the mountain? The path to her cave? They aren't fanatics," Allie said. "They're pilgrims."

"Fanatics—pilgrims. Tomato. Tomahto." Milt pulled out a chair for Allie, then for me. With a sly grin, he took the middle seat. "I can see you both climbing . . ." He wiggled his eyebrows at me. "Climbing up that mountain, no problem. You're both very fit. Well, the parade's next week."

Allie and I were facing each other, but she was avoiding my questioning looks. When Milt turned around to look for a waiter, I peered directly at her. "There's going to be a parade?" I asked.

"Oh!" She giggled nervously. "Just a local custom. Ask Milt."

"Once a year, the locals get together," he explained, "and the real diehards climb to the top of the Sainte-Baume mountain. The rest of it's a mystery to me. But you have to admit, we do crazier things in New York. Saint Patrick's Day, for example! Allison knows more about this than I ever will."

"Not *much* more," Allie said. "Duncan's the real expert!"

The very sound of his name made me want to hurl the sugar bowl at her. I took a deep, painful breath. "But they told you the footpath is closed. The mountain's not accessible."

Allie frowned and looked from side to side, like a trapped animal. Is she feeling guilty about Duncan and Lucho again?

"Then maybe they'll postpone the celebrations this year," Milt suggested.

"Maybe!" Allie said in a small voice. "But I don't think so!"

"Are you okay?" I asked. "What's wrong?"

"Nothing! Oh! That's sooooo nice," she sighed, as the waiter arrived with our snacks. Onion tart for Milt, a croissant for Allie and a slice of chestnut gateau for me.

I turned to Milt. "While you were detained in . . . Paris, we took a lovely ride to the mountain. We were planning to visit the grotto, but the path to the cave was closed. For security reasons?"

"Right!" Allie agreed, breaking off a small piece of croissant. Again, she looked rather uneasy. "Maybe I'll—I think I'd like a glass of white wine."

I sipped some Vittel, and said nothing. Allie has no business drinking *anything* after a night of rosé, Armagnac, foreplay in the SUV, and four missing condoms. "Just one!" she said. "Unless they have a nice rosé. It can't possibly hurt." Then, it hit me. OMG. Is she freaking out because—? But of course.

"I'll be back in five," Milt said, after attending to Allie's drink order. "I'm going to pick up a newspaper and call the office." At this hour? It's almost midnight in New York. But bankers—a shadow crossed my mind as I thought of my husband—do keep late hours. "Don't let them take my onion tart!"

As Milt rounded the corner of the Avenue Albert 1er, I leaned across the table. "Look, you have to talk to me about this." Allie's eyes were wide with fear. "It's okay. I know all about Plan B, and I have a supply."

"What?" That trapped expression again as she sipped her wine. "I don't know what you're talking about!" She was being ridiculously vehement.

"Look, it happens to everybody—once."

"*What* happens?"

"A broken condom. You were drunk. You probably weren't paying attention. But if you take two pills tonight, when we get back, and two more—"

"I'm fine!" she squeaked. "Where did you get the idea that—that—" She gulped some more wine. "Maybe you think I'm stupid, but I do know how to use a condom! I led TWO safe sex workshops in Barcelona, you know."

"I don't think anything of the sort!" I protested. "But you seem so nervous and upset! I'm trying to help! What's bothering you?"

"Nothing!" she sighed. "I guess I just have a lot on my mind."

"Well, try not to let this thing with Duncan affect you so much." I tried to sound simpatico. "You have a job to do, and so does he. If you don't control yourself, you might jeopardize his situation with Milt."

Allison was half-listening, gazing into the Place Malherbe. Two middle-aged women were standing together in front of the fountain, leaning into each other, while a third—young and wiry, with spiky hair—took pictures of them. The two older women consulted a map while the third one waited, arms crossed. Then, as we watched, they wheeled their luggage through the square. The oldest, wearing a long denim skirt, led the way, pulling a hard gray suitcase behind her. Her hair was dark, almost black, mixed with white, literally salt on pepper. The youngest, in cargo pants and a blue T-shirt with some white lettering on it, was wheeling a duffel case large enough for an army. As they approached the café, I closed my eyes. I felt dizzy.

"Are YOU okay?" Allie said.

Was I hallucinating?

"I don't know!" I looked toward the busy square, frozen with shock, for the leader of this trio, in a tie-dyed shirt and brown Birkenstocks, looked exactly like my mother. Her outfit was on the baggy side, her pace was brisk, her posture impeccable. "It—it's very strange, but that woman—that shirt and the way she walks. It can't be—she reminds me—"

The three travelers were in a hurry to get somewhere, and the woman who looked like my mother was staring straight ahead. As they neared the café, I could hear suitcase wheels rattling loudly. Instinctively, I bent down to look inside my handbag and hide my face. Then I heard my mother's voice.

"Goodness!" she exclaimed. Both mother and suitcase came to a halt. Her companions looked at each other, puzzled. Then, still wheeling the case behind her, she propelled herself to our table without missing a beat or allowing her suitcase to falter. A small dog scurried away in fear.

"Why Nancy!" she said cheerfully. "Fancy meeting you here!"

"Fancy!" I breathed. "How did you know I was here though? Did Matt—"

"I didn't!" she said. "What a coincidence!" She turned to Allie. "I'm Helen," she said, extending a hand. "Nancy's mother. How lovely to meet you."

"Allison! Allison Rogers! Nancy's my neighbor in New York!" Allie was burbling aerobically. "Can we offer you something? Have a seat! Are you hungry? Wow! This is . . . so cool!"

It's so NOT. I looked around in panic. Where's Milt? Isn't he due back at any moment? How will I explain HIM to my mother? I glanced at her unpainted toe nails and took in her speckled hair. If my favorite customer sees this Birkenstocked figure, looking like me on fast forward, sans all the maintenance, going happily gray . . . Will he ever look at me the same way again?

"How kind," Mother was saying to Allie. "But we can't stop! We've just seen the rooms at the Plaisance and had the good luck to find something more suitable at the Couvent Royal. They've had two cancelations. If we don't get there soon, we might lose our room. It's a busy time of year here. Dodie and I came down to keep Ruth company! We're going back to Mortagne-au-Perche after the Magdalen's feast day, to close on the goat farm." How did Mother get so interested in Mary Magdalen? Isn't she an atheist? "You'll have to come and visit us! We're selling the B&B—if I don't, Sebastian will try to move in, and we can't have that."

"No," I agreed. "That would be—"

"Ruth's taking over the bookstore. Next month, we drive back to Wales and fetch Dodie's wheel. And we'll have to see about her kiln." Mother, full of chatter about her move to Normandy, was talking as though it were the most natural thing in the world to run into her daughter in the middle of a remote French town in July. "And what are you up to, my dear?" But this was an afterthought and not a real query.

She waved to her companions. So that's Dodie, whom I've heard so much about. Pottery teacher with a used bookstore. Welsh Nationalist from Saskatoon. Lives down the street from Mother's B&B. The one with all the eyebrow rings must be Dodie's daughter, the former addict. She had on a sky blue T-shirt—the color of heaven on a good day. The letters, bright and white across her chest, were clearer now. TAKE BACK THE MAGDALEN. ST-MAXIMIN 2002.

While Dodie introduced herself, Ruth watched over her mother's battered-looking suitcase, impatiently ignoring us. Her mind was on something else, incapable of distraction. Milt's words echoed in my head: "Fanatics—pilgrims." My mother's more of a pilgrim. Ruth, however, strikes me as some sort of fanatic. There's a grim look around the jaw which she didn't inherit from her mother.

How did such a good-natured personality produce a daughter who comes across as a profound harridan? Dodie, like Mother, is doing the natural look, but she's less gray and more playful. Her hair is a mousy mess of curls framing a round childlike face, and her Birkenstocks are bright purple. Around her neck, against a

147

striped tunic, she was wearing a large lavender-colored ceramic pendant—two linked female symbols—which, I'm willing to bet, she baked herself, in that kiln. So this is Mother's best friend!

"You're looking for the monastery?" I finally said. "I can help you find it!" And it's one way I can prevent Milt from meeting Mother. I prepared to slip away from our table.

"Don't be silly!" Mother said. "Dodie and I are seasoned travelers. We know exactly where we're going," she added briskly. "When we're settled in, I'll call. You have your phone with you?"

"Of course," I said. "Shall I call your room in an hour?" Mother always keeps her phone shut off, to preserve the battery.

"Oh, good. Yes! It's been a long day." And with that, my mother turned around, dragging her suitcase behind her. As her friends resumed their trek to the Couvent Royal, I noticed the back of Ruth's T-shirt. END ALL SEX TRAFFICKING. STOP THE OPPRESSION!

"Omigod!" Allie gasped. "They're early!"

*Early for what?* Milt, coming back from the Avenue Albert 1er with a small collection of magazines and newspapers, was still on his phone as he approached the café. Mother, Dodie and Ruth were growing smaller and fuzzier, as they continued across the square. I kept an eye on them, hoping, praying, that they wouldn't turn around. As Milt was putting his phone away, they disappeared into the Boulevard Bonfils. It's a rather long indirect route—and I do know the shortest way to the monastery—but try telling that to a seasoned traveler, especially when it's your mother.

## Thursday morning

Yesterday wasn't exactly Milt's day of rest. Flying back from Luxembourg, swimming those extra laps, hosting a three-girl orgy. Plus, having to drive on Duncan's night off. I thought Milt would want to take it easy this morning, but no such luck. "Why not get it over with before Duncan returns?" I told Allison. "It's easier when we don't have to worry about being discreet. And then we'll have the whole day to ourselves."

By now, it's obvious to Duncan what we're doing here, but I like it when Milt has his privacy and we girls can preserve what's left of our mystery. When Duncan's not in the house, I don't have to worry about how much noise we're making.

## Later

We climbed into Milt's bed half-naked, dressed in identical crotchless panties. Allison sat over his face, with her ass cheeks parallel to his forehead. She was frowning in a distracted way while I prepared both ends of the double dildo.

Our purple toy was ready, covered in latex and lube. "MMMMmmmm," Allie announced, "Milt's *so good* at this! He's getting me ready . . . I'm nice and wet!"

Her speech was a little canned but Milt wasn't bothered. When he's got two or more to keep track of, the physical proximity of one girl's pussy is more than enough to keep him happily occupied. We got ourselves into a position we almost never try because it requires real insertion. It's one of those things you just can't fake. Allie was on her hands and knees when I slid the dildo into her pussy from behind. She reached between her legs, clutched her end of the toy, and moaned intensely.

When Milt tried to assist, I gave his hand a light slap. "Ladies only," I told him. "You get to watch." If Milt takes hold of the dildo when Allie's not looking, he might get carried away.

I turned around on my knees, facing away from Allie and pushed my end of the dildo inside very slowly. Breathing through my mouth, I was able to take more of the dildo, but it was almost too uncomfortable. In this position, it's hard to relax completely, and the head's rather imposing. The view, for Milt, was even more pornographic than he's used to. He was staring directly at two similar-sized bottoms, bordered by shiny black fabric, and two sets of lubricated labia. We wriggled our pussies obligingly, and I felt the black satin fabric of my crotchless panties digging into my groin. My right knee was doing something strange, but Milt's cock was doing something entirely predictable.

"Omigosh I'm ABOUT to COME!" Allie exclaimed. "Are YOU coming?"

I threw myself into slutty, orgasmic build-up, closed my eyes and—"Now! Now! Do it now!" I moaned.

"Oh, but she's just getting started!" Allie told Milt, "I'll eat her pussy while you fuck me from behind."

I got onto my back and slipped a condom onto Milt, while Allie fondled his balls. Then I spread my legs wide and peeked to make sure Allie's long hair was falling over the right parts of me. In real life, it's impossible to eat a girl's pussy with any kind of skill while also giving in to the wild sensation of getting fucked from behind.

When you put on a threesome, go for the implausible. As I writhed and gasped, postponing my next pseudo-orgasm, my thoughts meandered. The purple dildo had rolled beneath my back. I dislodged it. Funny how this sleazy-but-functional device is exactly the same color as . . . Dodie's lavender pendant. Which is the very opposite of this double-ended tool. Two decorative, wholesome circles: I wonder if Dodie has an entire studio filled with handcrafted granola lesbiana. Will she take the lot with her to Normandy?

*Wait.* Why did Mother say *we're* selling the B&B? Who is We? Is my mother's restored Tudor cottage jointly owned? I had no idea. So . . . is Dodie . . . the other half of We?

*And they're buying that goat farm together.* How many of these cross-Europe car trips have they taken over the last ten years? Ten, actually. Once a year. Mother hasn't, since the divorce, so much as been on a date with a man, has she? Well, she never talks about men . . .

*Those couple-ish snapshots at the fountain.* Ruth was taking their picture. Is she in on my mother's secret? Of course. She wouldn't find it strange at all. *Her* mom's not hiding anything.

*But neither is mine.* I've just been horribly *obtuse.* Could Ruth and I end up in some sort of squabble over the goat farm? I mean, what if my mother—her mother—*This is no time to be contemplating your hypothetical inheritance.* I tried to focus on Milt's thrusting motions instead.

I removed a condom from one end of the dildo and pressed the bulbous head against my open mouth. Looking directly at Milt, I made sure he could see the movements of my tongue. My lips enveloped the largest part. I willed my mouth to relax completely. Still staring directly at him, with my mouth completely occupied, I was emitting a helpless wanton moan. There was a faint taste of the condom, alas, but his noisy reaction helped me to ignore that.

*When I called the hotel last night,* I was a little surprised to find that Mother's room is registered under *Dodie*'s name. I was expecting Dodie might share with Ruth. Apparently not. My God. It's all starting to add up.

Here I am, faking a great big over-the-top orgasm with *my* best friend, while Mother and HER best friend are, um, *the real thing.*

Christ. How, for the last ten years, have I totally missed that? For some reason, I just don't—didn't—want to know. Just like Mother! Who never challenges a cover story. Lives in total denial about how I survived during my teens, made good during my twenties. But I certainly don't want to think about all this NOW when Milt's about to—Christ! No!

151

I moaned some more, removed the dildo from my mouth, threw in a spasm, and made as much of a racket as possible, hoping to wipe clean from my horrified mind the realization that my mother . . .

. . . has a sex life? But she had sex with Dad, she must have, so what's the big deal?

I've been so busy hiding *my* sexual reality—especially from Mother—that I long ago stopped thinking about hers. Why do our own secrets—no matter how slick, worldly or decadent we imagine ourselves to be—cause us to lose sight of the most obvious facts of life?

## Later

Duncan says he'll drive me into town for *un brushing*—what the French call a blow-out—at that walk-in salon across from the Couvent Royal. If I told him what I'm really up to he would never believe me: sneaking out of the house to visit my mother?

For some reason, Allie has changed her mind and declines to join us. "Don't you want to check out the reliquary?" I asked. And doesn't she want to hang out with Duncan?

"I—I do," she said. "But not today."

Lover's tiff, perhaps? Knowing Allie, she's sulking because Duncan didn't call her every half hour while he was off-duty. But what does she expect? She's the guest of his client. In other words, she's almost a client herself. A concierge needs his space!

She, of all people, should know how *that* goes, but I decided not to pursue the topic. We were sitting by the pool—she in a striped bikini under the sun, I in my gauzy jellaba under an umbrella—just two feet away from Milt who was going through his pile of news.

He wasn't really listening—but still, I didn't want to risk an outburst. It's not like Milt to look so *studious* after an orgasm. He was frowning intensely, systematically combing each daily. For what? He rifled through the *Herald Tribune*, folded it carefully, then started on the *Telegraph*. Is he looking at the same section of each paper? And how did Milt manage to track down a copy of *USA Today*? That's not his usual fare. Then he proceeded through *Time*, *Newsweek*, the *Economist*.

Could this be connected, in some way, to his sudden trip to Luxembourg?

## Thursday, later

As I sat next to Duncan in the SUV, I remembered, suddenly, the afternoon when he reached for my seatbelt, how his hand against my breast seemed like a gay boy's oversight. Then I remembered Allie's seatbelt-assisted orgasm, and I had to look away.

My gaydar's truly out of whack. In addition to misreading this thoroughly heterosexual twenty-eight-year-old, I've spent my entire adult life oblivious to Mother's increasingly lesbian lifestyle. I mean, she doesn't carry a banner, but she's never hidden it from me.

"We'll rendezvous in front of the basilica," Duncan said. "Just call when you're ready. I might be en route from Brignole. I'm . . . picking up some newspapers."

"In Brignole??"

"There's a big international newsagent, and Milt's trying to find a *Wall Street Journal*. Is there something you'd like me to get for you?"

He gave a warm, parting smile as I left the car—a confusing smile that made me feel reconnected. As if nothing could break the flow of our unacknowledged flirtation. A smile that suggested he was about to kiss me. I walked past the half-empty hair salon toward the *hôtellerie*, thrown off-balance by that phantom kiss.

When I knocked on the door of Mother's room, I was greeted by Ruth, wearing yesterday's T-shirt—in black. "Oh sorry! Have I got the wrong room?"

"They're downstairs ordering lunch," she informed me, in a dour voice.

"That's . . . quite a T-shirt! Weren't you wearing one like it yesterday?"

"I have them in five colors. Would you like one? I've got—" Ruth opened the door and gestured toward my mother's—her mother's—unmade bed, now the repository for a pile of TAKE BACK THE MAGDALEN END ALL SEX TRAFFICKING T-shirts. "Come in. You look like a small."

"Oh, I don't think—Th-thank you!" I said. "Yes, the black one will do nicely. How kind!" I sound, eerily, like an echo of my mother. "So! We're all having lunch?"

"I'll be down in a sec," Ruth mumbled, turning to the laptop. "Don't let me hold you up."

I found my mother in the converted Chapter House, sitting at one of the large square tables with Dodie on her left. Dodie was sipping an amber-colored aperitif while Mother poured her own pick-me-up from a small teapot.

"And how was your morning?" Mother asked. "How is Allison? What have you two been up to?"

"Oh, I . . . we . . . very uneventful." The purple dildo was now resting in Allison's bidet, in a special antiseptic solution which, she assures me, kills anything that might afflict jelly rubber or human flesh. "We decided to sleep in."

"So did we!" Dodie chirped. "The real activity begins tomorrow."

"We're documenting Ruth's conference," Mother told me. She reached into her knapsack and held up a digital camera. "For their website."

"Ruthie is the cofounder . . ." Dodie's voice trailed off into maternal vagueness, something mothers do when the details of your life are getting to be a bit much.

"It's a women's group," Mother explained.

Omigod. "What *kind* of women's group?" Every T-shirt tells a story!

"Well." Dodie exchanged a sheepish look with Mother. "They're an offshoot. Ruthie joined a Protestant youth movement when she went into rehab. Then she broke away and formed a women's group. Something to do with The Female Christ. Take Back The Magdalen Dot Org. Tee-bee-teemorg!"

"They're planning some sort of alternative event," Mother said, "for her feast day. But we're not involved with Ruth's *religion*," Mother pointed out. "We're just helping with the website. We came for the architecture. Have you seen the wood carvings in the basilica?"

"It's hard to believe," Dodie said, with a sly titter, "that our room was once a monk's cell! But you can see little remnants of the austerity. And your friend's uncle has a house nearby?"

"Oh it's . . . on the outskirts," I riffed. *No need to tell Mother that Villa Gambetta's just down the road from here.* "Nice but rather small," I lied. "And it's filling up with new people every day. It's a relief to get away from all the other guests—and Allison's relatives! I think the rental agent was rather misleading."

"Oh dear," Mother said. "One of those situations." Surely, if Mother finds out the "uncle" isn't quite as advertised, she'll pin the carnality on my bubbly single friend? "If you're up in time, you can join us tomorrow for breakfast!"

"I'm uh . . ." *That's cutting it a little close!* Serge arrives at eleven-thirty with Natalia, so she can get back to St-Tropez in plenty of time for her next date. "I don't think that's a good idea," I said, nervously consulting the lunch menu. Natalia has a standing appointment with a fortyish man from Monaco who, Izzy claims, is famous for being supported by his well-born—and somewhat older—wife. Yet he's been booking Natalia for multiple hours each Friday. Seems dangerous to have a regular who's such a successful gigolo. If his wife catches on, won't she be furious with him for spending her loot on a younger woman?

Or am I being hopelessly provincial?

In any case, breakfast with Mother is out of the question under these circumstances. "What do you think of this blood orange salad?" I asked. Knowing full well that Mother would pronounce it "horribly trendy." But it got her onto a new topic, thank goodness.

Ruthie's seat at the table remained empty. "She gets a little intense at meal times," Dodie confided. "She's an ethical vegan these days. Gets all her protein from cashew nuts. Helen made the awful *mistake*—" Mother pursed her lips. She doesn't like that word! "—of inviting Ruthie to the international *boudin* competition. They have it every year in Mortagne-au-Perche."

Hmmm. The annual black pudding bake-off—a Norman tradition—must be a vegan's worst nightmare. Ruth, clearly, is one of those high-maintenance offspring who can't stop involving Mom in the minutiae of each new drama, whether getting off drugs, eating cashews or . . . "taking back the Magdalen." Why, she's even got her mother (and mine!) *taking pictures of her* "taking back" the Magdalen.

As I bade my mother farewell for the day, I congratulated myself for keeping her sheltered from my problems. I protect her from any HINT of drama. It's not always easy, but I make the effort. I bet Ruth doesn't even try.

While *I'm* forced to grapple with the reality of my mother's personal life, she's still in the dark about most aspects of mine. As she should be. Daughters, not mothers, belong in the catbird seat. In the eighties, when cocaine tested my sanity and threatened my looks, she never knew. She would be shocked to learn that, in addition to being seduced by freebase, I've been hustled by professional pimps, pursued by vice cops, terrorized by a bondage freak, and threatened (once) by a call-girl-turned-blackmailer.

Mother senses that my marriage is a safe harbor, but she has no idea why, exactly—and doesn't want to know. As far as she's concerned, I'm her "surprisingly conservative" child who always knew how to take care of herself. A mother's denial mechanisms are a form of emotional genius. A daughter's? Not so much. The self-centered hubris of a liar can really trip you up.

I passed beneath the high arched walkway of the deserted cloister with my phone turned off, at home in the dead zone— not with God, of course, but with my past. With the conflicting pieces of my life. And my smug assessment of somebody else's daughter.

In the reception area, I switched on my cellphone. A startling vision emerged from the elevator. Her profile was unmistakable. The precision of her cheekbones, the glossy black hair, the perfectly formed figure, taut yet girlish. Today, in a simple orange T-shirt and a pair of jeans, she looked almost wholesome. But Tini is too regal to be taken for merely wholesome. She sailed right by, heading for the street.

What the hell is SHE doing in the monastery hotel??

That day, after our session with Milt, when I asked Allie what she was doing in Tini's room, she denied exchanging phone numbers, but she was obviously lying! Is Allison thinking she might sneak out to the monastery and do a session with Tini and Milt behind my back? She'd better not! Or is this place becoming Sapphic Central?

But Tini said she wasn't into girls.

Something does not compute.

I followed her through the gate. She paused outside the stone wall of the *hôtellerie* to light a cigarette. *Why does everyone here—even a 2000 euro call girl!—smoke so much?* As she walked ahead, I kept my distance from the trail of smoke.

We were passing the parking lot behind the town hall, but she was too far ahead and when she turned left, I couldn't catch up. By the time I reached the town hall, she had disappeared. On the wall were announcements of impending marriages—name, address, occupation of each spouse—and hours of the *office de tourisme*. I looked around. Tini could only be in the town hall or the basilica.

Suddenly, a loud, familiar voice—from *New York*—nasal, female, completely out of place in this poky town was calling my name.

"NANcy!"

I froze when I saw Roxana Blair, two feet away, her arms extended in a gesture of solidarity. Time to deliver one of her righteous hugs! She was wearing a red T-shirt with black letters on the front. This was a T-shirt no English-speaking person could look away from. Did it really say . . .

*W* e

*H* onor

*O* urselves with

*R* espect &

*E* mpowerment

?

Yes. It really did. The first letter of each line was in grotesque Gothic caps. The O in Ourselves fit squarely, so to speak, over Roxana's right breast. Her hair, as usual, was a mess, and I noticed some glitter on her cheeks. *Why is she wearing body glitter in the middle of the day? This is so typical of the activist mindset.*

I stared at her T-shirt. I wanted to flee. Then I realized: the Gothic font—in a small French town where few speak English on a daily basis—won't be so easily read by the locals.

But my mother is right next door!

"I'm SO GLAD YOU COULD COME! I knew Allison wouldn't let us down," she told me.

"What are you—why are you—"

"Come with me!" she said, releasing me from her scary embrace. "Everyone's waiting—well, we were expecting Allison, but now I feel blessed by the unexpected!" She gestured toward a cluster of girls in identical, red WHORE shirts, close to the door of the basilica. "We really need your perspective around here. *And* we need to get you a T-shirt! Before the meeting starts! Did you bring the maps?" she asked.

"Maps?"

"And the camera? I think we should do a group shot for the website! To document our experience. I'm so glad you're getting involved. Is Allison okay? Her message was really weird! It's not like Allison to miss a meeting!"

"Allison," I said, "is doing just fine. Would you please tell me what's going on? Since Allison can't be bothered to?"

"What do you mean?" Roxana was bewildered—we both were.

"I came into town to get my hair done. I don't know why you're here or what you're talking about. Would you please tell me what this is about? And what you're doing here?"

"Oh." Roxana looked crestfallen, but how crestfallen can a zealot be? After a second, she recovered her optimism and beamed at me, oozing benevolence and pride. "Bad Girls Without Borders has come to St-Maximin. We claim ownership of Mary Magdalen's narrative. We're here to preserve her bad reputation because it's good for all sex workers. And we're defending Provençal culture from the sex-negative extremists who have no respect for indigenous traditions."

So. This is why Allison's been so jumpy. *This is what she's been hiding from me.* That phone call in the library. Emails to Roxana. Her obsession with Mary Magdalen's "reputation." Those maps?

Did Roxana say something about maps? But Allie didn't count on me going into town today! Her decision to stay away must be a last-minute ploy, her idea of damage control.

"So . . . you're having a meeting? A conference of some sort?"

"Well, it's more of an intervention," Roxana explained. "The Paris whores told us about Ruthie Page when we were in Barcelona. They asked us to support their intervention with a statement. Then Allison had a better idea! Since she was coming here anyway, we came up with Plan B! Representatives from four different regions—on the ground. What I really hope is that Ruth will dialog with us. We don't want a confrontation, but we don't want forced rehabilitation either!"

Ruthie. I caught my breath. "Plan B?" The other day, that look on Allie's face when I thought she was in dire need of the morning after pill! "Allie told me about the cave, and I've seen the relics. But I didn't realize—"

"What Ruthie is planning to do here is nothing less than cultural genocide!"

"Does this Ruthie Page have access to weapons?"

"I don't think so. But if she *did*," Roxana warned me, "I wouldn't put anything past her OR her followers. There she is now. Behind you."

Ruthie, in the Rue du Général de Gaulle, was flanked by two teenage girls lugging too many Casino grocery bags. They were a curious-looking trinity, walking down the main shopping street in their black TAKE BACK THE MAGDALEN shirts. Ruthie was carrying a bag from the *boulangerie*.

I didn't want her to see me standing with the red-shirted opposition. Roxana's comrades were moving away from the church door. Eight or ten bodies, labeled WHORE, were advancing toward us, moving as one to protect Roxana from the feminist Christians. Or were they just making their presence known to Ruthie?

*I don't want to be caught in the middle.* What if Mother has a sudden urge to photograph the basilica? Stranger things have been known to happen.

"Listen," I said, in as steady a voice as I could. "I cannot afford to be spotted by Ruthie. Do you understand?"

"Where are you going? What about your T-shirt?"

"I'll get it later!" I gasped. Then I bolted in the direction of the hair salon and ducked into a dingy, narrow cobblestoned street.

Walking past doors with peeling paint, exposed stairways, drying laundry, I turned a corner and found myself on another small street. Now there were brass name plates, lace curtains and the cobblestones looked clean.

When I called Duncan, he picked up on the first ring. "Where are you?" I asked, unable to hide my panic.

"Very close to the basilica," he said. "Are you all right?"

"I wasn't able to get a hair appointment. I'm—I'm hiding. But I'm okay."

"Hiding." There was a pause. "Where?"

"In . . ." I looked for a street sign. "Omigod. I'm not sure where I am! Wait. Wait. I'm in the Rue Raspail. Duncan?"

"I'm right here."

"I cannot, must not, return to the basilica today. I'll explain everything later."

"Well, if you follow the street to the next corner and turn right, you'll see some low arches under a covered sidewalk. There's a sign that says *ancien quartier juif*. Walk away from that toward a house that has Lucien Bonaparte's name on a blue and white plaque."

It's hard to believe Duncan's only twenty-eight! He really knows how to make a girl feel handled . . . in a way that some guys NEVER can, at any age.

"Make a left. You'll be in the Place Hoche. There's a house with a very tall birdcage on the second floor balcony. I'll be parked in front." He paused. "Suzy?"

"Y- yes?" I could just see the medieval arches of the Jewish quarter coming into view.

"No need to explain. I'm here to help."

Now safely back at Villa Gambetta, but dreading my next meeting with Mother. Perhaps I can persuade her to meet me at a distance from the *basilique*? Someplace where Roxana won't be dialoguing with Ruth?

Allie—surprise!—has been resting in her bedroom with the door locked. But she can't stay in there forever. Who does she think she's kidding?


## Midnight

Duncan, true to his word, hasn't asked me to explain a thing.

This evening, as I was sitting by the pool, watching the sunset with a worried look on my face, wondering how to get Allie to end her wildcat strike, he appeared with a tiny shot of ice cold *poire William*.

"Really?" I said. "I don't know . . . it does smell wonderful though." Essence of orchard; soupçon of airplane fuel.

"When it's this small," he assured me, "it's medicinal. By the way, there's a hair salon on Rue Gutemberg. You can't see the basilica from there, and it can't see you. I'll take you tomorrow, if you like."

CHAPTER TWELVE

# France: Two or Three Things I Know About Her

## Friday morning, early

Allie's work ethic has kicked in.

At dawn, I heard the blow-dryer going in her room. Readying herself for our midday adventure with Natalia. I must not confront Allie until that's over and done with. It would be unprofessional to let personal issues affect our session.

## Ten minutes later

Last night, when I called Isabel to confirm Natalia, her normal voicemail picked up. So far, there's been no response. And now, Izzy's outgoing message has changed to something generic—her phone number invoked by an efficient French robot.

## Later

Breakfast by the pool was nerve-racking. Allie sat on a sun chair, meekly sipping her coffee. Now that I know that she knows that I know . . . the grounds I have for being thoroughly annoyed with her . . . she's avoiding all eye contact! Roxana must have called her and told all.

But Allie doesn't know I'm onto her arrangement with Tini. WHY does Allie have to complicate everything? Can't she just keep her mind on the business at hand? I recruited her because I felt, on some level, I could trust her. What was I thinking?

Milt, studying his *Wall Street Journal*, was oblivious to the atmosphere of suspicion and panic circling his hired companions. I sat beneath a table umbrella, with one eye on my phone, chewing nervously on some blueberries. When I got up to call Isabel from the library, Allie began chattering to Milt about the beauty of his herb garden. "It's a gorgeous lay-out," she gushed. "We're really at one with our environment!" She sighed with undisguised relief as I disappeared into the house.

Where I discovered that Izzy's outgoing message has changed *again*! And now I can't understand a word of it.

Duncan was in the kitchen, wearing a striped apron over his jeans, peeling some very ripe tomatoes. I called to him in a low voice, almost a whisper. "I think I need your help with something!"

He put down his implements, hung up the juice-splattered apron, and rinsed his hands. Then he followed me into the library where I was perched on the edge of a chair. Yes, that chair.

*On that carefree afternoon, when Milt was fucking me from behind, I almost came thinking about*—I looked away from Duncan, embarrassed by my unreadable thoughts. Well, I hope they were unreadable.

I dialed Izzy's number and gave him the phone. "*Vive la différence*," I said, trying to keep it light. "But I don't like the way these robots keep changing sex. It was a female before. Now it's a guy. And I'm not sure I understand what he's saying."

He listened, frowned, and handed the phone back. "Turned off at the owner's request."

"But—but—Serge is supposed to be here at eleven-thirty. With Natalia. And they haven't confirmed."

Duncan's eyebrows shot up to his forehead. "Were you dealing directly with Serge?"

"No," I said.

"I didn't think so." But he refused to pry.

A madam turns her phone off without warning, in the middle of doing business with you, and it only ever means one thing. I know because, unbeknownst to Milt, I've been through this before. Twice.

But this kind of thing "doesn't happen" to girls like me. My connections are supposed to be impeccable. And I've taken as many precautions as I could to prevent it. Or so I thought.

"Something happened. I know it." I placed my phone on the table. A book fell to the floor. My hand was shaking.

"Just take a deep breath," Duncan said.

"Serge is someone's driver. Did he talk to you about her?"

"He wasn't talkative that way."

"She wouldn't just *disappear*," I said. "She has a reputation to protect. I wouldn't deal with just anyone—"

"I'm sure you wouldn't."

"People like that don't just disconnect. Do you know what I'm talking about?"

When I looked up into his eyes, I felt like I was drowning.

"Well, I might. But I think it's best to assume I don't know anything." There was a long silence as I digested this. "When did you last speak to her?" he asked.

"Wednesday, after Katya left. You were in Tanneron. But Serge was here. I spoke to her that night."

"That's not even two days. Well," he agreed. "It sounds like—something bad may have happened."

Oh God. I'm in her phone records, too! That's REALLY bad.

"Please don't tell Milt about this? It would wreck his vacation!" *And make me look a little cheesy, perhaps.* Customers tend to disappear on you when things like this happen—to you, to your friends. You can't let them hear about it. "Anyway, look, there are things he doesn't WANT to know."

"I know what you mean," Duncan said.

"I'll—" *bet you do*, I almost said. I bit my lip. "I'll have to talk to him though." Then, to my surprise, my phone began vibrating. I stared at the number. "It's—it's New York." My husband! The call went into voicemail, and I switched everything off.

If Izzy's in trouble with the law, it's a good time to make myself hard to reach.

But—

Maybe Tini's trip to St-Max has nothing to do with Allison, and everything to do with Isabel's sudden silence.

When I returned to the pool, Allie had vanished. If Duncan found some "inappropriate" way to keep her occupied, I just don't want to know.

I settled into the chair next to Milt, grateful to be alone with him. "I just heard from Isabel."

"And?" He was still looking at his newspaper.

"Um . . . there's been a slight change of plans," I said. "Natalia was supposed to return from Rome last night. And she had to stay over. Something involving her mother! Izzy feels terrible of course because she wanted to surprise you with someone gorgeous—someone *equally* gorgeous . . . but she doesn't want to send just anyone. She's very particular," I riffed. "Probably TOO particular, but I think you'll agree that it's better to err in that direction than the other. And she PROMISED she'll do her level best to make this up to—to us, just as soon as she has someone special for us."

Somehow, I felt that "us" was the magic word that would smooth everything out.

"Kiddo . . ." Milt put his newspaper on the stone surface next to his chair. "Girls called Natalia who hang around St-Tropez in July are *supposed* to get delayed in Rome. Whether it's a problem with her mother or a private appointment with the Pope himself! Isn't that half the fun of dealing with one of Isabel's girls?"

Poor Natalia. At this point, she might be calling Izzy in a panic. Dodging the police. Or simply wondering where her next date is coming from. For the sake of my customer's peace of mind, though, I smiled sideways and said, "I like the way you're thinking."

"You, on the other hand, more than make up for the absence of any number of Natalias. And I'm kind of particular myself!" He picked up his newspaper. "When Duncan goes into town," he suggested, "let's lock ourselves in the media hut and watch some porn movies. You know what? I miss being alone with you."

Perhaps I overdid the hand-wringing. Now he wants to reassure me by devoting an entire session to "us"—a situation I've done *my* level best to avoid during this Viagra-fueled sojourn.


### Later

Alone with Milt in the media hut. There's something about watching porn on an eight-foot screen that I, for one, could do without. Repeated mechanical insertion at life-size (or smaller) dimensions is graphic enough for me.

"No disrespect to your decorator," I told Milt, "but I prefer watching stuff like this on my rickety little TV set. Be it ever so humble."

He smirked and patted my knee. "Just humor me a minute— there's a great scene coming up."

"Okay . . . but the human clitoris loses some of its inherent cuteness when it gets to be the size of a *cabbage*."

"Hmmmm. I see your point."

"Thank you."

He waved the remote at the wall—"Bye-bye for now!"—then placed his hands between my thighs. He coaxed them apart, gently, and slid a finger beneath my panties. I twisted my hips— fractionally—to keep him from getting too close to my inner lips. Milt is such a veteran john, he's almost a pro. When a working girl moves her pelvis a certain way, he knows how to pull back. Just enough to make her relax, so he can remove her panties.

I lured his hands away from my pussy toward my breasts. I don't really mind his fingers, but I don't want him to make a habit of using them. There are things I like done to me when I'm not working. Things I allow a john who's a runner, because I won't see him again for a year. *None* of these actions can be permitted with my regulars.

Sex with a regular shouldn't be intrusive. Even though he's just a john, there's a chance he might become an important part of your life—a part that needs to be carefully managed. A finger in your panties? Thin end of the wedge. Needs watching.

After many days of threeway acrobatics, our porno tryst in the converted dairy shed was a simple pleasure. Mostly for Milt, of course. For me, the pleasure comes from knowing HE's happy.

Just checked voicemail and found a hang-up from my husband, followed by a message. "I'm having dinner with Elspeth tomorrow and I'm worried. She sounds kind of weird. I'll let you know how it goes. AC went out at the office, so I'm home now, working on this deal."

Should I call back? It's not like Matt to worry about Elspeth.

But I can't bring myself to call him from this house—even when Milt's napping.

## Friday, later

I was showering when Duncan's SUV pulled into the driveway. Peeking out of my bathroom window, I saw Allie look around quickly before stealing a kiss. The nerve! Well, she was responsible enough to check if Milt was around. But her mouth lingered a second longer than it should have before she scurried into the house. They're both playing with fire. And driving me insane.

I dried off quickly and wrapped a towel around my naked body. When I heard her bedroom door, I dashed across the hall and knocked sharply.

"We need to talk," I said. One frightened unblinking eye was staring through a crack in the doorway.

"Open the fucking door," I hissed. "Are you alone?"

"What do you mean?" she gasped, as I pushed the door open.

Closing the door behind me, I said, "You know exactly what I mean. You'd better not invite Duncan in here!"

"You're the only other person who's been in this room since I arrived." This might be the one true thing she's told me in days.

"Did you go into town to meet Roxana?"

"Rrrrrrr . . . um . . . Roxana?"

"I know all about it! Roxana told me everything."

"She did?"

"I know what you've been up to! Roxana was standing around in front of the basilica with a bunch of your friends. Wearing these insane scary T-shirts! Do you understand what a catastrophe you've created? Inviting all these people to St-Maximin?"

"It seemed like a good idea!" Allie sat on the edge of her rumpled bed. "I have to admit, it never occurred to me that your mom . . .!"

Now she looked cornered. Beleaguered. "Do YOU understand? What Ruth is trying to do?"

I leaned against the door, clutching the towel to my breasts, willing myself not to give her an inch of sympathy as she argued her case.

"Ruth says Mary Magdalen's identity as a whore is part of a damaging misogynist centuries-old conspiracy, but she doesn't understand that she's part of this conspiracy herself! You can see for yourself why she has to be stopped. It's all on her blog!"

"On her WHAT? You brought Roxana here because of something Ruth says on her blog?"

"Ruth gets a hundred visitors a day! And she's part of a much larger movement. Their goal is to eliminate sex work! We had to do something," Allie protested. "Ruth says the world will be healed when the Magdalen's sexual virtue is restored. She's wrong, of course. I mean, she's *right* about Mary Magdalen being the equal of Jesus and a victim of misogyny, but she's wrong about sexual virtue. WE are society's healers! And we're here to defend indigenous Provençal culture! Against sex-negative Christianity."

"Listen to me. You're here on business. You did not come here to plan some multicultural version of the Second Coming! You'll have to do that on your own time." I was so angry I was losing control of my towel. "Have you seen what Roxana's wearing?"

"Of course! I picked out the fonts! Roxana chose the colors. Anyway, have you seen what Ruth's *followers* are wearing? If we don't respond in kind, they control the discourse." Oh God. The battle of the T-shirts. "Ruth needs to meet a real sex worker," Allie added, "in order to understand the issues!"

"I've already MET Ruth." I decided not to mention Ruth's T-shirt, sitting in my tote bag. "Do you realize she's the daughter of my mom's best friend? She grew up in the village where my mother lives, and I know far more about her than she does about me. I'd like to keep it that way."

"You should come out to Ruth! It would make a huge difference if she understood that sex workers aren't just an abstraction," Allie said. "We need to educate her about who prostitutes really are!"

"No we do not! I can't have Ruth spilling the beans to my mother! Would you want her spilling the beans to yours?"

Allie frowned. "Well, I haven't resolved that particular, um." She looked away, suddenly misty-eyed.

"I bet you haven't! Your glorious liberation movement is a total sham!" I was tempted to slam Allison's door on the way out, but it would be profoundly uncool to let Milt overhear one peep of discord.

Standing barefoot in the hall, I almost dropped my towel when I saw Duncan on the staircase.

"I thought, as Milt's having a swim, I'd bring you these," he said quietly. "*Var-Matin*—it's a local tabloid. A bit like your *Daily News*. And there's something in the *Daily Mail*. About Serge." He stood on the top stair holding a bundle of newspapers, taking in my exposed shoulders.

"Th . . . ank you," I stammered.

"It's no trouble at all. I had to pay another visit to that newsagent in Brignole anyway."

I was horrified by the sensation spreading across my damp skin. His eyes flickered as he took in my uncovered legs. My pussy, completely bare beneath my towel, was swollen. As were my nipples. "I—um—can't really use my hands," I pointed out, holding the towel tight. For some reason, the cotton against my thighs was almost excruciating. My nerve-endings were now alert to every movement of the fabric.

"I'll just leave these here," he offered. "You can get them when you're dressed. But I think you should keep them somewhere safe.

In your room." I nodded stiffly and tried to breathe normally. "I have to warn you, there's a large picture of our friend. You might find it upsetting," he added. "I'll be in the kitchen."

As I collapsed onto my bed, allowing the towel to fall away from my torso, I had to touch myself to see . . . if I was really that wet. I was. Am still. Omigod. Why can't I stop feeling this way?

Even the sight of Serge on the front page of *Var-Matin*, looking more scruffy than swarthy in handcuffs, bathrobe *and slippers*, can't quell the hunger between my thighs.

CHAPTER THIRTEEN

# France: Shopper of the Year

*Friday, later still*

But the photos of Serge are cringe-inducing.

If you know what he really looks like, those lumpy images in *Var-Matin*—taken during an early morning bust—are bad enough to arouse pity. What happened to the hard-bodied, smooth-faced driver we met—his clean muscular lines? Flawless posture? In a dressing gown, arrested at dawn, he looks less like the slick *proxénète* and more like . . .

Who would have guessed?

He's Isabel's *husband*, but there are no pictures of Izzy in the French paper—just a photo of where they were living when the arrest went down. And it's not in St-Tropez. It's a massive apartment complex, designed to look like a cruise ship, in the newest part of Villeneuve Loubet, just outside Nice. Filled with middle class families and retirees who have been chatting to reporters about what a quiet couple they were. The window of Izzy's apartment looks onto a sandy playground, complete with swing set and see-saws.

And now that they've both been arrested, they are—according to the *Daily Mail*—offering to rat on *each other*. I locked the bedroom door and flipped through the *Mail*. The only picture of Isabel so far is a dated black and white profile taken in front of Harvey Nichols in London. Izzy, wearing a head scarf, looks convincingly Sloane-ish, and you can't really see her hair. Under a big headline—SHOPPER OF THE YEAR—the *Mail* explains: she was arrested *first* because her husband, "a French citizen of mixed background fourteen years her junior" informed on her to the authorities. Scotland Yard may investigate due to multiple bank accounts and a house in Maidstone, Kent, which he "insisted on putting in his wife's name."

If a straight guy did that, he'd be viewed as a *saint*.

"A source close to the couple has told the *Mail* that Isabel Morgan's only recourse is to shop her husband, Serge Dolmy, the mastermind and enforcer in their St-Tropez escort service." According to the *Mail*, he ran a brothel in St-Tropez, procuring girls from the "shadowy corners of a global network specializing in desperate beauties from Eastern Europe and Asia." Izzy was introduced to "a deceptively glamorous" lifestyle when she came to Nice on holiday, haunted by memories of an abusive marriage. Within a year, she discovered she was "trapped" in yet another such marriage—only much worse, as she was now "caught in the web of an international trafficking network" and terrified of leaving because "her new husband's links to a Prague syndicate would, he told her, incriminate them both."

There's something in this story that rings true, yet not. Izzy's phone manner was so bossy. And she kept her maiden name? Nowhere do I see her called Isabel Dolmy, not even in the French tabloid account. Wouldn't a guy like that make her adopt his surname? Or am I being ridiculously naive? All I really know about guys like that is how to avoid them.

Didn't Liane say her old friend Hillary was doing business with Izzy in London? But Isabel Morgan claims that she came to Nice in a state of innocence! Even if she lies about THAT, *could* she have become the mental slave of this . . . bathrobed "enforcer"? Well, he's much better-looking in real life. And he did have a masterful way with Katya. When I saw them flirting in front of the car, Katya looked so docile. *Was she afraid?* I can't say for sure that she wasn't.

But Liane will be horrified when she hears about all this. And embarrassed by her gaffe—introducing me to this shady couple! Will she freak out? At seventy-something, this could send her over the edge, but she has a right to know what the papers are saying. Especially since the *Mail* claims Serge Dolmy was sending girls to L.A. and Palm Beach! Florida's dangerously close to New York.

Just switched on my phone. More messages from Matt, working from home, tugging at my heart strings. "Babe? I can't find the ink jet cartridges! Did you HIDE them? Would you call me, please?"

What hooker in her right mind wants to chat with her husband at a time like this? Reading about Isabel's marriage in the *Daily Mail* makes the most innocent spouse seem totally ominous.


## Friday, much later

This is one hell of a way to learn about another girl's marital status. Let's hope MINE never comes to light in this way.

I sat in my room, re-reading the horrifying news stories. Then crept downstairs where I found Duncan, standing in front of a large copper pot pressing dried cloves into a small onion.

"I'm looking for some of that poire William," I said. "Just a tiny hit. Is—is Milt around?"

"I haven't seen him for an hour and that usually means he's in bed." I winced at this remark, and tried to cover my reaction with a polite smile. "In repose," Duncan added, "when it's this late. He's a very early sleeper." He handed me a shot glass and opened a shimmering steel drawer beneath the counter, stocked with bags of ice and other provisions. "You can always feel free to raid the deep freeze." I could feel my shoulders relaxing as he poured. "I'm not the nanny, you know. Just the cook."

"I don't know what to do!" I sighed. "Everything's going wrong. And I have to make some difficult decisions."

"Are you saying—" he turned on a faucet and lowered his voice "—that you need legal advice?"

*Gosh. Does he really mean that?* He was peeling a carrot, and the faucet was still running, muffling our conversation.

"Nothing that serious," I said, moving closer to the water. I peeked into the stock pot and saw an entire chicken, split in two. "Maybe it's safer if I go home! The thing is, Milt would never understand. He would take it the wrong way. And I can't possibly tell him about . . ."

Duncan nodded. "I see what you mean."

"Was there anything in the *Herald Tribune*?"

"Not yet. It's a very local story, don't you think?"

"Not local enough for me."

But let's say it does appear in his daily paper, would Milt notice? With all the emphasis on Serge Dolmy's misdeeds—since Milt never heard of Serge—maybe it will go right over his head. He might skip past that particular bit of news, if we're lucky. But if he DOES read it, he's sure to notice Isabel's name. Some coincidence!

"Speaking of local," I confessed, "there's one person in New York who might be able to help. But I'm afraid to call."

Duncan put down his paring knife and leaned back against the counter, arms crossed, head cocked toward the running faucet. "Afraid because?"

"Embarrassed, really. Someone I've known for years. We quarreled last month. I guess it's a girl thing. I haven't spoken to her since. And I miss her sometimes." I gazed at the soup greens on the shiny counter tiles, then sniffed my glass. "I don't know why I'm telling you this, but I just realized an hour ago that I've stopped talking to one of the few people I can actually trust. A guy wouldn't understand. She's kind of tactless!"

"It's all right," he said. "But you're in an awkward spot and you can't talk to just anyone. When you say she's tactless—?"

"She's discreet about the important things. She's just tactless about—" I felt foolish admitting this "—about things that don't matter in the long run."

"Right! One of those. Well, maybe you just needed a break."

"Promise me you won't discuss this?" I can't come right out and ask him not to tell Milt—can I? Milt, after all, is his client— mine too. How much do we owe each other at this point? How much loyalty do we owe the client?

"Everything we discuss is strictly entre nous," he said. Again, I had the eerie feeling nobody could come between us. Except that . . . the person who HAS done that very thing is upstairs, giving herself a mini-pedicure! And I certainly don't want HER to overhear us.

"There's no reason for either of us to ruin anyone's vacation," Duncan said. "Especially since neither of us is on vacation."

Allison, I was dying to point out, is certainly ACTING like she's on vacation, but I decided not to mess with a good thing by bringing her into it. I'm also, for once, oddly grateful to her for coming downstairs and spending the night in his bed. Clarifying for Duncan that I'm the one who WON'T.

It's better this way. Duncan's no prude, but I have a sneaking suspicion he's easier to talk to because I haven't fucked him. Didn't he leave for an entire day—and night—after they made love? That's not a coincidence.

"I can't possibly understand it the way you do," he said, "but it sounds like you know on some level that it's time to get over whatever hassles you've had with a longtime friend. These things happen."

We looked at each other and I wondered, *Does he realize what I'm feeling?*

If I were a decade younger, starting all over again, an ambitious twenty-something hooker, and I met someone like Duncan—streetwise yet discreet, good-looking, well-mannered. Someone I can talk to. Fall for. Capable of giving me decent advice. Willing to look out for me. A strategist I confide in . . .

Would my life have turned out differently? Is this what Milt means when he tells me, once a year, how he feels about "us"?

I suddenly imagined making it work with Duncan—like Serge and Izzy without all the ugly problems. We would buy a small house, keep each other's secrets, launder our money intelligently.

What am I thinking! I've never entertained such ideas about a guy. Why now? My heart, for a moment, was breaking over the impossibility of it all. A dream that never occurs to you until it's passed its sell-by date. He's having a summertime fling with my best friend—and I married a guy I'll never confide in. But Matt can't betray me the way Serge betrayed Izzy.

"Are you okay?" Duncan said.

"I'm going upstairs," I gasped. "It's getting late. I'd better call my girlfriend—but I think I need one more."

I returned to my bedroom, fortified by that second shot . . . and called Jasmine. If I have to apologize for my long silence—well! I swallowed my pride with the rest of my eau-de-vie.

"So," she said, as blasé as ever. "Where the fuck are you?"

"The south of France," I said meekly.

"France. Huh." She sounds more impressed than miffed. Not what I expected at all. What drove us apart—she has no CLUE how I've been feeling and doesn't really care—is what brings us back together. She's oblivious to my nervousness about losing face.

"I think Allison said something about a gig—are you in France TOGETHER?"

"Yes," I told her. "And it's the biggest mistake I've ever made in my entire life."

"You sure about that?"

"Pretty sure."

"Well, don't speak too soon. The worst is yet to come!" Jasmine said with a knowing cackle. "What else is new?"

"This trip is turning into a disaster. I might need Barry's help."

The cackling stopped. Invoking the name of our lawyer, Barry Horowitz, made Jasmine turn quite steely.

"Is this *Allison*'s fault?"

"No! It's someone I met through Liane!" I told her about Isabel, then Serge, and read a few choice bits from the *Mail*. "Has this reached the New York papers?"

Jasmine, a daily consumer of all the papers nobody admits to reading, believes that the real news almost never appears in the *New York Times*. She's got a point. If you define real news as being about . . . people like us.

"Well, there's nothing in the *Post*," she said. "I'll take another look at the *News*. You met this chick through Liane? That's incredible."

"And now I'm afraid to tell her! But she needs to know. I can't tell her like this, out of the blue. The phone seems *wrong*."

"Totally," Jasmine agreed. "Liane might have a stroke! But listen. I have to go see her. She says it can wait till Monday, but I do owe her a cut. So I'll tell her I want to drop off the money this weekend, and I'll break it to her gently! I'll see if I can find the *Daily Mail* online and show her—"

"Don't!" I pleaded. This is Jasmine's idea of gentle? "Those pictures of Serge will totally freak her out. And the headlines! You know how she is."

"True. But doesn't she have a right to know about Isabel's pimp?"

"Don't say that word to Liane! I don't want to be responsible for—what you said about a stroke! Jesus."

"Fine, I'll call him her image consultant!" Jasmine said. "I just hope Allison doesn't say anything stupid in front of your customer. You know how these guys are, they want everything discreet, and they don't like to think they did business with some AIRHEAD who ends up in a newspaper complaining about her pimp! All we need now is for Allison to organize a protest in front of the prison gates!"

"She doesn't know! And she's never met Isabel, thank God. But she's caused enough trouble as it is! I'm not telling her a thing."

"Good move," Jasmine said. "But . . . she has nothing to do with Isabel. What are you talking about?"

"You have *no idea* what she's done!" I lowered my voice and stuck a pillow over my head. Allie is dangerously near—across the hall. "She invited the entire membership of her international movement to THIS TOWN, and those lunatics are staying in the same hotel as my MOTHER. And they walk around in bright red T-shirts that say WHORE in big black letters! And Allison has the nerve to tell me she picked out the font!"

"*What?*"

"You heard me."

"Have you been drinking absinthe or something?"

"I swear to God, I am totally sober," I sort of lied.

"Did you just *make up* that entire thing about Isabel? I think you're going crazy."

"I am not hallucinating! Do you think I would be foolish enough to drink absinthe at my age? Wait." A call was trying to get through. I stared at the phone number, relieved it wasn't New York. "It's my mom. I'll call you later."

"Well, I have this guy coming tomorrow at EIGHT in the fucking morning, can you believe it? So don't call too early. I'll be catching up on my Booty Sleep. But we'll talk about your situation tomorrow. I don't think France agrees with you."

As Jasmine hung up, Mother went into voicemail. When I heard the message, my heart froze:

"I just spoke to Matt." Omigod. How did he get through to her? Mother always keeps the phone turned off. To save the battery. I've been counting on her predictable frugality. "Anyway," her message continues, "we're looking forward to seeing you tomorrow! Maybe you'd like to bring Allison. Ruth will join us."

Omigod squared.

At the very least, I owe my husband a phone call. Do I also owe him an explanation? I can't possibly deliver THAT without knowing what Matt and Mother actually *said* to each other. I can't let on that I'm hiding something from my husband or using her as an alibi. She's never been the kind of mom you involve in your secrets. Though I've heard that such mothers exist, that was never Mother's MO. This is neither the time nor place to chance it. All those stories I told him about Mother's quest for a Provençal home-stead—did he get into *that* with her? Did she tell him how we met in the town square?

When you owe your husband an explanation—but don't quite know what that should be—email's the safest course. Well, Duncan did say it's okay to raid the Sub-Zero, and I don't have to see Milt until morning. So can I allow myself a third?

Just a small one.

## Saturday morning

No message from Matt. But a voicemail from Jasmine came in while I was sleeping. "I just called Liane. I'll let you know after I see her. Let's hope she doesn't go into a coma! What was all that about your mom? Did I hear you correctly?? I'm going to the newsstand FIRST thing in the morning. Well, as soon as that guy has his clothes on."

### Later

On my way to breakfast, I delivered my empty shot glass to the kitchen, and quietly buttonholed Duncan. "I need to go to the internet café kind of soon! Can you take me later when I—" *get done with Milt*, I almost said. After last night, it seemed like the most natural thing to say. ". . . when I go to the hair salon? I have a few things to do in town today."

"Perfect," he said. "I've got to pay a visit to Pasquale. The rabbit breeder. Allison's got some errands to do as well. I'll swing by and pick you both up on the way back from Draguignan."

Errands to do?

"Has Allie told you . . ." Uh-oh. This is very questionable terrain. I SHOULD find out what she's told him about Roxana and Ruth, but I can't ask Duncan to tattle on Allie. ". . . how she feels about rabbits?" I asked.

"Don't worry," he said with a cheerful wink. "I've got the entire meal sorted."

If I went down that road—more a back alley than a road—it would ruin what I now have with him.

An hour later, from Milt's bed, I could hear Duncan rearranging pool furniture while I rubbed my left nipple against Allison's pussy.

"Mmmmm," she said, approvingly, "That feels good on my clit!" She giggled like an excited schoolgirl, then turned her face toward Milt's cock.

What exactly do we have, Duncan and I, that I hesitate to ruin? I should be afraid to confide so much—I hardly know him—but I tell him things I could never tell Matt or Milt. Or Allison. She hasn't said one word about Isabel. If Duncan told her, she wouldn't bother to hide it from me. That much I know.

As I slid into position, teasing Milt's latex-covered erection with the opening of my pussy, Allie slipped her fingers between my thighs and held my lips apart. I felt a light, perfunctory flick of her tongue, more contact than I'm used to. Milt wasn't expecting to see that. Caught off-guard, he began thrusting. It seemed too good to be true, but soon enough he was coming—way ahead of schedule.

Thanks to Allie's well-timed excess, I can get to the cibercafé and email my husband before they close for lunch.

CHAPTER FOURTEEN

# France: Arrested Developments

*Saturday afternoon*

Foiled by the whimsical ethics of those people at the cibercafé. Not yet twelve-thirty, and Ste. Maxiphony was already closed for lunch.

Coiff' Cassien, the hair salon on Rue Gutemberg, is more businesslike. Not only are they open when they promise to be, they're doing a big promotion on . . . nail extensions. I negotiated a colorless manicure instead—no thanks on the *ongles américains*—along with *un brushing*, while Allison arranged her next BGWB strategy session.

"You are *not* having your lunch with Roxana at the monastery," I told her. "We can't let her see me there with my mother! She has no idea my mom's around, and I'd like to keep it that way. Why don't you tell her to meet you at the Renaissance? I think it's *the least* you could do, after everything you've put me through."

Allie shot me a guilty look. "I'm sorry!" she sighed. "I never imagined that your mother—! And Ruth—! How was I to know! Do you think it's . . . a sign?"

"Oh please." I was trying to suppress my bitter tone. *I never imagined it either!* "A sign of *what* exactly?" The *coiffeuse* gave us a curious look. She beckoned toward a row of basins at the back of the shop. "I have to get my hair washed. Remember," I said. "You can't say anything to Roxana about how I know Ruth. Not. One. Word."

"Okay," Allie replied, in a small but sincere voice. "I promise! The Renaissance is nicer for a meeting anyway." Her appeasing 'tude—like Milt's early orgasm—was much too good to be true.

"It's me again," I heard Allie saying, as my scalp submitted to a soapy massage. "LISTEN! I have an idea." Hot running water drowned out the rest of her call, which I was straining to hear. When I emerged from the back with my head wrapped in a towel, Allie was gone.

Forty minutes later, I approached the Place Malherbe feeling like a new woman, fully blown-out and ready for (almost) anything. Braver, too, about tackling Mother on the question of Matt's phone call. I must remember I am no longer ten years old. I have a natural right to know what my husband and mother have talked about. A wife who's not sneaking around would take that right for granted. For God's sake, play the part.

To be on the safe side, I passed by La Renaissance on my way to the monastery. From the doorway of Crédit Agricole, I caught sight of some girls in militant red T-shirts sitting at an outdoor table laden with food. I could see the back of Allison's head. Roxana was talking on her phone and eating at the same time. Suddenly, a girl at Allison's left turned around.

My God.

Is that Tini? Did Allie recruit her to the cause right after our session??

Incredible.

I put on my sunglasses, fluffed my hair up to cover my face and tried to get a better look without being recognized by Roxana.

Tini and Allison, it can't be denied, are the best-looking girls at the table. That controversial T-shirt is the uniform du jour. Everyone was wearing it. Except for Tini—in a revealing denim vest—and Allie, who *would* be flying the flag . . . if only she hadn't come to St-Max on business.

Five minutes later, in the monastery lobby, I spotted Ruth's teenage foot soldiers dressed in *their* T-shirt—sky blue today, instead of black. I made my way to the dining room where an entire table was occupied by women wearing the sky blue TAKE BACK THE MAGDALEN END ALL SEX TRAFFICKING T-shirt.

Now I see why Allie takes them seriously. They coordinate their colors like an army! Did Ruth tell me the T-shirt comes in five different colors? One for each day of their conference, I suppose.

At our own table, I detected some role-reversal. Mother sipping an aperitif, Dodie drinking tea.

"I'll have what you're having," I said to Dodie. All those pilgrimatic feminists! I was longing for a sip of wine to steady my nerves, but it seemed wiser to keep my wits about me.

Mother was making small talk about why the basilica's plus-size organ wasn't destroyed by rampaging mobs during the Revolution: "Napoleon's brother rescued the church organ for secular reasons—he liked playing *La Marseillaise*." Well, that makes it okay then! Mother, always looking for an atheistic silver lining.

"I've been trying to reach Matt all day," I told her. "I think there's something wrong with his phone." Technology can be your friend AND your scapegoat—in fact, these two categories needn't be mutually exclusive. "How, uh, was he sounding?"

"As he usually does."

Thanks a lot. Can't she offer some hint of his mood? Drop a clue? "Did he seem *upset*?" I asked.

"Upset! Why?"

"We're having communication problems."

"You are?" Now I had my mother's attention, and Dodie's too. They seemed to be peering at a medical specimen, trying to decide whether I was an important new mutation or a familiar variant.

"Yes, actually. We—I prefer you don't discuss this with him." I was affecting a kind of adult stoicism. "We've been seeing a relationship counselor. We ARE going to make this work."

"Oh dear," Dodie murmured.

"We're trying," I said. "I don't want to ruin your lunch with the details, but his call last night—do you mind if I ask what you talked about?"

"Sometimes I think your generation is too self-involved," Mother said. "It's possible to overanalyze a relationship. But you've never asked me for my opinion about this, so I won't offer it!"

"Well, therapy was HIS idea, not mine." I couldn't keep up my act without getting testy as I would have done had any of this been true. "What was he *calling* about?"

"To tell you that he found the inkjet cartridges. He said there was something wrong with *your* phone."

"That was it? You didn't—discuss real estate, did you? The farmhouse?"

"Goodness. No. It didn't come up."

"We were demolishing a lovely spaghetti at L'Imprévu," Dodie explained. "They do it with steamed *palourdes*. It wasn't conducive to a chat."

When Ruth appeared in HER blue T-shirt, Dodie's juicy *bifteck* wasn't entirely "demolished," but Mother was almost finished with a chicken breast. Ruth's vegan scowl took in the carnage on their plates. Without missing a beat, Dodie asked, "Shall we get you a dessert menu?"

Bribing her grown daughter with sweets? *My* mother would

never do that, not even when I was small. Sugar was the alien substance permitted by other moms, who were to be viewed with pity and suspicion because—she once explained—they simply didn't know any better. It never occurred to me that Mother, in her search for "adult companionship," would consort with one of *those* moms. Okay, it never occurred to me that Mother would search for "adult" companionship, period. Is Dodie the *floozy* in this relationship? OMG. This is weird, you can't go home again and I definitely want a drink!

But if I start drinking in the afternoon, I've lost my professional bearings. I guess, when you have adult kids and you're still in the mating game, you don't make identical parenting techniques a precondition. I peeked at Mother from the corner of my eye to see how she was reacting to the sugar bribe.

She was, of course, gazing at the twelfth century arches framing the side entrance to the basilica. If only I had inherited her knack for studying the architecture whenever something awful is happening! And speaking of inheritance, is Mother really buying a goat farm in Mortagne-au-Perche with this child-centered flake??

Why do I resent the way Ruthie's whims are being fussed over? Mother seems to tolerate from Dodie's daughter what she would never tolerate from her own.

I had to leave the table *fast* to avoid ordering a glass of wine. When I came to St-Max to see my favorite john, I knew I would have to be businesslike about my drinking habits—but I didn't know my professionalism would be tested in this completely unthinkable manner. Ruth's sweet tooth—a trait shared by former druggies and practicing vegans—gave excellent cover to my departure.

"There's a counter-conference taking place," I heard her telling Mother as I left. "Did you know? We might have to take a different route up the hill. I think they're planning a counter *action*."

"That won't affect my assignment at all!" Mother said. "Action shots are what I do best."

When I got to the cibercafé, I headed for my favorite cubicle in a corner near the back. I was startled to find it occupied—by Tini. She was hunched over the keyboard manipulating a mouse, muttering rapidly in a language I didn't recognize. I slid into the chair to her left and peeked across the low partition.

Tini *would* have all the latest phone gear. She appeared to be talking to herself, but I could see a bright pink phone next to the mouse pad, and a slim black wire snaking across her bare collar bone, toward her shimmering hair. There was just enough cleavage in that sporty denim vest to suggest she was on the prowl.

Scrolling through my emails, I listened with half an ear, trying to figure out what language Tini was cursing in. Certainly not French. Her voice was low but there was audible wrath—". . . abogado . . . Isabel . . . bilangguan!" Spanish?

I dashed off a quick, almost groveling, reply to my husband's various messages:

*Honey, I'm sorry you had trouble locating the printer cartridges. I moved them to keep them away from the AC! Then stupidly forgot to tell you.*

*Some new developments here regarding Mother and the hotel. I think it's best you avoid calling Mother just now though, she has lots on her mind. My phone is working again! Have to run. I miss you terribly and I love you.*

But I deleted the last sentence, afraid to sound like a cheater who's overcompensating. Instead, I wrote:

*Love you.*

Blameless and bland, but passion in a spouse is very suspect!

Tini sighed with irritation. I couldn't be sure what I was hearing, but some of it was too loud to ignore. "Dalawang libo…minsan." Is she speaking Tagalog? "…dalawang beses? Anong oras? Kelan?" Could she be from the Philippines? Passing for Malaysian? After a few seconds of silence on her end, I heard a knowing laugh. "It's not a fucking GIRLFRIEND EXPERIENCE."

There's no trace of a Filipino accent when she switches to English. It's a hybrid that reveals nothing.

Wait. Did Tini just say "girlfriend experience"? That's a dead giveaway. These website girls have their own strange words for things we've all done for years. As if they invented it yesterday and now have licensing rights.

When I coughed, Tini just kept talking. I coughed again, and she swiveled around with a sharp look. Her expression changed to disbelief.

Holding a finger to her lips, she ended her call, then said in a near-whisper, "I've been trying to get your phone number from Allison!"

"You *have*?"

"I don't understand. In Barcelona, she was very reliable. But now I get to know her better, I don't trust that girl's judgement."

They were both in Barcelona? At the shadow conference? Allie's a better actress than I imagined. I would never have known, during that three-on-one with Milt, that Allie and Tini were acquainted.

So *that's* why they were convening in their underwear, right under my nose. After Milt came . . . with Tini's cock in his mouth . . . didn't I overhear Allison telling Tini about "some stairs?" *Those stairs in the church leading to Mary Magdalen's skull.* Allie's reaction, when I asked if they exchanged phone numbers: it's all starting to make sense.

"We need to talk about Isabel!" Tini insisted.

"Does Allie know what happened? To Isabel?"

"Do you?" Tini's right eyebrow was twitching. "Allison said—"
Her eyes narrowed, I looked at the ceiling, as we both contemplated
respective conversations with Allison.

Allie has probably known about Izzy's arrest ever since Tini
arrived in St-Maximin—but she never thought to tell me. "Never
mind," I whispered. "We should go somewhere else and talk
about this!" Tables were starting to fill up with potential eaves-
droppers.

"Okay," she agreed. "But—look at this."

I closed my screen and got up to look at Tini's monitor. The
interior of Mary Magdalen's cave—a large white cross, some church
pews—dominating one corner of the screen, next to a balding
priest in white robes. In large red letters: *A La-Sainte-Baume les
chiens et le chwingom sont interdits.* Dogs and chewing gum
forbidden on the mountain. Huh.

"What's all this?" I asked. "Are you involved with the procession?"

"That business on the mountain? I'm keeping an eye on it. So
far so good." She fiddled with her mouse. "But you have to see
these pictures of Isabel. And Serge."

"I've seen the *Daily Mail*, you know."

"But Allison told me—." Tini's peevish squint, followed by
flaring nostrils, made me realize she has less patience with Allie
than I do. "Why did she—?"

"Never mind that—what Allison told you. I called Isabel on
Thursday because we had a date with Natalia. I never heard back."

"Natalia was called in for questioning! I haven't seen her since."
A Swedish newspaper popped up on Tini's screen. Only a few
words made sense. *Isabel Dolmy . . . Izzy Morgan . . . St-Tropez . . .
Interpol.* "I think they have her phone. We managed to get her
service switched off, so they can't monitor incoming calls. What
kind of message did you leave?"

"Oh God no." Is my voicemail to Izzy now the permanent property of Interpol? "I don't want to think about it."

"You don't *what*?" Tini was frowning at the computer screen. She turned to me and spoke in a harsh whisper. "You're in somebody else's country. You can't afford to stop thinking! One of the girls got deported already. What did you say on your message? If you called on Thursday, maybe they heard it. Isabel's in a lot of trouble. Her bank accounts are frozen. They might take her flat." Tini shook her head. "Look at this. *She was gorgeous.*"

The first clear picture I've seen of Isabel—posing for the camera, hands cupping her chin. A beguiling smile danced around her lips. There was a directness about her eyes that made me wince. Her golden-brown hair was arranged in a luxurious but informal updo. "How old was she?"

"Eighteen maybe? Izzy's first husband took the picture. Malcolm ran an agency."

"But she told the *Mail* that Serge introduced her to the business!"

"She can't help herself. Malcolm died in a car crash on her twentieth birthday and she never got over him. It was Malcolm who taught her the business." Tini touched the monitor with a manicured index finger, and gave the teenage Isabel a light tap on the nose. "Isabel tries to turn all her men into Malcolm because he 'discovered' her. You know her type."

If Izzy's first husband had lived, she would have outgrown him. As a widow, she's stuck.

"How does she look now?" I asked.

"Not bad." Tini shrugged. She clicked until a picture of Izzy's new husband appeared. "Did you see *Var-Matin*?"

"Yes." I looked away from the screen. "I never thought it was possible for Serge to look like that."

"I know," Tini agreed. "They humiliate a man in public. It's not right."

"But he informed on his *wife!*" I said.

Tini looked around the room. Only a few tables were occupied, and those customers were ignoring us—for now. Her mouth was next to my ear. I felt her thick silky hair tickling my neck, noticed a light citrus aroma emanating from her skin. The combination surprised my body. A tingling sensation in my breasts made me sit still.

"If it weren't for that bitch Katya," she hissed, "none of this would have happened. I hope she gets deported." Tini closed her screen, and picked up her woven leather shopping bag. "Let's pay. I know a place where we can talk."

On the Avenue du 15ème Corps, Tini's cleavage was turning heads—male and female alike. Do you need to secretly possess a cock to have this kind of supernatural effect on the public? Tini takes this reflexive reverence for granted—she tossed her hair, adjusted her sunglasses, walked a little faster. "You met Katya," she said. "Didn't you do a session with her?"

"I could tell she was involved with Serge," I told her. "I was kind of shocked!" I didn't want to admit that I was also turned on by what I saw. "I never realized he was married to Izzy. Then I saw the papers. But Serge and Katya look like a natural couple. Their body language . . ."

"Those three!" Tini scowled as she reached into her bag for a cigarette. "Serge is an idiot. Isabel should never have encouraged him to do that with one of the girls. But Katya's a little bitch. What she asked him to do was wrong. And what he did was stupid."

"What did he DO?" Besides ratting on his wife? She inhaled energetically, angrily. I turned away from the smoke.

"They were spending weekends together, all three. Isabel thought she could control him this way. She left them alone in St-Tropez. Well, she didn't count on Serge falling for Katya, only Katya falling for him! This last month was hell. Always bickering. Never work for a married couple!"

Tini guided us into a side street, toward a deserted café with metal tables on the sidewalk.

"Let's sit out here," I suggested. She showed no sign of being finished with her cigarette. "Fresh air."

"Nobody comes here," she assured me. "I don't know how they stay in business. At least we can talk."

"So the place in St-Tropez?" I asked. "The papers say Serge was running a brothel."

"She rents a flat in St-Trop five months a year," Tini explained. "Serge took care of it while Isabel stayed at their place in Villeneuve Loubet, and Katya got these ideas. She wanted Serge to leave Isabel. It's one thing you want the man to leave his wife for you. But Katya wanted him to take from Isabel what was never his and share it with HER."

"Take what? The apartment? The car?"

"Everything! The business mostly. The Lexus probably. The apartment—well, I overheard him tell Katya that the property is in his wife's name. When Katya's fantasies don't come true, she decides to make trouble for Isabel. It's just a mess."

Why is Tini telling me all this? She was so cool toward me the first time we met.

"If Katya weren't such a selfish bitch," Tini said, "we would all be making money and Isabel would still be answering her phone. The place in St-Trop is closed now. We can never go back there."

"Where's Katya?"

"No idea. Out of work, nowhere to live, and her lover's in prison!"

"But she . . ."

". . . caused all this to happen! Even to herself. Katya's the stupidest girl I ever worked with. Girls like that have eyes too big for their brains. But," Tini said. "I don't blame her for sleeping with Serge. Falling for him."

"No," I admitted, recalling his perfectly formed biceps. "I guess not."

"He's not my type, but he's a gorgeous man."

"But Katya was working for his *wife*," I pointed out.

"Yes, but Isabel encouraged Serge. She wanted him to cultivate a relationship with someone new to the business. Katya's the same age Isabel was . . ."

". . . when she met her first husband! Omigod."

"It's what they call arrested development," Tini said. "Izzy's a menace to herself and everyone she knows!"

I can't believe the havoc her first husband's death is creating more than two decades later.

"So it's not *all* Katya's fault," I said.

Tini sipped her rosé while I stirred my lemonade.

"Katya went too far!" she objected. "What if she calls you looking for business? How long can she live on the money she stole from the apartment? There's nothing Katya won't do. She might tell the police all about you. I've been telling Allison you need to be warned, but Allison pays no attention. All she wants to talk about is Mary Magdalen's cave! And the relics."

Unwilling to defend or criticize Allie, I tried to reassure Tini. "I haven't heard from Katya, thank God. I wonder who she's been calling."

"Desperate girls are dangerous. This is what Allison doesn't understand." As Tini lit yet another one of her cigarettes, I tried not to inhale. If only Europeans and Asians were a bit more excited about living forever. It would be easier to breathe in this town.

"There's a lot Allison doesn't understand," Tini continued, "but I hope she's right about that cave. The girl in the tourist office says the mayor of Plan d'Aups is coming Monday with the Archbishop of Toulon, for the grand opening of Mary Magdalen's cave! And we have one chance to get everything right. No dress rehearsal. Allison didn't tell you? I'm surprised."

*I'm* not. "Do you mind if I—" Reaching into my tote bag, I switched on my phone which was tucked beneath a black TAKE BACK THE MAGDALEN T-shirt. Allie *might* understand how I ended up with some enemy swag, Tini would not. And though I've done nothing wrong here, I don't want Tini to know about the T-shirt. It will only confuse things. "The lady who introduced me to Isabel. She's rather elderly, you see, but she needs to be told. So we've been trying to break it to her gently."

"We?" Tini asked.

"My best friend in New York. She's supposed to call back." I felt a twinge of dismay. Allie would be hurt to hear me put it that way, but I don't trust her. And I can trust Jasmine to do, if not always say, the right thing.

"What's wrong?" Tini said. I listened—with growing horror— to the only message in my system.

"I—I don't know." I forced myself to listen once more . . . to the last person I was expecting to hear from today.

"I think we have something to discuss." Elspeth, very icy, without even a hint of her usual rasp. I stopped breathing and tried to make sense of her message. "I wonder what my brother will do when he finds out." I was stunned. "How long did you think you could play this game?"

Has Elspeth been tailing me? How did *she* find out? And for how many days? What's SHE involved in? A covert investigation? Involving Isabel's connections in Palm Beach and New York? Involving Liane?? If so, it must be *very* covert. Omigod—it never occurred to me that my sister-in-law, the former prosecutor, could keep HER job a secret. Elspeth never said a thing about going back to work.

"If Interpol has my number," I said in a shaky voice. "Could they—?" I was too frightened to continue. Could they have traced, that quickly, my conversation with Jasmine?

"Calm down," Tini was saying. "Don't panic. Who called you?"

"I'm sorry." I shook my head numbly. Where is Jasmine? Did something happen to Jasmine? Why hasn't she called? "I can't talk about it! Could you order a glass of wine for me?"

"Of course." Tini sprang into action like a military nurse. "White or red?"

CHAPTER FIFTEEN

# France: Return of the (Not So) Repressed

### *Saturday, continued*

Tempted to drown my fears in a second glass of wine, I cut myself off, and called Duncan.

"I'm ten minutes away from St-Max," he said. "Can you meet me in the Place Malherbe? Across from the fountain."

"I'd better not have more to drink," I told Tini. "I'm having dinner with, um—" *That guy we did last week*, I almost said, but that sounds so trashy and immature.

"Your sugar daddy?"

"He's just a customer." Then I backtracked, suddenly possessive, not wanting Tini to think of Milt as fair game. After that phone call, he feels like the only sure thing I've got! If Elspeth tells Matt, well, at least my marital meltdown comes at a time when I have some serious money in hand—thanks to Milt. "He's been very good to me," I told her. "I've been seeing Milt for ten years. But he doesn't know about Isabel. I hid the newspapers."

"Good," Tini said. "Don't involve these men in our problems unless they have a way to help. He can't help with this, no point telling him." Her bold, concerned gaze made me think twice about lying to her. "Who called you before?"

"Someone I know in New York." I felt a knot in my chest. Elspeth's message was replaying in my head. Does she actually know about Isabel? Or only know about Milt? Am I in trouble with the law, with my husband, or both?

"New York?" Tini looked relieved, and pulled out a business card. "If the French police bother you, call Renaud. Immediately. Say I told you to."

"Renaud?"

"Renaud Rety. Our lawyer. Tini Avelino sent you. This—" she pointed with one of her impeccable white fingernails "—is his mobile."

"He's representing Isabel?"

"Yes. Not Serge, of course. His lawyer is a rascal. He will outsmart himself, if we're lucky."

"Serge?"

"The lawyer. Serge could not outsmart even himself." Tini rolled her eyes heavenward. "Serge never had it so good. And he never will again."

Now back at Villa Gambetta, checking messages in vain. Did Elspeth find her way to Jasmine? Involve *her* in some kind of investigation? If Jasmine gets a call from any manner or form of law enforcement, she'll be on the phone to her lawyer yesterday. I know she can protect herself, but it wouldn't be wise for us to talk under these circumstances. It's unwise to call ANYone at this point. Even Charmaine.

Unless . . .

### Later

Duncan was in the den—alone, thank goodness—organizing some magazines on the coffee table. "Would it seem strange," I said, "if

I borrow your phone for five minutes? I have to call New York and I'm afraid my number could be . . ." I can't bring myself to say out loud that my phone number is now tainted—damaged goods.

He nodded sympathetically—"No need to explain"—and reached into his pocket. "You'll get better reception in the library."

Charmaine was surprised to hear my voice. "I didn't recognize your number," she said.

"You never saw this number, okay? Don't call. Has anyone been bothering you?"

"You mean, like, a stalker?"

"Well, it might feel that way. I can't get into it now, but you need to be careful. Don't talk to people you don't know. Especially a woman—"

"Nancy! For God's sake, tell me what's going on!"

"Go to the web and google 'Isabel Morgan St-Tropez.' There was something in the *Daily Mail* this week. If you see anything in the American papers, I need to know. Send me a link, I think that's safer than the phone. I'm away from the computer now, but I'll check tomorrow."

"Okay," Charmaine said, rather tersely. "But keep me in the loop. Don't leave me exposed! Do you really think email's safer?"

"In this case, yes. I really think so. Listen. I need to stay in the apartment when I come back."

"*What*?"

"I know it's a change from what we agreed, I'll sort it out with you. And I'll try to find somewhere else, but I need to know I have a place to sleep. I'll stay out of your way. I'll sleep on the couch—we'll work out a different financial plan. I know it's inconvenient, I don't want to mess up your business. I promise I'll make it up to you—"

"It's okay! We've never had a problem with money. But—can't you tell me what happened?"

"I'm not sure yet." And now I realized my voice was getting shaky. "It's hard to say. It's not how I wanted things to go. I've only been married two years . . ." And it's embarrassing to be telling my twenty-something roommate how badly I've botched things. Begging her to let me sleep on my own couch.

"I think I get it," she said. "Look, if you need to sleep here, we'll just work it out."

"I'll call in a few days," I told her. "I'm sorry. I can't talk anymore. I have to get ready for dinner with Milt." I turned Duncan's phone off, and collapsed into the armchair—where my favorite client fucked me two weeks ago—feeling like a complete failure as a wife.

I keep hearing Elspeth's voicemail in my head: "I wonder what my brother will do when he finds out. How long did you think you could play this game?"

What exactly was my game? And what did I want to prove? That I could have it all?

All I've proven is that I can't.

### Later still

What about Matt? Will he ever be the same after discovering that his wife's . . . a hooker? Could he ever understand? "I've been unfaithful in my fashion," I want to tell him, "but only to you." And the person you tell the biggest lie to is the one who really matters. The man you're cheating on is the one you care about.

No, my husband wouldn't understand, nor should he have to. Didn't I tell Allie that the emotional cost of cheating is OURS and we pick up this tab ourselves? Here I am, stuck with a huge tab and no-one but myself to blame.

Dressing for a poolside dinner, I kept one eye on my phone. Sitting at my desk, waiting for the serum under my eyes to dry, I reached over to check my voicemail. The silence in my message bank was maddening. I stopped myself from dialing Jasmine and turned the phone off, afraid to let it ring—what if Matt calls?

A familiar dish was making its presence known throughout the house. Duncan, at work in the kitchen, having his way with my senses. That fragrant combination—young olive oil seeping into sweet peppers while they roast—sent my mind elsewhere. This aroma that went swirling through my head ten days ago, when I allowed Milt "just this once" to get me off . . . while allowing myself to think of Duncan. A breakthrough in my sex life, you might say—my inner sex life. Always off-limits to the man I have in mind or in bed.

Instead of returning to New York and having to explain myself to Matt, what if I could stay here forever, sustained by Duncan's cooking and Milt's money? Sneaking off to the media hut once a week to sample Duncan while Milt plays golf. Paradise + Salvation. Better together.

I slipped into raw silk pajama bottoms, pony skin flip-flops, then assessed myself in the mirror. Casual, relaxed—reassuringly expensive. My nipples were alert, pushing against a transparent black bra.

There was a light tap on my door. "It's me!" Allie whispered. "Can I come in?" She was clutching a fluffy bath sheet around her naked body, and her hair was wrapped in a small white towel. "My blow-dryer just died! I don't understand. It's brand new!" Once inside, she grew wary. "Are you—ummm—mad at me, Nancy?"

"Now why would I be mad at you." I made no effort to retrieve my dryer and continued playing with my pajama top, experimenting with the buttons.

"Well, Tini's mad at me." Allie, uninvited, took a seat at the edge of my bed. "But she says you KNEW about Isabel."

"We're not here to discuss Isabel. And it's not something Milt needs to know about. If you let one word slip out around Milt or Duncan—"

202

"Don't worry," she said. "I won't!"

"I want to know what you plan on doing Monday afternoon. Tini says you're part of a procession to the cave! And you're the coordinator? Why didn't you tell me?"

"I'm going to, I mean, *was* going to!"

"I can't trust anything you tell me anymore. We'll talk about this later. Here—" I handed her the dryer. "Do us both a favor and do not under any circumstances move the settings. If it's on the wrong setting, it will overheat and *die*. And then we'll be stranded here on a SUNDAY without any alternative means of—-"

"I know!" she gasped. "That would be awful!"

When I appeared poolside, Milt was in one of the upright wooden armchairs, immersed in the *Daily Telegraph*, sipping Pernod. Yesterday Isabel was in the *Mail*. Today, a story in a Swedish tabloid. Could she also be fodder for the *Telegraph*? I suppressed a violent urge to snatch the paper out of Milt's hands. Instead, I snuck up behind him. Allowing my hair to tickle his face, I leaned over his right shoulder. My breasts grazed the back of his head as I studied the paper. Nothing about Isabel so far. Why is Milt so focused on those Barclays bankers up on Enron charges?

Milt made no effort to move. He spoke in a quiet voice. "Kiddo, your hair on my neck is reminding me of something you did this morning. My cock is harder than it's ever been. If Duncan weren't twenty feet away I would ORDER you to sit on my lap."

"Would you like . . ." I kept my voice equally quiet. ". . . my panties on or off?"

"I'll try it both ways."

"He's so near," I murmured, looking in Duncan's direction. "But so far," I added, "he hasn't seen a thing." Milt twisted his head around, and his brow brushed against my breast. "Twenty feet?" I caught a glimpse of Duncan through the kitchen doorway and drew a sharp breath. I didn't have to fake my reaction. I was almost embarrassed to be sharing, for the first time, a feeling Milt and I never talk about. "How many meters away *is* he?"

"Good question. I'm lousy at conversion. But—" he folded his paper and tossed it aside "—maybe I should start thinking metric."

"Oh?"

"I might have to stay here. I don't think I'll be returning to New York right away." Allie was now standing barefoot on the other side of the pool in a flowery wrap-around dress, sipping a glass of white wine. "Let's talk about it later when we're alone," he said. That low insinuating growl made me wonder if he was up for an after-dinner session. That would be a first.

I grabbed the newspaper, then perched myself on the arm of Milt's chair. Facing away from him, I wriggled a bit and kept my eye on the kitchen doorway. Milt couldn't help noticing that my ass was inches from his lap. I imagined myself complying with my client's "order," then being caught by Duncan's curious gaze, and felt grateful to be wearing panties. A wet spot on my silk pajamas would be awkward just now.

I did my best to impersonate a casual unmotivated reader, enjoying a pre-dinner round-up of current events lite. For one thing, if MILT's monitoring the news for personal reasons, I don't want him to think I've noticed.

That trip to Luxembourg. Isn't that where all the secret bank accounts are? Now that Switzerland's become rather notorious? Could this explain his inclination to stick around St-Max and learn how to measure in French? He's so preoccupied. Isabel's arrest would be the last straw. I must never become the kind of girl who reminds Milt of other people's sordid, unsolvable problems—especially if he's trying to solve a few of his own.

After dinner, I turned my phone on and felt my throat closing up when the voicemail robot announced two messages. First, a call from Jasmine. Finally. "Liane canceled last minute." Uh-oh.

But Jasmine also sounds like she's been drinking. "I got a little paranoid," she admits. "Turns out she was showing her apartment! The broker had to come early. Did you know she's selling her duplex? She might have a buyer. Anyway. I just saw her. She knows what happened. There's nothing in the paper, but I told her all about it. Says it's a sign from the universe. Sell the place sooner, not later! I told her wait a few months, the market's too soft. Call me!"

Do I dare call Jasmine from this phone? She sounds nothing like a girl who's been sitting under a bare bulb fending off interrogators. More like a girl who's been sitting under a hairdryer with a martini in her hand. So that's one less thing to worry about.

But my husband's voicemail is one more, and I keep replaying it for clues. "Honey?" He sounds subdued. Definitely subdued. "When you get a chance—" suddenly, he takes that brisk tone, the one he sometimes uses to critique my *grocery list* "—check your email." Is this what a man in the market for a nasty divorce sounds like? Maybe so. God. "I don't want to talk about it until you've read the email. But we need to talk." Is he worried? Angry? I don't get it. Could it be that he doesn't believe his own sister? And how long could *that* last?

Who's worse? His sister, for telling him? Or his wife, for letting him find out?

## Sunday morning

Allie and I were ingesting our first dose of caffeine when Milt surprised us with a sudden change of plans. "I'll have to take a rain check on our threeway. Emergency golf date at ten!" he announced, stretching his arms in front of his chest. "Anyone care to accompany me?"

Allie, beneath her umbrella, couldn't conceal the panic on her face. This messes up our entire routine—we'll have to do him later in the day, when we'd rather be getting dressed for dinner. And does he want us to join him on the golf course? Neither of us is prepared for that much sun.

"But I've never played," I said faintly. "I'm a golf virgin!"

"I'm passing through St-Max," he explained. "I was thinking you girls might like a ride to church."

"Oh!" Allie perked up. "I just LOVE Sunday Mass. That would be so cool!"

"You might get a chance to photograph the relics for your scrapbook," Milt said.

I frowned at Allie. "Photos are . . ."

"Forbidden in church," she said agreeably. "I don't want to get thrown off the premises," she told Milt. "I'm waiting until Monday for—" My cup clattered on its saucer as I threw her a warning glance.

"And *I* need to send some email," I interrupted. "That would be perfect."

With a regretful grimace, Allie rushed upstairs to change for church.

"This came up last minute," Milt said quietly. "There's something I have to sort out if I stay in St-Max the rest of the year."

"How can—you're really staying till December?" I wonder who he's meeting. I didn't dare ask.

"It's possible, but I can't make a decision yet. What's wrong, kiddo?"

For some reason, Milt staying in France when the summer is over makes New York seem unsafe, less familiar. Less like home. Well, I can't say THAT to a john. And that's what Milt is. Always will be. But he's always been there for me! Or so it seems, as my marriage comes screeching to its disastrous conclusion. Was I counting on a familiar signpost to make the landing less bumpy?

Some sexual and emotional landmarks? You should never count on these guys. They're not landmarks, they're customers. What was I thinking?

"Nothing," I said lightly. "New York won't be quite the same. We girls will just have to manage without you." I smiled slyly. "Wait for you to change your mind. Get bored with France."

"I'm flattered!" he said. "Well, you never know." His silence on the subject of a return visit made me bite my lip. His wife must be coming over to spend the rest of the year with him. But this is a strange order in which to arrange your year. Shouldn't his family be here during the summer? Leaving him free to bring his play-mates to Villa Gambetta in the off months? But nothing Milt does these days quite makes sense.

Nothing adds up. This oversized, overly renovated hideaway, in this out-of-the-way location is large enough for three families. But why didn't he buy in La Garde-Freinet, or some obviously chic spot? Aside from the books in the library, everything's brand new and just so. Sometimes too much so. That media hut feels like the inside of an eighties limo!

I stared at the stone tiles bordering the pool. He can't possibly sell this place at a profit, can he? It's far more luxurious than anything I've seen around St-Max—including the monastery hotel. Without the historic buildings, St-Max would merely be tacky.

If he's madly in love with the locale, why no interest in its lore? What reason would Milt have for buying in a town like this, if he's not completely fascinated with its history? Milt couldn't care less about that old basilica, and Monday's procession is just "that crazy parade", for fanatics.

"Let's get you to the internet café," he said. "And when I know more about my situation, I'll take you somewhere for a quiet lunch."

Something about his confiding tone made my face feel warm,

my heart beat faster. After more than ten years, are my feelings for Milt becoming less manageable? Or is this just one of those opportunistic moods? How it feels to be on the verge of losing your husband while trying to hold on to the most reliable guy in your stable?

### Sunday, later

I joined Allie in the back seat of Milt's BMW where she was perusing a floor plan in *Revue de la Basilique*. "Where's Milt?" I glanced around quickly. "Listen, he's not dropping us at the church, okay? The last thing I need is to run into my mom when we're with Milt. If anything goes wrong, tell my mother Milt's your uncle. She thinks we're visiting your family."

"MY family?" Allie looked startled. "But nobody would believe . . ."

Milt was strolling toward the BMW, a golf bag over one shoulder, wearing a pair of wraparound shades. "It doesn't matter what my mother would or wouldn't believe about YOU. All that matters—" I stopped talking and placed a hand on Allison's thigh so that, as he got closer, he couldn't help seeing, through the open door, a furtive gesture. Allie giggled and covered my hand, her lap, with the open book.

Milt peeked into the back seat. "One of you has to sit up front," he insisted. "You're liable to get carried away back here and cause a distraction while I'm driving. You can't do that to a guy!"

Sitting next to Milt, I toyed with the buttons on my blouse and turned my head just enough to flash a discreet smile. He was approaching the Boulevard Bonfils when I said in a polite but clear voice, "We'll have to finish what we started when you come back from golf." His eyes lingered over my schoolgirlish outfit— a false skirt that opens when I move my legs, to reveal short culottes and a glimpse of thigh. "Why don't you drop us both at the ciber-café. We'll take care of our email and go on to church together."

"Good idea!" Allie piped up, anxious to show her cooperative spirit.

Remembering Tini, I backtracked. If Milt pulls up in front of the café, what are the chances of running into her? Would that be a good thing or a bad thing? I don't want to risk it, unless I know how to deal with the outcome.

"Actually," I said. "Why don't you drop us near the fountain. It's a nice day for a walk!"

As I exited the front seat, he caressed my hip. "Save this for later," he said. "And call Duncan if you need anything."

As I made my way toward the Avenue du 15ème Corps, Allie followed. She began walking faster.

"You don't have to come with me," I said. "I'll meet you after church. I just said that so Milt would—"

"No!" Allie said, in a high nervous voice. "I'm coming with you. Quickly," she added, as we reached the café. "Get inside! Close the door!" She dashed toward a table in the back. Now I was the one following.

"What's wrong?" I asked.

"I just saw someone we shouldn't—Don't look!" I turned around. "I can't believe it!"

"What are you talking about?"

"You didn't see him?" She moved into a corner table and gazed back at me like a woodland creature with a very short life span facing premature demise. "He didn't see you?"

"Who are you hiding from?"

"That priest!" She couldn't look me in the eye.

"Did you . . . did you pick up a priest?" I was horrified yet impressed—it's not like Allie to be so enterprising. "You're not supposed to be doing business with local guys! What if Milt finds out? Where did you do it? How much did you GET?"

"No!" she gasped. "Father Philippe is helping Bad Girls Without Borders protect Mary Magdalen's relics."

"He's helping YOU to protect the relics? Shouldn't it be the other way around? I want to get some coffee and a day pass. Take a deep breath! You can't let some lecherous priest intimidate you."

But when I got to the cash register, I saw what Allie was hiding from—and what she was hiding *from me.* Two men on the sidewalk were engrossed in conversation. The priest, tall and dark-haired with somewhat large ears, was more animated. Where have I seen his face before? Yesterday, on the Dominican website that Tini was looking at. The other man, nodding earnestly, was consulting a small book while they spoke. When he turned his head toward the window, I panicked. *Jason? What is my brother-in-law doing in St-Maximin?* Then I ducked.

I hurried back to the corner cubicle, where I found Allie hunched over her phone. She looked up. "Is he gone?"

"Why didn't you tell me about Jason!" Is THAT how Elspeth found out? Could Jason be spying for his wife? Or did he spill the beans accidentally? What has Jason seen?

Allie covered her face with her hands. Her shoulders were trembling. "I'm sorry!" she exclaimed.

"You knew he was out there! You let me—"

"I tried to stop you! Did he see you?"

"I don't know. I fucking well hope not! How long have you known about this?"

"About what?" she squeaked.

"About my brother-in-law. How long have you been hiding THAT from me?"

"It's not what you think!" Allie said. "Roxana told me a NYCOT supporter was flying in from Paris, but I had no idea who it was! He's driving us to the mountain tomorrow."

"You promised you would stay away from him. We had a deal."

"I kept my promise!" Now she was looking me in the eye, oddly enough. "But I can't control what Roxana does. You know what? Jason shows up every year around the same time. He tells Roxana he wants to make a difference. And then?" Allie shrugged. "He just disappears."

If she broke that promise and met with Jason, I bet NYCOT would NEVER be rid of him.

"He's a married man with twins. And a partner in his law firm. He's busy." Why am I defending Jason to her? And why does he get obsessed with hookers—in this completely inappropriate way!—whenever the weather warms up?

I was sure, when Jason became a father, he would get over NYCOT and I would never worry about him running into Allie, or finding out my secrets, again.

CHAPTER SIXTEEN

# France: Revelations

*Sunday afternoon, continued*

Matt's emails are mostly FWDs from Elspeth. That's no surprise,
but the content sure is.

> *Honey, don't freak. What you're about to read is kinda weird
> but I have to show you. I desperately need your advice.*
> *Matt:*
> *>> WAKE UP AND SMELL THE CAFÉ AU LAIT! Your
> darling wife is screwing my darling husband in the south of
> fucking France and has probably been doing him on the side ever
> since I HAD THE TWINS. He is not, I repeat, NOT in Paris—
> I don't care WHAT you say. You spoke to her mother? Well, has
> it ever occurred to you that her mother might be the perfect cover
> for a rendezvous with MY HUSBAND?—Elspeth*
> *>>Matt, You are obviously in total denial, my dear. Have
> you ever noticed that my husband and YOUR WIFE are
> always unreachable around six o'clock? I HAVE. Not once
> have I ever seen your wife ANSWERING HER CELLPHONE
> when YOU AND I have dinner with her. Don't you think*

*that's strange??? Why do you think she always has it turned off? To save the battery? She's hiding something from you BIG TIME and she's hiding something from ME. That two-faced bitch has you wrapped around her finger but I AM ONTO HER. E.*

*>> I almost can't believe those two would do something so blatant. Let me just explain. Criminals like to HIDE THINGS IN PLAIN SIGHT. Adultery is no longer prosecuted in New York State but the ADULTEROUS MENTALITY has never changed. Ask any criminologist. E.*

*>>MATT: Just had a meeting with Raoul Felder. You'd better be prepared to provide my son with a masculine role model because his father won't have a functioning set of balls when Felder and I get done with him. I'm glad I kept my maiden name. E.*

Omigod. Elspeth is farther off the mark than I ever imagined. Jason's not even my type! Sex with my brother-in-law has never crossed my mind. For once, I'm in the clear, even with myself.

Elspeth's always been nosy, but this is something new. I've never seen Elspeth get angry. To think I was worried about her *going back to work* and getting involved with Interpol.

But how does she know where Jason is? Matt's next message offers a clue.

*Honey, see what I mean? I'm really sorry to make you look at those crazy emails. I don't know what got into my sister. She called my office and tried to get them to interrupt a meeting. Last night, she woke me up. I'm worried. She says she "found out" he's not in Paris because of his GPS. She says he called from the airport in Marseille but they never spoke. Dunno what to think. Is she imagining all this? When I question her, she screams.*

*Refuses to call Jason. I tried. Says he'll have to talk to her lawyer. Could use some advice from a sensitive intelligent woman and you're, um, the first person that comes to mind. xoxo*

Am I off the hook here? My marriage is stronger than ever, and my husband is pestering me for advice! Breathing a sigh of relief, I typed back, almost joyfully:

*Has there been an incident like this before??? What provoked it? Were they having problems of any kind?*

Re-reading Elspeth's last message, I felt a twinge. Only a woman in deepest pain would say such things about her husband's testicles.

I don't know WHAT to make of Jason: has my worst nightmare become my new best friend? Well, not quite.

"You cannot be seen with me," I told Allison. "You have to go out there and distract those guys. Jason and I can't have any contact." *Not if those emails are for real.* "Get him out of my radius while I call Duncan. Be careful what you say! If Jason runs into me, I'll pretend I don't know you're here. Can you keep all that straight?"

Allie was massaging her temples. "I don't know!"

"Don't forget, Jason thinks I'm one of your straight friends. Just think about how you would act if I *were*."

"But I don't really *have* any straight friends," Allie said.

"I hardly do either," I admitted. "But having straight friends is a useful skill. Just pretend you're hiding your business from me! This way, if Jason runs into my mother, he'll keep your job a secret from her, too."

"If we just told everyone the truth, it would all be much simpler."

"It would NOT," I pointed out. "Remember, Matt thinks I'm staying with my mother in the monastery. And my mother thinks

214

we're both staying with your uncle. I want Jason to think I'm staying with my mother. And you're staying with your uncle."

"What if Jason talks to your mom? He might get the idea you're staying with my uncle!"

She's right! And what if he tells Matt? Elspeth's accusations will start sounding entirely credible. Yikes.

"We have to make sure that doesn't happen," I said. "You have to do everything in your power to keep Jason away from my mother."

I can't believe I've created such a deadly trap for my brother-in-law. It was never supposed to be like this!


## Later still

Sitting under an umbrella with an iced *tilleul* infusion and the latest *Nouvel Observateur*, I felt the phone vibrating in my lap.

"I'm in Plan d'Aups with Jason!" Allie was talking in a low, nervous voice. "We're at Father Philippe's museum. Should I ask him to drive me back to Milt's place?"

"No! Are you crazy? What are you doing all the way up there?"

"Well, you told me to keep away from your mom, but I keep running into her! I was in the church trying to get a close-up of Mary Magdalen's skull and she was doing exactly the same thing."

"That's why I'm not showing up for any of your festivities tomorrow. I wish you would both put your cameras away! I'm liable to end up on some Godawful website surrounded by people wearing embarrassing T-shirts."

"Remember that little altar girl? She came downstairs and caught us taking pictures. So I went across the street to that nice tea shop. Jason was in there interviewing Father Philippe. Jason's doing some very serious historical research. It's for his novel. And since Father Philippe was the caretaker of Mary Magdalen's cave . . ."

Oh no. That novel he was writing when he first met Allie. About Mary Magdalen surviving . . . a real estate boom.

"Then your mom and Dodie came into the tea shop and Dodie took a seat RIGHT NEXT to us! Father Philippe asked Dodie if he could practice his English with her!"

"Omigod. Did my mom meet JASON?"

"No," Allie assured me. "She was upfront, looking at the artisanal vinegars. So I asked Jason if he would take me to Father Philippe's museum. It's the only way I could keep everyone apart! Well, it turns out Jason is actually staying in one of the spare rooms, and Father Philippe says I can sleep in the OTHER guest room. He says the Sodomites' real sin was being unfriendly to visitors and he prefers to practice his English with a sex worker."

"We need to deal with this before Milt gets back from the golf course. Don't turn your phone off!"

I looked for Duncan in the kitchen, the library, the media hut. Finally, I tried the exercise room. I found him lying on the carpet, examining the underside of the exercise bike with a flashlight. Screwdriver and pliers lay on the floor, framing his torso. I couldn't help staring. His navy T-shirt, completing the effect, was immaculate.

"Who's there?" he said. Temptation stunned me into silence . . . I could walk right over and carefully straddle his pelvis in these culottes. The fabric on my thighs feels so loose and light. I can imagine the outline of my pussy pressing against him, the lips opening beneath my panties. I like the way his knees, slightly bent, cause a ripple in the front of his jeans. But if I were sitting on him like that, his legs would be straight.

I caught my breath. He was concentrating on the bike.

"It's me," I said quietly. My lower lips were swollen and I was afraid to move.

He slowly pulled himself away from the machine and looked up. "Is there something you need?"

I looked right back. My knees were trembling. He switched off his flashlight, holding my gaze. I could hear ringing in another room.

"Isn't that's your phone?" I said. "It might be Allison." His expression gave nothing away. Have they fucked again? How does he feel about her? The conflict in my culottes became more manageable. Duncan's phone continued, but he made no effort to leave the room. "Allison's in a bit of a jam," I told him. "She's stranded in Plan d'Aups. I'm afraid we need your help! I'd rather not discuss all this with Milt, of course."

"How did she—" He rephrased his question. "Do you know where in Plan d'Aups?"

"She's at a museum. With a priest. I think we'd better call her."

"La Maison Marie-Magdeleine? The founder is Pasquale's uncle."

"Pasquale?"

"The man I buy the rabbits from in Draguignan."

"So you know this Father Philippe?"

"Before he was chased away from the mountain, he was *père gardien* of the cave. He claims to have daily conversations with the Magdalen. How did Allison end up in his museum? Shall we go together?"

"Father Philippe has a houseguest from New York! Someone I need to avoid."

"Oh?" Duncan collected his tools from the floor.

"Allison's under strict instructions not to mention me to him." I followed Duncan to the SUV. "I wish I could come with you, but . . . there's something you don't know. About me."

He turned and smiled. "Is that so?"

"Milt doesn't know either! Father Philippe's houseguest is my brother-in-law. I can't have any contact with him because his wife thinks we're having an affair. She's completely deluded! He doesn't even know I'm in the area," I explained. "If I keep it that way, we have deniability. His wife went crazy last week and retained a celebrity divorce lawyer! I can't afford to get caught in the middle. It's bad enough that she thinks I would come here to be with her husband!"

It takes a lot to surprise Duncan.

I was blushing now. "Yes, she's my husband's sister." The look in his eyes unnerved me. Is he turned on because I have a husband? "Milt has no idea I'm married. And my husband has no idea I'm here. In this house, I mean. He thinks I'm staying at—" I looked away, embarrassed "—the Couvent Royale."

That's all I want Duncan to know about THAT. If I tell him about my mother, he'll think *I'm* delusional.

He opened the car door. "It's a lot to keep track of." His eyes lingered over my now-flustered appearance. I blinked, suddenly close to tears, having unraveled so much of my tale. "I'm very flattered you felt able to tell me," he said. He touched my arm gently, and leaned toward me. I closed my eyes and felt, for the first time, his lips delivering a gentle deliberate kiss. On my forehead.

"Any man who takes your confidence for granted would be extremely foolish," he said.

As I watched the SUV turning right, onto the Chemin du Moulin, Allie's call was coming through.

"What exactly is your mom doing here?" she asked. "Is she part of Ruth's plan?"

"Mother and Dodie are atheists. They won't be participating in Ruth's RITUAL. They're just taking pictures. It's a Mom Thing. They'll have a nice day on the mountain, documenting the event for Ruth's website."

"Your mom's documenting cultural genocide!" Allie was getting shrill. "Do you know what Ruthie's planning to do? They're going to kidnap those relics from the local worshipers! Taking Back the Magdalen is *forced rehabilitation!*"

Omigosh. When Allie spelled out Ruth's bizarre intentions, I was speechless.

"Of course, we could never tell the police!" she told me. "But this isn't just cultural genocide—it's theft! We're committed to nonviolence, but there's no guarantee THEY are. If the police get involved, your mother might be arrested."

"I don't think Dodie and Mother have any idea! They think Take Back the Magdalen is some kind of metaphor. Like the communion wafer."

"Well it's not! It's as *real* as the communion wafer," Allie said.

"But where will Ruth TAKE the Magdalen once they've got her? I mean, her relics."

"It would be very wrong to take the relics—they belong to the Church and the people of St-Maximin." The world is changing too fast for me. Allie's radical harlots are evolving into upright citizens before my eyes. "Tini overheard Ruth talking about a safe house. It's a goat farm in Normandy."

Mother's new farmhouse? But she would NEVER condone such irresponsible, superstitious behavior.

"There's no way my mother can be involved in such an anti-social plot," I declared. "She's an innocent accomplice."

"Well, you'd better tell her! She might end up being a witness. With evidence of a theft on her camera," Allie warned me. "If you think your mother's so innocent, you'd better call her!"

But just as Mother's phone began ringing, Milt's BMW pulled into the driveway, forcing me to hang up. If I tell Mother that Ruth is setting her up to harbor contraband relics, will she believe me? How can I explain my knowledge of Ruth's plot? Without telling her way too much about Allie and myself? It's hopeless! And Milt needs my attention.

Do I have time to change my outfit? Make that poolside fantasy—well, part of it—come true before Duncan returns from Plan d'Aups? For some reason, giving al fresco oral to another man feels like a fitting retort to Duncan's chaste kiss. My lips were *so ready* for him.

Now they're ready for business. And there's something I need . . . from the gardening shed.

CHAPTER SEVENTEEN

# France: Rite from Wrong

*Sunday, later*

While Milt was showering, I took a quick yet thorough "hooker bath" before changing into a short knit skirt and a bikini top. I scampered downstairs with my supplies wrapped in a towel, and organized a comfortable spot for my customer next to the pool. Then I fixed him a drink.

It took a few minutes for Milt to notice how empty the house was. Eventually, he came outside in polo shirt and khakis—and found me lying on one of the loungers barely clothed. I beckoned and pointed to his drink, waiting on a small table next to his favorite chair.

"Remember what you said the other night at dinner? When you were sitting right there?"

"I do," he growled. "Where's Duncan?"

"I asked him to take Allie to the museum in Plan d'Aups." Now I was standing in front of Milt and his palms were sliding up my thighs. His fingertips caressed my loins, discovering my lack of panties. "So I could have you all to myself."

"Nice." Milt was lifting my skirt higher. "You've always had a gorgeous pussy."

The breeze made me tingle. He wanted to lick me but the position was awkward and it was easier to watch me fingering myself. Then I turned around and sat on his lap. I reached around and rubbed his hard-on through his pants.

"If we had more time," I said, "I would unzip you and ride you backwards."

Milt made a protesting sound. "How much time do we have, baby?"

I pulled the gardener's stool from its hiding spot. Milt was too absorbed to notice. His hands were exploring my bikini top and my ass was wriggling against his fly. I pushed the stool toward the front of Milt's chair. "Enough time for this," I said, getting up.

"Suzy, you're a genius. Where did you get *that*?"

"Never you mind." I was kneeling in front of him, unzipping his pants, still wearing my skirt and bikini top. But the top had slipped quite a bit and he was trying to reach my nipples. No such luck. It gives me some mischievous pleasure to know that parts of me elude him, while I have full access to all HIS relevant bits. I pulled my skirt to my waist and stared up at him, massaging his erection with my hands. "I can feel the breeze on my pussy lips. They're so wet." He moaned. I hadn't even started sucking him but he was extremely hard. Arching my ass for emphasis, I said, "Do you think we can hear the car from here? I think we'll hear him arriving, don't you?"

"What an amazing view that would be."

"What are you talking about?"

"You know what I'm talking about. Can you open your legs a little wider? Stick your ass in the air. That's right."

Milt was staring behind me. Imagining . . . I was reluctant to ask what, though. I let his mind wander while I unpacked a condom. As my lips drove the condom downward onto his shaft, I remembered Duncan's well-behaved kiss, and felt so deliciously profane that I didn't want to stop.

I came up for air and said, "You bring out the slut in me." I heard a car engine. "We don't have much time," I murmured. "I feel like such a dirty little slut showing off my pussy like this." Then I sucked harder and Milt, unaccustomed to such language from Suzy, started coming.

As the sound of Duncan's SUV grew louder, I removed the condom, gathered up my supplies and skipped upstairs with the gardener's kneeling stool, leaving Milt to zip up and finish his drink.

## A bit later

Finally tracked my mother down in her hotel room. "I was wondering. What kind of shoes do you think I'll need if I want to come with you to the mountain?" Mother is THE authority on sensible shoes, and this is one job that calls for them. "I thought it might be fun to meet you at the hotel and go with you."

"There's been a change of plans," Mother told me. "Ruth decided the logistics of her ceremony work best in town. So they're joining the procession in St-Maximin. Dodie and I agree. Not that we were asked!"

Ruth must be planning to grab the relics during the parade in town! The long march to the mountaintop is impractical. Easier to disappear if you're on a flat surface in the *vieille ville*—it's filled with hiding places.

"Why don't you meet us for breakfast in the dining room?" Mother said. "Bring Allison and her uncle."

"Okay," I said warily. "I'll find out what they're up to."

Gosh. Ruth has both moms totally fooled. What nerve!

Trading in my Juicy Couture micromini for a striped jellaba, I returned to the pool where Milt was reading his *IHT*. "Where's Allison?" I asked him.

"Upstairs." He turned to the business section. "Kiddo, your timing was brilliant."

"They say it's everything."

"I haven't done it in the open air since I was a teenager."

"Me too," I assured him. Installing my covered body in a nearby chair, I tried not to be overly conscious of Duncan when he came outside to straighten the table umbrellas. I threw him a shy grateful smile, which he returned. If he knows Milt was being serviced during his impromptu absence, he's not letting on.

When Duncan disappeared into the house, I said, "Tomorrow's the local procession, isn't it?"

"Sure is," Milt replied, without looking up from his paper.

"I would love to be there," I said. "The Sainte-Baume mountain is really beautiful! And it's quite an important tradition. What do you think? I know Allie would too and I think it would be a shame to miss it. Unless . . ."

"I'd rather be golfing. But you girls should definitely partake, if that's what floats your boat. Ask Duncan! I'd drive you there myself, but I have another meeting."

"It won't interfere with your day?"

Milt laughed softly. "I'm putty in your hands and you know it. What else would you like from your Uncle Milt?"

"Actually," I said. "I'd like you to return to New York in the fall."

"Oh really?" He put his paper down and turned to face me. "I guess I should tell you." I sat up straighter. "Can you keep this between us?" he said. "I've been thinking about moving here permanently. I might become a French citizen."

"You can't," I blurted out. "That's crazy!"

"Suzy." His voice was gentle. "I know you have a life and we both know this is your business. But I'm flattered—well, more than flattered."

How can Milt become a French citizen? He doesn't even speak the language.

### Later

After dinner, I cornered Duncan in the library. He was sitting at the small desk taking care of some household bills.

"This is going to sound completely bizarre," I told him. "I desperately need your advice."

He looked up from his paperwork with a startled expression. Then he looked like a man who can't quite believe his luck. For about a second.

"It's about my mother," I began. "Yes, I know. First my brother-in-law, now my mother. I've been afraid to tell you. I was trying to get away from everybody. Now my worlds are colliding. And tomorrow they're going to collide right in front of the basilica. My mom is being set up by irresponsible zealots! Have you seen the two conferences taking place around town? The dueling T-shirts? Did Father Philippe tell you? My brother-in-law will be hanging around the church taking notes. I don't know how I'll keep him away from my mother. And Allie's up to her EYEBALLS in this—I have no idea what she's told you and I—I won't ask."

"Let's have a small drink," Duncan said. He tugged on one of the bookshelves, revealing a small collection of bottles and glasses embedded in the wall. "Allison told me very little when I picked her up at the museum. She seems quite worried." Handing me a snifter, he asked, "Is it possible you're both worrying about the same thing?"

"Yes," I said. "For once we're on the same page." I explained the situation, adding, "I can't tell my mother any of this! It's too far-fetched. And don't tell me to try talking Ruth out of this—I don't think she's open to persuasion."

"You can't negotiate with zealots," Duncan agreed. "By the way, Father Philippe says Bad Girls Without Borders won't talk to the police."

I sipped some Armagnac. "Can you blame them? One of the Bad Girls Without Borders is Tini! Remember the day you met Serge?"

"Officially, I remember nothing, but yes. Between us, who can forget Tini? She's striking. Of course she'll want to avoid the police. But even if that weren't an issue, Father Philippe sees the Church as a sanctuary from the authorities. Everybody's committed to an extra-legal solution."

"What should I do?" I sighed. "I can't let Mother walk into this situation, but I can't tell her what I know. She has no idea about my two lives."

Duncan was very calm for a moment. Then, looking inspired, he quietly tapped my snifter with his own. "Are you ready for 'Plan Dope'? Sorry. It hasn't got much to do with Plan d'Aups, so it's not even a good pun. Finish this and go upstairs. You need to be fully rested when you meet your mother for breakfast."

## *Monday, July 22, 2002 8:00 A.M.*

Can we really get away with this?

I'm holding my breath. And Duncan's waiting for us downstairs.

## *Monday, later*

In the car, Allie suggested I sit next to Duncan. "No thanks," I said. "I have my reasons."

Well, one reason—folded neatly in my tote bag. I unbuttoned my plaid blouse while the car was moving, and popped the black

T-shirt Ruth gave me over my head. An important part of my look at the breakfast table.

At the doorway of the hotel dining room, I reminded Duncan, "Don't forget to call me Nancy!"

Mother and Dodie were mildly surprised when I introduced Duncan, Allie's "bilingual cousin" from New Zealand who lives here most of the year. "Allie will be along in a few moments," I lied.

Allie's expat "cousin" knows all the locals, of course. "L'Imprévu? The owners are from a little fishing village in Italy," Duncan said. Mother and Dodie were impressed. When he mentioned "some curious rumors about Mary Magdalen's relics," they pumped him for more.

"I've heard through the grapevine that the reliquary will be empty this year. When they march through the Place de l'Hôtel de Ville, they carry her relics in a large copper head. The plan was to convey the reliquary all the way to the Sainte-Baume mountaintop for the re-opening of her cave. It's quite an important event."

"We're taking pictures for my daughter's website," Dodie chimed in. "But why is the reliquary empty this year?"

"A local priest was informed—he won't reveal how—that the relics are endangered," Duncan said, reaching for a piece of toast. "In the middle of the night, someone took the relics out of the tomb for safekeeping."

Mother was listening intently. "When did all this happen?"

"At two A.M. last night," he told her. "The relics were taken to a monastery in Burgundy. The locals haven't been told. Nobody has to know they're marching around with an empty reliquary goes the reasoning."

I turned to my mother. "Shouldn't we tell Ruthie? I think she'll want to know about this."

"I'm not so sure." Mother poured some tea. "Religion is symbolic, after all. What difference will it make? I don't feel like trekking off to Burgundy, do you?" She ignored Dodie's frowning response. "I was looking forward to a nice meal at L'Imprévu tonight! And *I* don't mind taking pictures of an empty reliquary. What Ruth doesn't know won't hurt her."

I shot Duncan a panicky look.

"We don't have to go to Burgundy," Dodie said. "But I won't be part of a plan to deceive my daughter. Ruth has a right to know."

"Oh for goodness sake." Mother was muttering into her brioche.

Ruth was heading toward us holding a small bowl of fruit. I spotted two of her companions at the buffet table.

While Ruth, in a bright yellow TAKE BACK THE MAGDALEN T-shirt, listened to her mother, Duncan and I appeared not to notice her agitated reaction.

"So where did they take her relics?" Ruth demanded. "To the mountain?"

"No," Duncan said. "They're in Vézelay now."

"Vézelay?" Ruth was trying, without success, to stay calm. "But that's where the relics were in the first place, before the Church hierarchy brought them to St-Maximin."

"That's right," Duncan said. "St-Maximin took over in 1270. I wonder how they'll get her relics out of Vézelay this time. When something comes back after nearly a thousand years, you might want to hold onto it."

"How do you know for sure that her relics are in Vézelay?" Ruth gave Duncan a flinty look.

"This is very hush-hush," he said. "My friend Pasquale was in on the plan. He breeds free-range rabbits in Draguignan. They used his delivery truck to transport the relics."

"It figures!" Ruth grumbled. "A male *rabbit butcher* absconding with a female saint's relics!"

Duncan raised an eyebrow. "Absconding?" he repeated. "Pasquale's family has been here for three hundred years. His uncle's the retired caretaker of the Magdalen's cave. When Pasquale heard about a plot to steal the Magdalen's relics, he took it rather personally." Ruth's face was twitching. "But now they're safely installed at Vézelay," Duncan continued. "Secretly, of course. Thanks to Pasquale."

Ruth stood up. "I'm calling an emergency meeting!" she announced. And before we knew it, she was gone.

"You're right," Duncan said to Mother. "A ritual is no less compelling when it involves an empty reliquary."

"Exactly. If Ruth wants to be such a fundamentalist, I'm afraid she'll have to take her own pictures," Mother said. "I think we should stay here and enjoy the parade."

"Maybe we'll get a chance to meet Pasquale," Dodie said. "He's part of the parade?"

"He called from the N7," Duncan told her. "He's on his way back from Vézelay, so he'll have to miss the procession."

After the two moms had gone upstairs, to fetch cameras and prepare for the annual procession, I asked, "Was ANY of that true?"

"Ten percent of what I told them was a hundred percent true."

"But the relics? Are they—?"

"Where they've been for the last millennium," Duncan said.

"I was getting convinced," I admitted. "And so was Ruth. I wonder where she is."

"I'm going to look for Father Philippe. Turn on your phone, in case I need to call you."

When I got to Ruth's floor, I knocked loudly on her door, but there was no response. Three of Ruth's followers, in bright yellow T-shirts, were hurrying toward the staircase with duffel bags and knapsacks.

"Excuse me?" I called out, thankful for my camouflage. They

gave my TAKE BACK THE MAGDALEN T-shirt a puzzled appraisal. Wrong color, right message. "I'm looking for Ruthie."

"She took the first bus. There's another minibus coming."

"Oh!" I did my best imitation of a happy believer embarking on the next leg of a perpetual pilgrimage. "Are we going to Vézelay? When are we leaving?"

"Thirty minutes!"

"Don't wait up for me," I said, as they disappeared into the stairwell. "I think I'll take the train."

I took the elevator downstairs and dashed across the cloister to the side door of the church. In one of the abandoned confession booths, I pulled off my T-shirt. Half-naked, I was sitting in the wrong part of the confessional—the priest's side. I dressed as quickly as I could.

When I emerged, the altar girl was standing before me in her long alb, staring at my unbuttoned cleavage. "Madame," she said earnestly. I adjusted my buttons.

Hurrying toward the exit, I looked back and saw her small head peeking into the booth, doing a quick inspection.

"Nancy?" I looked up. Jason was standing next to the baptismal font holding a notebook. "What are you doing here?"

"We need to talk!" I told him. "I should be asking YOU that."

"Matt said something about a holiday with your mother, but I had no idea . . ."

"Do you realize how much trouble you've created?" Jason's confused smile made me want to slap him. "I'm serious! Does your wife know you're here? Have you spoken to Elspeth?"

A cloud of self-doubt replaced the smile. "We'd better talk," he said.

In the Maison de Thé, Jason told me about his secret novel, but he was skirting the issue. Only when I pushed a bit did he mention a Mary Magdalen theme.

"I'm staying in Plan d'Aups at a small folk museum. It's run by Father Philippe Devoucoux. He's got a large collection of Magdalen-related postcards from all over Europe going back to the invention of photography."

To my relief, he said nothing about Allie or the other modern Magdalens milling around St-Max. As long as Jason feels he has to hide those details, I'm safe. If he stops lying to me, life as I know it will be over.

"Mary Magdalen?" I said blithely. "Well, you've come to the right place. Does Elspeth know you're writing a novel? She's never mentioned it."

"Well, no." He looked embarrassed. "She wouldn't understand."

"I think you should return to New York."

"I'm returning later this week. Flying back from Nice."

"Change your flight," I said. "It's a bad idea to linger here."

"I hope you don't think I'm in any danger of joining the priest-hood."

"Why would I think *that*? You're Presbyterian."

"In college, my roommate converted and went to Latin America, to work with the Jesuits." He was getting wistful. "I was a different person in those days. Before I met Elspeth."

It must have been Jason's idea to name their son after a Roman Catholic anarchist!

"For Berrigan's sake," I begged him, "please get on the next plane back to New York. When did you last speak to your wife?"

"About five days ago. But we're in constant touch. Voicemail."

"Is she returning your voicemail?"

"No," he admitted, "but that's usually a good sign."

"Well, this time it's not," I told him. Should I repeat what Elspeth said about the fate of his balls? "Raoul Felder might be contacting you."

"Did you just say—?" Jason was now completely disoriented. "Raoul Felder?"

"Elspeth thinks you're having an affair. She's telling Matt you lied to her about being in Paris."

"I was in Paris for a week, working on a deal. I didn't—" He looked down at his cup. "I didn't lie to Elspeth, but I haven't told her where I am," he added. "Yet."

"Elspeth thinks you're having an affair with ME." Jason stared numbly at my upper body. He's never thought about me that way, but now—just hearing those words—he's forced to reconsider. "She knows you called her from Marseille. She already knew I was here with my mom, and she put two and two together. Or so she thinks."

"Are you serious?"

"She intends to communicate with you through Felder from now on."

"Felder! How the—"

"You must have given her a reason to suspect. How exactly does a wife get an idea like that?"

"Maybe she shouldn't have quit her job. Elspeth needs an outlet. She's a good prosecutor, you know."

"Well, her instincts in this case are all wrong! Mostly wrong," I corrected myself.

"What should I do?" Jason said. "Should I tell her about my novel? It's been a secret since we met."

"No," I said abruptly. *That novel leads to Allison, to NYCOT, to God knows what, but he doesn't know I know that.* "You never saw me during this visit, we never spoke, you were never here, and I never saw *you*. No mention of St-Maximin. And nothing about this novel of yours."

"Really?" The cloud was lifting from Jason's face.

"Only if you get on the next available flight and get your butt back to New York. I don't enjoy being the target of Elspeth's rage. She's scary when she's like this."

"I'm spending five more days at Father Philippe's museum."

Five more days contemplating what might have been. Day-dreaming about Allison. Consorting with Tini, Roxana, the members of Les Putes. While I try to hide in Milt's house, pretending to be at the hotel with Mother.

"You can come back next summer," I said firmly. "But first you have to patch things up with Elspeth. You can't stay here another day! Elspeth has Felder on a retainer. Do you want Berrigan growing up in a single parent household? If Elspeth files for a divorce—"

"Okay," Jason conceded. "Point taken."

"Will you take my advice? Do we have a deal?"

He nodded, still a bit incredulous.

"But you can't change your mind," I added. "If you 'never came' to St-Max, you can't break down two weeks later and confess. That will screw us both up for the rest of our lives! I'm willing to lie for you, but you have to promise not to tell a soul. Especially Matt. If you do that to me, I'll never forgive you."

"I understand. It's a deal."

"And turn off your fucking GPS." I sighed. "You'd better NOT be having an affair. You can't even tell a harmless lie and get away with it!"

Jason smiled sheepishly. "I promise. I'm not having an affair. And I won't mess this up."

## CHAPTER EIGHTEEN

# What Happens in Provence Stays in Provence

## Monday, continued

As I walked toward the Couvent Royale, I saw the last yellow T-shirts climbing into a crowded minivan. Father Philippe waved happily, and the vehicle pulled away. He turned to Duncan, shook his hand, then opened his arms to greet me in his unique blend of English, French and Latin.

"The double agent est arrivée! You came to St-Maximin to save our heritage! Blessed are the Bad Girls Sans Frontières. Beati qui persecutoniem . . ."

"*Blessed are those who have been persecuted,*" Duncan explained. "Book of Matthew," he added. "Eighth beatitude."

Father Philippe clasped his hands around mine. "Vous vous appelez . . .?"

"Nnnn . . . Suzy," I replied, looking sideways at Duncan.

"Vous êtes un beau couple," Father Philippe said.

*You*—I began to blush—*make a lovely couple.* Is that really what he said?

"Bonne chance," he told Duncan. He had one eye on the second button of my blouse. "Excuse me," he said. "I must fly toward the tea shop. I've an houseguest who needs help urgently. I hope I will practice my English with you one day."

As I watched the priest hurrying away in his black and white robes, Duncan said, "Father Philippe's very grateful to us."

To us. Did he say that with unexpected tenderness? I wanted Duncan to repeat the words, just to be sure.

A sound from the street made me turn around. A group of men in traditional costume—red sashes, white shirts—carried a square frame on their shoulders. A copper head with flowing copper hair was resting on top—mistress of the street, the center of everybody's attention. As the crowd passed, I felt a strong urge to salute the Magdalen's relics.

"Now they'll drive up to the mountain," Duncan said. "Every one of Ruthie's disciples is on her way to Vézelay now, so it's safe."

'I can't believe we did that. Did we really save the relics?"

"We did." He pulled me gently toward him, his hands resting lightly on either side of my waist. "How does it feel?"

*To be touched by you for the first time?*

Our bodies, which had never been this close before, seemed to be talking to each other. I felt something just below my chest, intense fluttering. My heart was beating faster, and the look in his eyes convinced me for a mad few seconds that he was my body's true owner.

In a quiet voice, I asked, "Do you think Ruth will ever find out what we did?"

"We may have started a new myth," Duncan said. "If all goes as planned, Ruthie will spend the rest of her days spreading the gospel, telling how the relics were taken back to their original home, but nobody wants to admit it. She'll convince herself that she intended, all along, to take the Magdalen back to Vézelay. She can tell her followers the T-shirt was a prophecy." He let go of me. "People need beliefs."

We walked in the direction of Place Hoche, where Duncan's

SUV was parked. "Careful," I heard him say. "I just saw Milt's car. It's better if we don't run into his golf buddy."

He pulled me into a corner, where he could watch the BMW without being seen. "You mean," I said, "if *I* don't run into him."

"Just doing my job," Duncan said. Then he turned to me. But now, in that tight corner, with his hands on my waist, he was leaning against my front, pinning me gently to the wall. "Is this what you wanted me to do?" he asked. "Out there on the pavement? When you looked at me like that?"

"We can't—I can't—"

"I know. But you can give me permission to kiss you." Without which he pressed his lips against my mouth, opening my lips with his tongue while his right leg pushed my legs apart. I felt my entire body responding with silent spasms, and I kissed him hard, allowing myself to come while he held my arms down. "Again," he insisted, pressing his leg against the zipper on my jeans. This time, I began to moan and he had to silence me with another deep kiss.

"We have to stop," I whispered. "Milt's too important in my life. I'm a professional."

I didn't dare tell Duncan how badly I wanted to make him come—right there in that alleyway.

"I understand," he said. "But I've been wanting to kiss you for weeks."

"Now you have." I smoothed out my blouse. "We can put it behind us. Go back to being . . ."

"Being what?" He had released my body, but his arms were blocking me so I couldn't just walk away.

"Colleagues?" I suggested. "We're both doing business with Milt. And I'm not—" *Allison*, I almost said, but didn't. I want him to think I fell asleep and saw nothing that night. "I wish we'd met under different circumstances," I told him.

His lips touched my forehead. "Me too," he said. Then he took my hand and led me toward the cobblestoned square. Milt's BMW was no longer there. A slender man, gray-haired, with excellent posture, was walking away from the parked cars.

"Omigod!" I whispered. "What is HE doing here?"

"Milt's golf buddy?"

"For a second," I lied, "I thought he looked like someone I knew. I guess my nerves are shot."

What is Etienne doing in St-Max? And how does he know Milt? Does he live nearby? He says he lives in Paris, but I've learned not to trust the stated whereabouts of a john. They're capable of lying about anything—name, occupation, marital status.

As long as they don't lie about your fee.

Speaking of which, Etienne has always been more frugal than Milt. I can't let them find out they both know me. They might compare notes!

### Monday night

My mother leaves for Normandy tomorrow to close on the goat farm. Duncan just heard that Father Philippe's houseguest—my brother-in-law—was summoned back to New York, due to "illness in the family."

"I need to sneak out of here tomorrow for a farewell lunch with Mother and Dodie," I told Duncan. "I can't possibly tell Milt I'm visiting my mother."

"I'll figure something out," he promised.

### Tuesday, July 23

Milt was up earlier than all of us. The BMW's gone. "Don't look so worried," Duncan said. "Your trip to the monastery has been simplified."

## Later

As I left the hotel dining room, I congratulated myself on managing Mother's visit with maximum discretion and minimum disorder. She never suspected a thing—not even about Allie—and sailed through her time here completely unaware of the dangers she was facing.

Dodie looks much happier, now that her daughter's out of her hair—staying at a Benedictine *hôtellerie* in Vézelay with her followers, trying to figure out where the relics are hidden.

"The nuns gave them a group rate," Dodie told me. "Ruth says she can feel the presence of the relics."

"You must visit the goat farm when we've settled in," Mother said. "Ruth might come for Christmas. Bring Matt!"

In the lobby, I picked up my phone to call Duncan. Halfway toward the front door, I looked up.

Milt and Etienne were sitting in adjacent armchairs, slightly sunburned from the golf course. As I walked through the lobby, they were vying for eye contact, the kind you make when nobody else knows you've met before. Each was a little too confident of the other man's ignorance. I tried not to look, but Etienne couldn't resist a forward smile.

"This town grows more exotic and beautiful with each passing summer." He spoke in a sage voice to Milt that was really directed at me.

"Too true," Milt agreed, loud enough for me to hear. "Too bad about the lousy plumbing."

Plumbing? Surely THAT wasn't meant for my ears. I walked briskly through the gates to the main street and stopped in front of the Maison de Thé, phone in hand—but Etienne's voice interrupted my call.

"It is safe to say hello!" Etienne announced. "Bonjour cocotte, what brings you of all people to this remote place?"

"Safe for you!" I told him, putting away my phone. "But not for me!" I looked around carefully. "I'm staying in that hotel with my mother."

"Ah." He looked miserable. Then his eyes lit up. "But I'm staying there alone. I have a suite. You stay on the premises? It's convenient. Your mother goes to sleep early, does she not?"

At the door of the tea shop, he gestured with his head to a table in the back. "Here, cocotte, for your trouble." He slipped a hundred euros into my open bag. "You should always carry a pretty bag like this. It's efficient. Order yourself a refreshment. We will not sit together. If your mother sees us, she sees only a very lonely person trying to chat up her beautiful daughter. Which is natural."

There is nothing quite so businesslike as a veteran john. I installed myself at the back table and began reading a magazine. Etienne, at the entrance, was looking out for Milt. When he felt secure that the coast was clear, he wandered into the shop, paused over the vinegar section, then made his way to the table next to me.

"You move like a panther," I said quietly. "Nice that these tables are so close together."

"It comes from years of practice," he replied. When a server came within earshot, he made a point of saying, "Vous parlez anglais? Where do you live?"

I nursed my linden infusion. "I never imagined *you* in a town like this."

"Nor I you," he said. "I came south to help my cousin's husband sort out some business matters. He got himself into a spot of trouble. I had a similar dilemma myself, a few years ago, so I'm trying to advise him on possible solutions. But I have to stay at the monastery for a few days because they're having the house renovated."

I almost choked on my tea.

"There was a plumbing disaster so he can't have me as a guest. When my cousin's mother died, I urged her to sell the house. Her husband insists on keeping it. I'll be very interested to see what a mess he's made of the renovation. You know these Americans, they overdo everything!"

"Indeed," I said, catching my breath. So Etienne's cousin is . . . Milt's wife? It never occurred to me that Milt would have access to French citizenship through his *wife*. And Milt . . . didn't buy that house. It's been hers all along.

"Do you have your own room or share with maman?" Etienne asked.

"Share," I said quickly. "And your cousin? She must be French."

I felt a twinge of guilt, snooping on Milt like this.

"Yes, but Cécile grew up in Boston, very American. Her mother inherited a rather large house—one of our uncles ran it as a small hotel for many years and he owned a vineyard. He sold the vineyard and kept the building. Céci's parents used it as a holiday place, but she always hated it. Being a fan of the best things in life, she found it rather lacking."

Even if the renovation was financed by my customer, I've been having sex every day with my favorite john in a house that technically belongs to his wife. Would it bother me if I weren't myself a wife? With womanly feelings about my own household?

All summer, I've assumed that Milt paid for this property the way he pays for everything else. It made me feel like a member of his harem, and it never occurred to me that Milt had married into property. Somehow that breaks up my harem fantasy big time.

"I will be in room 235," Etienne said.

"I'll try," I replied, "but it's almost impossible."

"You don't think it would be a tragedy for us to miss this opportunity?"

With a sad smile, I replied, "Life is littered with manageable tragedies."

## Later

Counting and sorting my euros. How to stash them safely for the flight home?

Milt has said nothing about another visit, or about returning to New York. If his problems have anything in common with Etienne's, then his solution—to relocate—makes sense. Milt, my bread and butter date, is becoming a foreign memory.

This visit was a generous way to tell me goodbye. I have to accept that nothing lasts forever.

Besides, I'm trespassing on another woman's real estate, and that just makes me homesick—for my marriage.

## Wednesday, Air France, Flight 3210

Allie is conked out in her seat, nestled into her inflatable plaid neck support, with a copy of *The Making of the Magdalen* on her lap.

Before falling asleep, she confided, "Lucho's meeting me at the airport. He doesn't know about that night with Duncan. Anyway, it only happened once."

"Only once?" I said.

"Only once," she repeated. "I don't have to tell Lucho about Duncan as long as Duncan knows about Lucho—isn't that what you said?" Since when does Allison follow my advice about men? "I made Duncan remove my number from his phone," she added.

"You did? Why?"

"I'm renewing my commitment to Lucho. Duncan wasn't as upset as I thought he'd be. In fact—" she was pouting just a bit "—he seems to be *relieved* about Lucho. Do you think I was imagining that?"

"Um, no. I mean, yes," I riffed. "Duncan needs time to get over you." Allie's face brightened up. "But . . . how do you know he deleted your number?"

"I was right there. I made him show me. This way, if I ever tell Lucho, I can tell him about that too."

"That was an *excellent* move," I told her.

Allie's discreet ladylike breathing—she even has a pretty snore—is audible enough to the businessman across the aisle. When he glances her way, he smiles indulgently.

The latest email from Matt was encouraging:

*Elspeth's doing better. She's liking the Prozac and Jason's back. So it's safe to come home. I miss you honey.*

The divorce is off, my sister-in-law no longer wants to "prosecute" me, and the wrinkles of her soul have been paralyzed.

## Thursday, July 25 New York

I'm home again, many euros richer, with all my secrets intact.

Last night, after three deception-fueled orgasms in the arms of my husband, I closed my eyes. As Matt wrapped an arm around my naked waist—the part of me Duncan touched through my clothes—I felt a shudder passing through my body. What was I thinking when I allowed Duncan to kiss me that afternoon? How could I let something like that happen?

My trip to Provence was a lucky dream that almost turned into a nightmare. While Matt began drifting off, my jet-lagged brain was still adding, subtracting, calculating the odds.

What will become of Izzy and Serge? Katya can't track me down in New York and embarrass me, can she? What about the police?

I held onto Matt a little tighter as I recalled Milt's parting words. "Do something practical with your money, kiddo." How some guys talk when your financial relationship is coming to an end.

The money makes it easier to let go. And he never, in all the time I knew him, found out my other name.

## Friday, July 26 New York

A call from Jasmine. Given the attrition rate around here, her business is more welcome than ever.

"Harry's gotta have it," she said with a chuckle. "He wants to see us together, Monday noon." At least her clients aren't fleeing to Europe—and they're quick.

"Sure thing." I was anxious to hang up and throw out the paper before my husband returns from the office.

I buy all the tabloids, searching for news about Isabel, and I'm turning into a regular at the foreign newsstand on Eighty-sixth Street. Matt would find the sudden shift in my reading patterns bizarre—and what if he mentions my new habit to Elspeth?

There's very little the French police can do to me here. I'm finally safe, truly out of their reach, but I can't stop wondering about Izzy. I'm haunted by what happened to her, not just this summer, but twenty years ago when she entered the business.

## Sunday, August 4 Easthampton, Long Island

Elspeth and Jason think they've found a solution to their problem: a house on the beach. Elspeth's moved out here for the rest of the summer with the twins and her Prozac. Jason spends as much time in the Hamptons as he can—which isn't enough, since he has to work in the city.

Last night, Jason and Matt cooked lobsters. I prepared a watercress salad with freshly toasted pine nuts and a parmesan custard—something Elspeth would never let me do alone. But now she's content to sit on the deck reading *Oprah* magazine while I take over her kitchen.

Elspeth has changed! Her voice is flatter and sweeter. Not one question about Provence or my mother. Nor has she acknowledged the scary things she said to me in voicemail.

At breakfast today, I announced to the table: "I just got a message from my mother. After *all that*, she completely changed her mind and decided to go house-hunting in Normandy. She's talking about a goat farm in Mortagne-au-Perche."

Elspeth was surprisingly unaffected by this turn of events. "I wonder—" her voice was sunny and vague "—if I could persuade someone to get those beach towels out of the dryer."

When she returned from her swim, she disappeared into the twins' bedroom, played with them for half an hour, and emerged with a placid smile on her face.

"I'm going to Briermere Farm to pick up a blueberry pie," she told me. "Want to come?"

In the past, I would have made an excuse but I actually felt safe sitting next to her in the car. The new Elspeth! But how long can it last?

Later, I gazed across the table at her while nibbling a piece of pie. After three years of dodging Elspeth's phone calls and questions, I'm not sure what to think. My pulse used to go up whenever she opened her mouth.

Can we really trust the new Elspeth? She needs to be a prosecutor the way I need to turn tricks. It's what she was born to do. If she doesn't pursue her vocation, she'll find other ways to prosecute—unless she's neutralized by Prozac.

I should be glad, but it seems wrong to win the battle this way.

And I can't help wondering, if Matt were to put ME on Prozac, would I totally lose interest in my profession?

I don't want to find out.

### Six Weeks Later
### September 6, 2002 New York

This morning, while my lips were savoring a new customer's hard-on, we both heard my phone chiming in the other room. His erection was firmer now, more sure of its goal. Does the idea of another client turn him on? I flashed him a knowing slutty look.

While he showered, I checked Call History. The phone began ringing again and I answered in a discreet voice.

"I can't believe my luck, kiddo. Getting you to answer at this hour." Milt! "Admit it, you're up to something. What are you wearing?" he growled.

With one eye on the bathroom door, I giggled. "Not much. I just came back from the gym. But . . . I need to call you back. Are you in town?" He's calling from a blocked number.

"I'm in Luxembourg for a few days."

"Again?"

"Have you ever been to the Cayman Islands? Leave your phone on, so I can reach you, kiddo. I've missed your body AND your voice."

It looks like my life isn't getting any simpler. If Milt wants to arrange a ticket from overseas, I have to tell him my other name. After being Suzy for almost thirteen years, that's a taboo.

I waited for my customer to dress and leave. When I retrieved the message, I was shocked to hear Duncan's voice. "I might be flying to the States next week. Something's happening in Southampton. Will you be in town? I'll try you again later," he said. "I promise."

Should I call back? I haven't thought about Duncan—much—these last few weeks.

Replaying his message, I remembered how close we almost were, that day in the library. Is that when he knew he wanted to kiss me? The way he looked at me when I stood before him in my towel—I keep trying to forget how that felt.

The memory of our kiss returns whenever I listen to his voice. Another voice responds, *Of course you won't call. You have to wait—because he promised.*

And we all know that waiting for a man to call is only the beginning.